Whispers Beneath th

By

Carla Kovach

Copyright

Copyright © 2014, Whispers Beneath the Pines by Carla Kovach

Disclaimer

All characters appearing in this work are fictitious. Any resemblance to real persons, living or dead, is purely coincidental.

Dedication

I would like to give special thanks to good friend Barbara Camelford for the IT training and to my wonderful husband Nigel Buckley for designing my book cover. Your help has been much appreciated.

I think at this point it would be appropriate to mention that my work is purely fictional. My love of Içmeler in Turkey drove me to use this location in my book. I have found the locals there to be nothing more than warm and hospitable and my crime gang could have been located anywhere in the world. I chose Içmeler because it is a beautiful location that is surrounded by magnificent mountains and pine trees which are perfect for my choice of crime. One last thank you to Içmeler, its beautiful scenery and its equally beautiful people. I hope to return someday soon.

Whispers Beneath the Pines

Chapter 1

As he dragged the woman by her feet his legs buckled. He fell to his knees gasping for air. Exhausting, Guz thought. She must have weighed at least two hundred pounds, the same as him if not a little more. The main beams from the car shone across the top of the burial hole, just a few more feet and they would both be placed together in the earth. Him first, her on top; she seemed to be a bit of a nagging cow throughout the day. Guz laughed at his macabre thought. By placing her on top, she would always be over him; nagging him; blocking his soul from making its departure; imprisoning it with her hefty weight.

    Dried mud, foliage and gravel got caught in her mousy blonde hair; her grey complexion was now scuffed with dirt marks from the dusty ground. He watched the skin on the end of her nose flap down. The skin that had easily torn as he'd pulled her dead weight over a tree stump before her nose had crashed down on to its splintered edge. It was, after all, too far to drag her around the stump, too much effort and too hot.

Sweat trickled into Guz's eyes, down his face and into his mouth. He coughed then spat a gritty bolus to the ground before standing and continuing to pull hard at her limp body. He felt his leg muscles tighten and with every tug he feared he might burst a blood vessel. Black dots clouded his vision, he stopped to let the light-headedness pass. The last few feet were the hardest; he needed a break, a proper break. He dropped her legs, stood tall and reached up to the sky for a good stretch.

He bent down and took a seat on the mossy ground before pulling out the pack of cigarettes he had grabbed from her pocket, he lit one. Looks like she smoked Bensons; better than his usual brand of unfiltered baccy that he got down the market. That shit had aged him. Sucking hard, he closed his eyes and savoured the cigarette's calming effects. The heat had been relentless that day, reaching the forties he guessed. What he wouldn't do right now to be sat in Sadik's little pool in Sadik's little garden, smelling the spicy aroma of Sadik's secret recipe Adana Kebabs grilling on the barbeque. Instead he was sat in the forest, with a pasty whale that was beginning to stink of shit. Shit, cigarettes and pine trees, interesting mix of smells. He stubbed his nub end out between his hardened fingertips and placed it in his pocket. No one was ever likely to come here in search of anyone but 'you never know,' and leaving cigarette ends next to burial sites was not a good idea.

Back to the job. He stood and grabbed her legs once again. Only a few feet, he reminded himself. 'A few more feet then I can go to Sadik's, get in that pool and have my kebab,' he thought. Music blared out. Guz dropped the woman's legs and dived towards the hard ground slamming his knee onto a jagged rock as he fell. He cowered out of the light beam and his eyes darted left and right. Heart pounding, he reached down towards his knee and rubbed the ache away. He gazed at his phone then laughed. His text alert was calling. Tarkan sang 'Kiss Kiss.' The music stopped before the phone beeped. Standing, he walked over to the car, took a swig of warm cola from the bottle that lay on the driver's seat as he checked his alert. A text from Sadik.

'3 credit cards, 700 euros, 2000 lira, Gucci bag, 2 drivers' licences. Jewels'

Sadik, straight to the point as always. No, hi Brother? How you getting on with the bodies, Brother? Is it okay to celebrate with your lady, Celile, Brother? He had seen the look they shared when they thought he hadn't been looking. A look he remembers all too well, the look he had once received all the time from Celile only three years ago. He threw the phone to the seat. Sadik and Celile would now be heading to the house to celebrate and that thought made him feel sick to the stomach. Next time, he would put himself first; him and him alone. Once the next job was completed, he would clear out, go and make a fresh start with the proceeds. In his mind he was clear. Stuff them both; they were welcome to each other. For now though, he still wanted to join them and have that beer and kebab. Cursing himself for his weaknesses he had another swig of the cola before placing it on the back seat next to the passports. Two German passports and driving licences, he grabbed them and placed them in the glove box, things were looking up. He would never mention the passports that Ilse had kept in her bag. As far as The Boss and the others were aware, they had only found driving licences.

All around him he heard the song of the crickets. As he moved and turned it would disappear only to reappear when he turned again.

Forcing his weary body back over to the woman he stopped and stared. She stirred and groaned. Opening up one eye she looked towards him, squinting as if she couldn't focus. His heart beat faster and his hands began to shake. She was dead, he was sure he'd killed her. Had he checked her pulse? No he hadn't, he'd been slack.

"Gerhard? Helfen sie mir," his German was lacking, Sadik had done most of the talking that day. He stared into her eyes, the eyes that thought he was her beloved Gerhard. Eyes that were blood shot and wet, his stomach turned. "Es ist Ilse, hilf mir," she cried. Hilf, hilf, he'd heard this one before. She said her name Ilse; he knew that her name was Ilse. Hilf, Helfen, help! He remembered. She was asking for help. 'She thinks I'm Gerhard and she's asking for help.'

He ignored her and walked over to the hole in the ground, wedged in the bottom was Gerhard. His face was now expressionless, no glint at all in his eyes. He hated it when they died with open eyes, he should've closed them but yuck, he shuddered at the thought. Killing them he could deal with but eyes and eyeballs were a thing he couldn't touch so he'd left Gerhard's eyes open. He could see speckled movements over the body, it was too dark to make out what it was but he guessed it was ants or insects of some kind. There was no shortage of insects in the forest.

In the distance he heard the crashing of the mountain waterfall gushing into the pool below. Earlier that day the couple had swam in it. He could tell they were cold, they'd come out shaking even though the temperature was so high that day. Why did it always surprise them that mountain water was so cold?

His hands shook at the thought of what he had to do next and his arm pits began to itch with sweat, then so did his groin. He scratched hard, first his groin, then his arm pit. He felt the burning of a rash begin to spread within these delicate crevices.

"Gerhard," she cried, louder this time. He didn't respond; from his lack of response she seemed to know that he was not her beloved. She knew that he wasn't there to help. She was disorientated but not dead as he had earlier thought. Cursing Sadik under his breath he kicked the tree that stood next to him. He flinched then rubbed his throbbing foot, the tree was harder than he'd thought. Insects scurried up the bark as he backed away from the tree; disturbed by being at the epicentre of the earthquake on their trunk.

The lights on the car began to flicker. The battery. Guz hobbled to the vehicle and turned them off. There was no way he could break down here, miles from anywhere. Sadik wouldn't come back for him that night. He felt a gentle piercing on his arm, slapping hard he then felt the trickle of liquid spread down his bicep and past his elbow. Mosquitoes. After a moment his eyes adjusted to the light from the half moon.

"Gerhard," she said as she sobbed. He could hear her snivelling and filling up with mucous. She screamed; her voice was getting louder.

"Fuck," he cried as he hurried over towards the hole and grabbed the shovel. Standing behind her he watched as her pleading eyes tried to focus on him. Although he had done this many times, it never got easier. Her wet teary face shone as the trees branches parted with the humid breeze, allowing the moonlight to catch her tears. One minute he saw her whole face, as clear as day; the next he saw only the glistening ridge of a trickling tear that had caught the light. Then nothing. The breeze dropped, she lay there sobbing in the shadows. He heard rustling amongst the leaves beneath him; she was on the move; now on her front she had dragged herself along the rough ground. Scraping her delicate swollen skin over the sharp limestone and grit, she grunted as she kept going. The breeze picked up again and the moon fully revealed her position. He could see the wound on the back of her head from their earlier assault on her. Blood had dried to her head and he was sure he could see a bit of exposed skull. His stomach turned and he heaved. The bubbles from the warm cola were repeating on him, causing him to belch bits of sweet cola. Without hesitation he drew the shovel above her head and hit the original wound again.

"Nein, bitte." Nein, he knew nein, no. She was still shouting. Why wouldn't she just die? Letting out a hefty grunt Guz brought down the shovel one more time onto her head, this time at a slant. It cut into her neck and she screamed. Deliriously rambling away the woman soon hushed before she was finally silent. He knelt down and checked her pulse, her breathing still persisted. Without hesitation, he grabbed her legs and with all his strength he hauled her over to the hole and rolled her in to it. Thud; she had landed hard on top of her Gerhard but facing upwards. He watched as her pupils disappeared into her upper eyelids exposing a red, veined eyeball. Acid rose up his wind pipe. He belched again to relieve the pressure. Why the eyes, why him? As the light caught her he was sure he saw her chest rise. She's dead; she has to be dead, he thought.

Shovelling the earth that he had earlier stacked next to the grave, he watched as it began to cover her body. It landed on her middle, her bare legs and her face. She spluttered. He hesitated, staring at the earth splattered body. He heard it again, she spluttered, her hand began to move. She wasn't dead but she wasn't shouting either. As good as? he asked himself. As good as, he answered. Without hesitating he shovelled more earth over the woman. Underneath the grit he was sure he'd heard a whine, a subdued whine. Ignore it, he thought, it didn't happen. Carry on, hurry up, and go to the barbeque.

Filling his head with thoughts of food grilling; the spicy aromas; the oily kebabs being turned; the coolness of the pool; the end of this job. 'They don't always die this hard,' he thought. This was an exception, it wouldn't happen again. He promised himself it would be quicker, more humane next time. He wasn't a savage; this was a means to an end. Maybe next time he could force his imbecile brother Sadik to do the clean-up. He continued to shovel the earth fast, panting with every movement.

Thoughts of hot meat; cold beer; hot aromatic meat. Salivating at those thoughts he began patting the top of the grave down with the shovel. Then, in his mind he saw the meat being cut, still rare; rare like the back of her head. Un-boned, the whiteness of the bone standing out brightly against the bloody meat; cartilage. Bloody, vacant eyes. Dropping the shovel he ran and ran until he'd got away from the grave. His heart was now in his mouth. Was it his heart? Toppling over the side of a mound he fell to the earth on all fours, sweat poured out of him. The meat still lingered; the greasy smell; the bone; the blood. Not just bone and blood but matted gritty hair; matted with congealed blood. He vomited onto the earth, letting all the disgust fall out into a heap beneath him.

His body trembled all over. As he sat up, he wiped the sweat from his brow with his gritty sleeve. With sweat now replaced by grit, he wiped again. As he wiped, the grit scratched into his skin. He whacked the ground, why couldn't he get rid of the dirt? Close by he could hear the water again, he needed to cleanse himself, to cool down, to regain momentum and get home. He stood, then he staggered towards the waterfall. Intoxicated by the moment he eventually reached the water's edge. Icy cold splashes flecked onto his face washing him free of his sins. Kneeling over the edge, he scooped some of the cold water up, drinking it and splashing it over his face, on his clothes and down his front.

In the distance he heard Tarkan singing again. His phone, he had to get back to the car; cover up the grave with some foliage, get the shovel and go. Standing, he admired the beauty of the waterfall for a moment and enjoyed the feel of the cool spray on his face before staggering back towards the car. The sound of the crickets seemed to be all around him, the moon's light barely showing him the way. To the left of the waterfall's peak he was sure he could see an outline, "kara kulak," he whispered to himself; a lynx. The creature's ear was touched by the light from the moon emphasising its points. Then it disappeared as a cloud interrupted the moon's light. Disorientated, Guz tripped on the undergrowth, a thorny stem pierced through his canvas trouser and into his leg. "Shit," he cried. He rubbed his leg and felt wetness gather around the area. He stood still, leaned over and pressed his hand against the wound to stem the blood flow. Appetite now all gone, all he imagined now was the cold beer. Stuff the others; he was going home to his apartment to crack open a beer. Beer and bed; a cure for everything he'd always insisted. He gazed up at the dark sky, the moon was still concealed. Where was he? Where was the car? He hoped Tarkan would sing again soon. He heard rustling all around him; the crickets' chorus became louder. Breathing fast he grabbed hold of the undergrowth, he squeezed hard, feeling for some clue as to how to get out of this predicament. Stop, think logically, he could still hear the water behind him and as long as the water was behind him he was going the right way.

After a tedious trek forward, the cloud had disappeared and through the gaps in the branches he could see the moon glistening off the bonnet of the car. Laughing with relief he hobbled towards the vehicle. Skin still bumpy from the coldness of the water, he hurried to the grave. He snatched the shovel from the ground and finished off by patting the earth down. After wrestling with some stringy undergrowth, he dragged it over the bare earth and placed some leaves over the top followed by a few pine cones and a couple of needled branches.

He grabbed the shovel, ran back to the car and got in the driver's seat. He turned the engine, it spluttered and hissed. He'd left the headlamps on for far too long. He turned it again and once again it spluttered. Wait, he would give it a moment to recharge. Placing his head on the steering wheel, he clenched his fists as he hit the dashboard. How could he have been so stupid leaving the lights on for so long?

Tarkan sang continuously, a phone call. He snatched the phone from the passenger seat.

"He keeps on about what we've got. He wants to talk to you and said your phone isn't on. He keeps mentioning the passports and I told him that we just couldn't find them but I don't think he believes me. You have to get back now and deal with this shit. He's well peeved," Sadik shouted without pausing to breathe.

"But, the car, it won't-" Sadik hung up. Guz smashed his fist onto the steering wheel. He looked at the phone to reveal two missed calls. He would've heard Tarkan; the signal must've dropped as he'd moved about.

Trying again he turned the engine, it spat and spluttered before it fired up. "Yes," he was on his way home. But he didn't want to go to Sadik's, he wanted to go home and drink. Drink to get drunk and drink to sleep. Drink to forget the bone, the eyes and the raw meat; drink to forget Celile and Sadik's betrayal. Their day would come. "I could cut them all out; stuff them all," he whispered. He then shuddered as he thought about the consequences if he got caught by The Boss. As he steered the car down the embankment he was determined to forget all his troubles. He smiled as he imagined opening a bottle of beer. But first he had to get home, quick and call The Boss.

Chapter 2

"Banana boat, ringo, jet ski, date with me?" the young man shouted. Eve smiled as she shook her head and turned away. The tout moved on to a middle aged man who sunbathed on a lounger in front of them. Her head was burning with the mid-afternoon heat and she squinted as she gazed towards the sun's brightness. Wishing she had unpacked her sunglasses before exploring she held her hand horizontally across the top of her eyes and gazed out at the still blue sea in front of her. The water lapped, barely breaking into much of a wave. A couple of ducks swam near the safety rope, a woman yelled before laughing and swimming in another direction.

"We should get back and bag ourselves a good room before the guys get in there," Selina said. A couple of stray blond hair extensions were beginning to stick to her friend's sweaty forehead. Selina lit a cigarette and stood, "Besides, there's someone coming, he'll probably want his five lira or whatever it costs for the sun lounger you're sitting on."

"You're right. I just had to see the sea. It's been a long time since I've been away, in fact it's the first holiday I've had without my parents," she laughed.

"And it won't be the last. Come on Evie," Selina said as she held her hand out to Eve and pulled her up. "We are going to have a fantastic week and it starts with bagging our room and then working our way through all the cocktail menus in Marmaris."

The young Turkish man stopped in front of them. "Massage, I am the best there is. Or Turkish bath, I make your skin glow, ready for the beach, I make you sexy ladies," he grinned. Eve stared at him as she twiddled her fingers, blushed and looked down at her feet.

"I wouldn't mind being given an orgasm by him," Selina whispered as she leaned towards Eve's ear. Eve giggled and slapped her arm. "What? I meant the cocktail." The man smiled as he awaited their answer. "Maybe another day," Selina said as Eve dragged her towards the edge of the thin strip of beach.

"But you want to look beach beautiful," he shouted.

"As I said, maybe tomorrow," Selina called. "You really have to be assertive around here," she smiled, eyes still fixed on the young man. She dropped her nub end on the floor and stood on it. "It really is the hard sell around here. I may take him up on the massage though," she said as she repositioned her breasts in her plunge bra before turning away from the man's distant stare.

They ambled along the bumpy cobbled pavements past an array of restaurants and cafes. The smell of the grill filled the air; rich and meaty. Chefs with open kitchens flipped and plated food, staff called orders and children ran around the tables shouting.

Touts beckoned them over with every step. "Boat trip, first cocktail free, jeep safari, best food in Içmeler, first time in Turkey?" Distracted, Eve stumbled on an upturned cobble and Selina grabbed her arm. Nearly there, she thought as she recognised the Karaoke Bar. They had passed it half an hour ago. She knew then that their villa was only a couple of minutes away.

At the end of the road they saw the little grey house surrounded by the unruly shrubbery and a rickety looking balcony. "How come we couldn't have a villa like that one?" Eve said as she looked at the neighboring villa with its clean white paint, newly stained balconies and its large pool. "Ours looks like it's going to appear on 'Holidays from Hell' one day soon."

"That would cost more than we could afford. One day, I'm coming back and having that one," Selina said pointing to an even grander villa across the road. Eve stopped and leaned up against a wall. Wiping the sweat off her brow she took a couple of deep breaths. Selina had carried on walking, Eve laughed to herself as she heard Selina continue to talk about all that she was going to do one day. A couple passed her and stared. Halting in the middle of the pavement her friend looked back. "What the hell are you playing at? I bet those people thought I was some sort of loon," she cried, eyes watering and laughing, "I'll get my own back tonight."

Selina grabbed Eve's arm and they turned, plunging Eve face first into a fast walking young man. She felt his clammy skin against her arm and cheek, he smelt sweet, like sweat mixed with aftershave. The man held out his hands and smiled. "I so sorry. English?" Eve nodded and the man took a step back. "I see you need a trip. I can do Jeep Safari, cheapest in village. I will do even cheaper for you lovely ladies," he said as he looked into Selina's eyes. "We work from there." He pointed to a small shop front that was shaded by a green canopy.

Outside the window sat a large older man in a white suit and hat playing a game. White Suit shouted at his scrawny opponent in Turkish, but then Scrawny put his hands up and the suited man sat back down. The table was low and positioned either side were two little chairs. Eve wondered how White Suit had managed to sit on the tiny chair without breaking it. A chequers board filled the table's centre and Eve could just about see that the last white had just been taken. "Is he always such a sore loser?" she asked the man.

"Him, oh yes. Take no notice. I'm Mehmet. What are you lovely ladies called?" Eve looked at Selina. Should she answer? Be more assertive she was told. Leaving the response to Selina she waited. Selina didn't respond, she smiled and looked at the young topless man who had so obviously impressed her.

Rolling her eyes, Eve replied. "This is Selina, I'm Eve."

"Jeeps did you say?" Selina said.

"Yes, we do the cheapest around. We can do, just for you or your group, a deal. One whole day with the jeep all for yourselves, can take up to twelve. You can have it, with a barbeque dinner for only sixty British Pounds. I can book you in tomorrow, only ten pounds deposit," Mehmet said as he pulled out a booking pad from the back pocket of his shorts.

"That sounds g-"

"We'll think about it," Eve interrupted. Selina stared at Eve. "What? We can ask the others and let him know later."

"Don't leave it too late, I may not be able to offer you this good deal if you wait too long," he said as he smiled at Selina.

Bang. Chequers flew against the shop window and White Suit stood up. He snatched an envelope from Scrawny and left him sitting alone amongst the turmoil. As he stood he stepped over the upturned table and placed the envelope in his breast pocket. "So you want it? It is good deal." Mehmet asked again. Another bang from across the road, White Suit kicked the little chair over. "Ignore him," Mehmet said. White Suit turned and paced before stopping and staring at Eve. Eve realised she had been staring at him; blushing, she looked away. Out of the corner of her eye she could see the white suit moving away from the shop front, another suited man ran out of the shop and walked three paces behind. White Suit then turned his head to Eve and grinned as he turned the corner. "Well, ladies, I can't do any better than that," Mehmet continued.

"I think you could do much better," replied Selina. She was now playing with her hair, coiling it around her index finger and occasionally pushing up her bra. Eve watched her in action and wondered if she could ever have the allure that Selina had. She looked back at the shop window. Scrawny was bent over picking up the counters that had been strewn across the tiled shop front.

"Excuse me." A veiled lady of about eighty years placed her bony hand on Eve's arm and steered her over to the wall. The lady pulled out several pairs of sunglasses that were attached to a cardboard frame from her bag.

"I don't need any sunglasses, sorry," Eve said as she turned.

"Shh," the woman said as she pulled Eve back and held her finger to her lips. "I see you watching over there," the woman pointed to the shop. As she turned her hearing aid whistled. Drawn to Eve's chest, the woman stared at the little heart necklace that said 'Mum' on it. "You are a mother. From a mother to a mother, you must be careful. Trust what you feel. Things are not always so good. People not always so good."

"I'm sorry?" Eve said.

Scrawny stood and looked across at the woman. Leaning on her stick, she stepped back and spoke. "You are a beautiful girl. You should protect your eyes, you need sunglasses," the woman took out several pairs and began to place them against Eve's eyes. "Only two British Pounds."

"What did you mean before?" Eve asked as she snatched the glasses from her face and placed them back in the old woman's bag.

The woman looked across at Scrawny; he continued cleaning up the mess from the floor. "Nothing. Young girls, you have to be careful. I just say, I am a mother. I look out for you. Remember what I say. Trust what you think. Trust your instincts," the woman said as she hobbled away. Eve leaned up against the wall. What did the old woman mean? White Suit, the stare, the old woman. She needed reality, the last few moments had all seemed bizarre. Even in the midday heat she shuddered.

Selina giggled at something Mehmet had said. Eve moved away from the wall and joined them. "We best go, got loads to do. Remember that room that we have to get back to and bag?" She grabbed Selina's arm and dragged her away.

"I be here later ...... and tomorrow, and the next day. Come see me anytime," Mehmet shouted as he walked across the road back to his stand.

"What are you doing to me?"

"That man," Eve replied as she looked around, White Suit had now gone. She opened the rusty gate and they headed down the uneven cobbles to their front door.

"Yes, he was really nice and you blew my chances," Selina shouted.

"Not him, the angry one in his shop window, the one in the white suit. Did you see the way he left? He stared me out." Eve shook as she banged hard on the heavy wooden door. She heard footsteps coming down the stairs.

"I think you're just being paranoid. He was probably eyeing you up," Selina replied.

"Whatever, it was a bit weird. Then the old woman said I should trust my instincts or something odd."

Selina grabbed both of Eve's shoulders and looked her in the eye. "It was just her patter. It was nothing. Listen to someone who comes on holidays more than you. Loosen up. We're going to have the best time. The best. I mean it."

The door opened. Ryan stood there with his tee-shirt slung over his pale shoulders and his shorts hanging low. Rachel walked past him and carried on up the stairs. "I see you're last to get a bedroom. I think you're both sharing the couch. It's okay, at least you'll get some pricks this holiday, from the dodgy springs in that sofa bed," he said as he walked away.

"Why the hell did he have to come? Knob," Selina said. "I'm not having it. I know he's my brother but I'm losing the will to live with him being around. He hasn't even paid me back for his share of the villa yet and he thinks he's bagging a bedroom all for himself. No way, that one is ours." Selina stomped up the stairs and a few seconds later Ryan's rucksack flew down. Eve jolted to the left missing the impact of the bag before it landed on the floor with a thud. "If that couch is so full of pricks, you can join them. You'll be right at home," Selina shouted as she stomped in her wedges down the stairs.

"Whatever Sis. You know you love me really," he called from the kitchen.

"Yeah right," she replied.

Eve grabbed her case that was leaned up against the far wall and followed Selina upstairs.

Their room overlooked the main road that they had just strolled down. It was now bustling with tourists. From her window she could see Scrawny approach Mehmet. He appeared to push him, shout and get into a car before driving off. Maybe she was a bit paranoid. They were probably all family. A few seconds ago, she had witnessed how family could drive you insane with anger. If Selina and Ryan were anything to go by, insanity should follow shortly. She could see Selina smacking him one before the week was out.

Smiling, she sat down and lay on the bed. The floor was dusty, the windows were cobwebbed in the corners and the bed, well that was lumpy too but she was on holiday; for the first time in her adult life, she was abroad. She lay with closed eyes, listening to children shouting and cars passing by. Horns tooted every few seconds.

"I hope you're not thinking of going to sleep, we're getting something to eat then going out on the town. You are so going to have a good time tonight," Selina said as she walked to the window.

"Look at him, such a perfect example of the male species. Be great to catch up with him again."

Eve walked over to Selina and linked arms with her. "Just be careful, trust what you feel." She found herself paraphrasing the old woman's words. She watched Mehmet sit behind his stand and stare down at the floor as potential customers walked by.

Chapter 3

Eve stood in her underwear as she observed herself in the bathroom mirror. Her previously infected caesarean scar was showing just above her knicker line. It brought back memories of the pain from the wound, then worse memories of not having the strength to comfort her new born son. It also screamed shame, the shame of her pregnancy that her family felt and in turn had bestowed upon her. The door knocked, she grabbed her knickers and stretched them over the thick scar line, covering as much of it as she could.

"Who is it?" she called as she grabbed a towel and held it against her body.

"It's me," Kevin said. "The other four are waiting downstairs."

"I'll be there in a minute." She heard Kevin walk down the stairs. On the toilet, folded, were her cropped jeans and a tight black dress. She slipped the dress over her head which ruffled her loosely pinned up tresses. Strands of sandy hair fell over her face; she clipped them back before zipping up the dress. Turning sideways to the mirror, she could see a slight tummy bulge, her pre-pregnancy size ten figure had never returned, not even after four years. Not a huge bulge but noticeable side on, it would definitely be seen when standing next to Selina. Unzipping the dress, she began to tug it back over her head and the door knocked again.

"Eve, we're waiting for you. If you hadn't conked out we'd be there by now," shouted Selina.

"Sorry, I'm struggling with this dress. I'm just going to put my jeans on and I'll be down. Two minutes, I promise."

"You dare take that dress off Evie," Selina called as she barged in. Eve grabbed the dress and pulled it back over her head and held her hand across her stomach. "That dress looks great on you. You're not coming out in those old jeans you always wear." Her friend stood behind her and pulled up the zip. She then unclipped Eve's hair and ruffled it up into a frizzy mess before spraying it into place. "There, now you look like you're going out, come on, let's go it's nearly ten o clock," she smiled as she walked away. Eve grabbed her bag off the bed, put the stilettos on that Selina had left for her to wear and walked towards the stairs. Wearing shoes so high wasn't as bad as she remembered.

As Eve's legs reached the step where the rest of the party could see, Ryan let out a whistle. "Ooh, Miss Prim has legs," he shouted.

"Leave it out," Kevin replied.

"Although she's not prim really is she?" he snorted.

"I said; leave it out," Kevin shouted. Ryan laughed back at him; gum making a slapping noise as he chewed, then he placed a wacky drinking hat on his head before leaving the villa.

"I know he's my friend but he can be such a knob sometimes," Kevin said as he shook his head. Eve smiled.

They all started to leave the villa. Eve stepped over the strewn clothes, the open pot of hair gel and half a squashed sandwich before finally reaching the door. The others had gone ahead, Kevin waited at the door with the key. Together they walked in the warm night air away from the beach front towards the bus stop where the others waited. Marmaris and its bright lights were beckoning and the Dolmus had just pulled into the stop. About ten minutes is all it would take and they would be heading for Bar Street in Party Paradise.

*****

Eve slipped off her shoes, now they were pinching. All she could hear was the pounding of several club classics all overlaying each other. To her left was a karaoke bar that was crammed with a group of men singing 'My Way' out of tune and just ahead were the multi-coloured neon lights of Bar Street. The music got louder as she got closer. Selina dragged Rachel across the path towards Bar Club Asylum. Rachel resisted as Selina ran in, preferring to stay outside with the smokers as usual. Her black lipstick was out of place on this street and her heavy facial piercings were being ogled with curiosity by the other smokers.

"I'm going to get me some of this. Get me some beer and watch out girls," shouted Ryan as he dragged Stephen into the bar with him.

"Cool," replied Stephen.

"Well," Kevin said. "Are we going in?"

"I'm not sure, I don't think this is my thing," Eve said as she swallowed. Her stomach twitched and her heart beat picked up in pace. The place was full of hot, sweaty, writhing bodies, dancing to tunes she had not kept up with. These days she was more likely to recognise the tunes from CBeebies rather than Dizzy Rascal.

"I'm not sure it's mine either. Shall we both brave it together?" he asked as he smiled. Eve looked at him. Kevin had a warm smile, one she had taken for granted all the years of knowing him. He held out his hand. She placed her shoes on the floor, stepped into them and took Kevin's hand.

Before she knew it she was then being dragged through the masses, cutting through the wall of people that blocked the way to the bar. "Free shot," shouted a man carrying a tray full of blue drinks in shot glasses. Kevin took two and handed one to Eve. The music blared out and a mass of black and red balloons were released from a suspended net above the dance floor. They floated down and landed on the rampant crowd who responded with shouts and cheers. Eve sipped the tiny sickly drink. Kevin threw his back and grimaced. After been trodden on twice, they reached the bar and joined the queue.

In the distance Eve could see Selina on the dance floor, bottle in one hand, phone in the other. She was writhing hands free with a young man. They danced and he turned; she had found Mehmet. She watched as the young man held Selina around the waist and pulled her close. She moved in closer to him. First she laughed, then smiled and finally she kissed him. "That didn't take long," Eve shouted with a smile on her face. Kevin looked across and smiled back at Eve, she wasn't sure that he had heard. He handed her a vodka and coke and had one himself. Kevin spoke and then shouted, she heard the odd word but could not make out the sentence. Kevin grabbed her arm and once again pulled her through the crowd towards the door. Fresh, warm air hit her. A waft of kebab drifted in the air. The hum of people speaking and the filtered club music is all she heard now. Taking a deep breath, she took a sip of her drink and placed the shot that she had not finished on a table. Rachel stood with several other people laughing and joking. It looked like they were passing around a joint.

"It's better out here," Kevin said.

"Yes, thank you. I don't think I can cope with that many people all in one go," she laughed. The vodka was starting to take effect. She felt her muscles relax and a tipsy warmth flow through her. She hadn't been out and drank for several months so the effect was fast moving. Liking it she took another sip.

"So tell me what you've been up to over the past few years. It seems like forever," Kevin said.

"It has been a few years. Some of it I'd rather forget but here goes," Eve said as she began her story. Kevin looked back, interested in what she had to say.

*****

A couple of hours had passed. Selina had come out for air once before going back into the club for more. Ryan and Stephen were trying their hardest to impress women and Rachel remained with the same group. Pupils now dilated she looked mellow as she sat on a bench with her feet crossed on the table. Others around her lounged about laughing and finding things funny that weren't really funny.

"I've really enjoyed tonight," Kevin said. "We were good friends once. I've missed you, as a friend I mean," his face flushed as he corrected himself.

"I've missed you too. We had such a laugh back then," Eve replied as she slipped down the wall she was leaning against. Three drinks and she was officially tipsy. Kevin caught her and held her up. His arms were warm and firm around her shoulders. He stroked her back as he steadied her. She sunk into his chest, it had been a few years since she'd felt the warmth of a man against her body. The only hugs she'd received had been from Harry, her little boy. She thought of him, on holiday in Florida with his Dad and his wife and she missed him. She always missed him, competing had been difficult. She nuzzled deeper into Kevin's arms and held him close. He then moved away from her creating a distance so that he could look at her.

"You are beautiful, you really are Eve," he said.

She laughed and looked away. "Don't be silly. You're drunk."

"I mean it, and don't you forget it," he said as he smiled back. "And I'm not too drunk." Worried he was going to kiss her Eve loosened their embrace and looked away.

"You haven't had enough then, how about another drink?" She smiled as she held her glass up. Obligingly Kevin took her glass and walked towards the entrance.

"Don't expect me back too soon," he laughed. As he turned to the door Selina crashed into him. She stumbled out of the door and dragged Mehmet towards the end of the street. They stood together against a wall laughing and dodging out of the way of street lamps. "You best keep an eye on her," said Kevin as he entered the club.

Eve leaned on the window ledge and once again removed her shoes. The cobbled path felt soothing against the soles of her feet. She looked at her watch, one in the morning. Still early for the rest of them, but she'd had enough. Selina was now writhing with her back to the wall; she pulled Mehmet close to her and kissed him hard. Eve watched, not knowing whether to get her friend and save her from doing anything embarrassing. She decided to leave it a while. They continued to kiss and grab at each other. Mehmet had his hand down the back of Selina's dress and she held his buttocks hard and pressed him into her. She slipped and then fell to the floor on her bottom. Mehmet helped her back up. They laughed and he stumbled as he helped her up. Both of them were now holding each other up. They began to kiss again then Selina grabbed a clump of Mehmet's hair and pulled him away from her. The young man stepped back and let her walk away. She took two steps away from him and vomited on to her shoes and the floor below.

"Have I missed anything?" Kevin said as he thrust a sparkling drink into Eve's hand; something red with orange slices attached to the side of the glass. She pulled the sparkler out of the fruit and placed it on a table.

"I think I need to take Selina back," smiled Eve. Selina was now leaning up against the wall crying. Mehmet leaned across and stroked her hair.

"Has he upset her?" Kevin asked.

"No, she's just been sick on her new shoes." They placed their drinks on the table. Kevin followed Eve closely behind.

"Come on party girl, we're going to get you back," Eve said.

"I love you Evie. Have I ever told you I love you?" she cried. Mascara smudged around her one eye and her hair extensions stuck across her face by the sticky sweat that she smelled of.

"I love you too and because I love you I'm going to take you back and put you to bed," she smiled. Kevin ran back and picked Eve's shoes up.

"Can I see you again, tomorrow?" Mehmet asked. Eve could tell he was disappointed that Selina was being taken home.

"Yes, I think so. I just need to fix my make-up and my shoes and I'll see you tomorrow," she replied. The man smiled back.

"And I'm not saying that just so you come on a trip in the jeep. I like you. Please remember me tomorrow," Mehmet shouted as they walked away, leaving him standing on the edge of Bar Street.

"We should go on a trip," said Selina, slurring every word. "But boats make me sick," she giggled.

"Don't you think about anything, we'll have you back at the villa in a minute," Eve replied. "Thanks Kevin, for helping me." She lowered Selina into the taxi before standing on her toes and kissing Kevin on the cheek.

Chapter 4

Pushing open the bar door, Guz was hit by the pounding music. He nodded at the barman who in turn nodded at the two men sat at a table. One of those men nodded at the man who stood at the back of the bar next to the DJ. That man disappeared down some stairs behind the DJ's box. Where was The Boss?

Guz looked back at Sadik. His brother's smaller frame had been concealed by his heftier frame, he grabbed Sadik's arm and pulled him along. Clutching his leather satchel, he took the walk along the bar floor. With every step, his shoes stuck to the carpet. If he could hear them over the music, he was sure they would be making a squelch noise. He inhaled the smell of beer, what he wouldn't do for a beer right now. His throat became constricted by his collar; he loosened it and cleared his throat. As he approached the mid way of the walk, drunken eyes turned and glared. Mostly men; well dressed men. As they approached the DJ's booth the man reappeared from the room downstairs. He waved them over. Guz swallowed hard as he followed. He didn't look at Sadik, didn't want to have an exchange of fearful looks. This gang knew fear, sensed it before you even knew you yourself were fearful. He was sure that every man he'd just walked past had smelt his fear.

As he got to the top of the wooden narrow staircase he lifted his arms away from his body to allow his arm pits to breathe. He hoped that his shirt was not one of those that showed sweat patches.

The man leading them was about six feet tall. As Guz followed he looked up and faced the back of his head which exposed a large bald patch, like that on a monk. It seemed unusual as the man only looked like he was in his mid twenties. He wore a black vest and had a muscular frame that stretched the material over his torso showing off his muscular frame. A young man with strength and speed was a better match than Guz's lager fuelled lazy body. He was still in pain from all the digging he had done the other night.

As they approached the bottom of the stairs, the light became more subdued. The portable lights that were hooked onto the brick wall flickered and barely lit up the next few steps. The balding man stopped when he reached the bottom of the steps causing Guz to bump into him, in turn Sadik bumped into Guz. Neither one of them complained. He led them down a dark corridor before turning to face them.

"He is in that room," the man with the bald patch said. "Just knock and wait." The man squeezed past Guz and Sadik maintaining eye contact all the time. So narrow was the passageway, Guz felt the man's solid body squash his own soft body against the wall. Once he had passed both men, the balding man walked backwards, maintaining his watch over the pair. As he reached the end of the small corridor he grinned before the lights clicked off. The only light they could now see was the light coming from under the door of The Boss's room.

The base from the disco thumped above them. Guz looked at Sadik, he knew his brother was looking at him but he couldn't see his expression through the darkness. He hoped that Sadik was keeping his nerves in check but he could smell his brother's sweat and knew from the pungency that his nerves weren't holding up.

It was always a different place for the meeting; a previous one had even been held in a public street at their stand. Other meetings had been in the library, but this one had taken him by surprise. He had always been aware that this was one of the bars The Boss operated from but he'd always hoped that he'd never have to come. "Remember, don't piss him off," Guz whispered to Sadik as they approached the door. An aura of light framed the door's outer edges almost creating a holy looking glow but Guz knew that there was nothing holy about the man who sat beyond that door. Guz took a deep breath, cleared his throat and knocked once. There was no answer. "Shall I knock again?" asked Guz.

"You said not to piss him off," Sadik said.

"I know but maybe he didn't hear." Clutching the satchel close to his chest, Guz knocked once more, louder this time. The door opened inwards with a force that almost sucked Guz into the room.

"I heard you the first time," the man bellowed as he slammed the door in their faces. Heart beating hard, Guz turned back to Sadik who was leaning against the wall. They stood in the dark and waited. It was all they could do. Behind the door Guz heard voices saying words he couldn't quite make out. The Boss shouted something about inefficiency before slamming his hand onto what sounded like a table. Beginning to shake, Guz joined Sadik in using the wall for support. Sweat began to pour down his face; it trickled over his nose and over his cracked lips. He licked them; the sweat left a salty taste in his mouth. He wiped his brow and took a deep breath.

"How long do you think we should wait?" Sadik whispered.

"As long as he wants us to, you idiot," replied Guz as he punched Sadik's arm.

"Ouch. I was only asking," he said as he rubbed his arm.

The room went quiet. "Shush," Guz whispered.

"You can both enter," said the gaunt assistant as he opened the door and pointed the way with his revolver. The man stood at Guz's height and was of a small build, scrawny in appearance. They had met on several occasions in the past, Guz never knew his name, he didn't know The Boss's name either. They weren't from around this region, preferring to travel to where business took them.

The battery powered light shone in Guz's direction causing him to squint. He could make out The Boss's signature white suit; he could also make out The Boss's signature icy glare from his hard piggy eyes. To his right, the scrawny man leaned up against some old metal filing cabinets; the rest of the room was filled with stock. Crates of beer and alcopops lined the back wall. Staring at Sadik and Guz, The Boss opened a bottle of Raki and poured it over a glass of ice before taking a large swig. Guz winced; he hadn't even put any water in the drink as a mixer for the Raki. The boss slammed the glass down. "You keep giving me old people. I have orders lined up for young people."

"I'm sorry," Guz replied. "We will get you some younger ones, I promise."

"The German, she was nearly sixty, disposing of her was your only option. Okay, not old, I am over fifty. But they are old for what I need. If you are not capable, I have others who are," he stared at Guz for what seemed like a minute. "You know what happens if I have no need for you."

Guz nodded. "We can deliver some for you. Tell us what you need and we will get it. We will won't we?" Sadik nodded. The scrawny man used his one hand to rub his facial stubble and the other to aim the gun. First at Guz's head and then across to Sadik's. Guz opened his mouth to talk, to plead, even beg if it came to it, but the words were stuck. He could still hear the thudding base above. If they were wasted here no-one would ever know. It's not like they would be missed.

Guz had been living under the radar since he had left his home town of Bursa five years earlier. He knew no-one would look for him. Same with Sadik. Celile would look but she was as guilty as them, they were all guilty. There would be no police, no search no happy ending.

"Bang," the scrawny man shouted, and then he and The Boss both burst into loud laughter. Guz slammed his body into the back of the door, pushing Sadik over as he jerked. Sadik lay there on the floor cowering and shaking.

"What have you got for me in the bag? If it's any good, I'll give you another chance. If not, you can go now and by go, I don't mean walk out and leave. Is that a deal?" The Boss laughed and revealed a few gold teeth at the back of his mouth and a furred tongue. Guz peeled his sweaty body off the back of the door, his shirt now drenched and his forehead once again dripping. There was no point wiping it, he had already revealed his hand. Besides, The Boss was good at games, even when he had a bad hand he always won.

Guz shuffled up to the table leaving Sadik still shaking on the floor. The man appeared to be in his own world, chanting some prayer under his breath. Guz's thoughts flashed to his Celile. What does she get from that coward that he couldn't give? He had to get through this, had to get out once and for all, had to deal with Celile. His brother would be harder though, blood is always harder. Now in a stronger frame of mind, Guz dropped the leather satchel onto the desk and began to undo the buckles.

Out of it he pulled a handful of gold bracelets and necklaces, wedding rings, the Gucci bag and Ilse's and Gerhard's driving licences. He had kept the passports; they would be his perfect escape. At the back of his mind he hoped he was wrong about Sadik and Celile. Ilse's passport could be for Celile if she proved herself to be worthy.

The Boss picked up the gold and examined it closer. Out of the drawer he pulled out some scales and placed the items on them. "Drivers licence? If you've searched everything they have, why do I not have passports?" The Boss stared at Guz. Guz began to tremble and looked away. "You shouldn't be holding things back. Are you holding things back from me? Have I not always given you a fair price?"

Guz nodded. "I only found these things. I swear, we looked really hard and this is all we could get hold of." He clenched his sweaty palms and tensed as he felt the weight of the silence that followed bearing down on his nerves. Maybe holding back the passports had been the wrong thing to do, they certainly weren't worth dying for.

"Right, because I would know if you were holding back on me. You know what happens to people who hold back." The Boss said as he continued to stare.

Guz nodded, praying in the back of his mind that The Boss couldn't tell. He remembered the massacre of the Muğla operation that had done The Boss a bad turn. "I wouldn't hold back. You have been very fair with us." Sadik looked up at Guz and began to shake. Sadik had been there, he hadn't known about the passports though. His brother whimpered on the floor and after a moment he was sat in a puddle.

"Get that fucking dirty mess of a man out of my office," shouted The Boss to Scrawny. The man obliged by dragging Sadik by the hair out of the room and into the corridor before slamming the door again. Scrawny came back in and went back to his post. "He's an embarrassment to you. If you don't fix him up, I'll put a bullet through his head myself. Sit," shouted the Boss.

"I will sort him. Don't worry about him. He gets the job done when he has to and you can trust him. You can trust me, you can trust us both," Guz replied as he wiped his brow and sat on the wooden chair.

The Boss pulled a dirty, red lipstick rimmed glass from the floor and poured another Raki. "Here drink."

"I don't drink Raki on its own."

"When I say drink, you drink. We are going to play a game, a drinking game to celebrate our understanding. We do have an understanding don't we?" He smiled.

"Yes, we do," Guz replied as he downed the Raki. Coughing hard he slammed the glass down and then smiled. There was only one way to play this out, let The Boss lead the game and let The Boss win the game. Scrawny filled his glass up with another shot of Raki; The Boss passed it to him.

"I best pay you. The driver's licence isn't worth that much. Firstly, it's for a woman and secondly she is mature. Not so much in demand. The gold is only nine carat, the gems are cubic zirconia and the bag; well it's a fake. I know because I export them," he laughed as he pulled out some cash from his pocket. "I hope US Dollars are good." Guz nodded. The Boss counted six hundred US Dollars and threw the cash over to Guz's side of the table. "That's your cut. Get me what I really want and you could be a very rich man. Drink."

Guz stared at the pittance he was being paid and knocked back the drink. Had he been selfish in keeping the passports? No, he needed them. Next time he would get girls then he would be paid thousands. He belched; the large undiluted measures were starting to create an uneasy burning in his stomach. "I would love to drink with you all night but I fear I may be ill," he laughed.

"That'll do then, your brothers already pissed on my floor," he laughed. Guz forced out some laughter in response.

"He'll learn to grow some balls," laughed Guz. He was building a rapport with this man and felt certain that he was going to get out alive. The only suffering would be an awful hangover in the morning. "So you're after young passports. I'll get my boy onto it. He is a hit with the young ones, handsome like his Dad," Guz laughed.

"Don't get too carried away," The Boss stopped laughing and stared at Guz. "I need women, young women. Bring them to me intact and you shall be rewarded beyond your wildest dreams."

"But, I thought-"

"Doesn't matter what you thought. I have some extremely wealthy contacts that need women. There is a big demand for young European women. We make on their passports, we make on their gold, we make on their bodies. Just think of it this way, at least you don't have to kill them. You can kill their boyfriends though unless they are young and pretty also," he laughed.

"Well, I err. I think I'd better get back," Guz said. "Get my wreck of a brother home."

"Just remember what I said. Get me what I need and you will be a very wealthy man, there is room here up the top for someone that can prove themselves. Cross me and you won't know what's hit you. You have until the weekend to come up with the goods."

Guz stood and scooped up the money from the desk before placing it in his pocket.

"Thank you," Guz said. Scrawny held the gun up to Guz and The Boss stared at him, his face giving nothing away. The thin man came closer and touched the gun's barrel on Guz's ear. He closed his eyes and he was sure he'd dribbled down the side of his mouth. The smell of the Raki began to overpower his senses, he began to sweat and shake.

"Boo," shouted the scrawny man. He and The Boss laughed hysterically. Guz needed to scream, he needed to exhale hard, he needed to shout, and he needed to be allowed to be alone so he could feel sick. Instead he laughed, he forced himself to laugh. They couldn't see his fear; he laughed as much as he wanted to cry and at that moment the door burst open. A woman who looked to be in her late thirties was pushed into the room. She was dressed in heels, bright red lipstick, a mini skirt and a bikini top. Her hair was a luscious brown. Long, cascading curls fell over her bosom. She staggered as she crossed the threshold.

"Get off me, tell them Boss to get off me," she shouted as she took a drag of her cigarette.

"You heard her," he shouted with a smile. The two men released the woman. "You lot, get out, we've got business to attend to haven't we Sweet?" The woman nodded as she stepped around the urine puddle and walked over to him. She then poured herself a Raki before sitting on The Boss's lap. Guz left, Scrawny followed and closed the door.

"Come on Brother, we have business to attend to," Guz said as he helped his traumatised brother off the floor. And they did have business to attend to. Money for their victims, not killing them but passing them on, this was going to be easier than the others.

The words, 'you can be a very rich man' rang through his ears. He was going to do it, get what he wanted and get out, become Gerhard, learn German and move away and never come back.

Chapter 5

It was only ten but the sun filled the sky with golden beams. Kevin led Eve to the small café opposite their villa and pulled out a seat for her. Sitting, she smiled. She picked up the menu. Was it a full English day or should she opt for something different?

A hot looking black and tan dog lay down on the pavement in front of the cafe and panted. The waiter came out with a bowl of water.

"That's Dolly. We all look after Dolly," he said as he placed the bowl of water in front of the dog and went back into the cafe. Eve stood, walked across to the dog and stroked behind her ears. The panting dog stood, wagged her tail and walked over to the bowl. Eve sat back down and looked back at Kevin who was studying the menu. She watched him as he looked the list up and down, his square rimmed glasses were perched low on his nose. There was something striking about his features; delicate, yet masculine. His lightly freckled face was smooth shaven and she caught the scent of his musky aftershave as he looked back up at her. Her heart beat a little quicker, had he noticed her looking? "I think I'll have the Turkish Breakfast," she said with a short burst of laughter.

Kevin placed the menu onto the side of the table, took off his glasses and placed them in his top pocket. "I think I'll go with one of them too, be nice to try something different." He nodded to the waiter who came over and took their orders.

They both sat and gazed at everything except each other. Eve began to pick her thumb nail; Kevin pretended to watch passers-by. Then, after a moment, the silence was broken. Kevin had started asking a question as Eve had started to comment on how wonderful the weather was. They both laughed.

"So what's life like for you now, you know with little Harry?" he asked.

"Routine, it has to be very routine. But he's four now so it's getting easier. He's starting school this September. He is really good I never have any problems with him, he's obsessed with boats," she blurted out. "I'm sorry," she replied realising that she may be boring him.

"Don't be sorry. Anyway, he sounds lovely. How come I haven't met him yet?" Kevin smiled.

"I didn't think you'd....." she paused and looked down. "We haven't spoken for such a long time."

"Well I am and I would love too. Is that a date?"

"Yes, I guess it is. Definitely." Eve replied.

"Great," he paused. He picked up his knife and began to rub it with a paper napkin. "What happened Eve? We used to be really good friends. I've missed you all these years," he said. This time his smile had vanished and had been replaced by a look of sadness. He took his glasses back out of his pocket and put them back on. This time he pushed them as far up against his eyes as he could and looked away.

"I'm sorry. I wanted to contact you but I thought ..., so many things had happened and I didn't think you'd want to speak to me." She placed her hand on the table and began to fiddle with her napkin as she looked down. "I screwed up Kevin. I was ashamed. I thought it was best if I just made myself scarce for a few years. My mother wasn't happy and I was having a load of hassle from his wife."

"His wife?"

"Yes, I fell for the charms of the married man as the whole world seems to know. Oh my marriage is over; oh I'm only sharing the house with her whilst the divorce comes through. I believed all the stories, every last one of them. He made me feel wonderful Kevin, but it was all a lie and I was stupid. I have been stupid. I don't even know why I fell for him, I'm not even sure I did. I just fell for the thought of him and the way he made me feel. Let's just say that I was young and stupid and leave it at that. Do you hate me?"

"I don't hate you; I just wished it had been me. I wouldn't have let you down," he said as he placed his warm hand over Eve's fiddling fingers.

"You never said anything; I thought you just wanted to be friends."

"I could see you were drifting away from me. Was scared you'd reject me." Eve placed her other hand over his and she could feel his soft skin. She thought of all their teen years, when he was her all, her best friend, her confidante. What had gone wrong? If only she had read Kevin's signals. A tear began to burst from the corner of her eye. How hard she'd had it, fighting for time with Harry. Dealing with a liar, a womaniser who'd humiliated not only her but the wife he had never left.

"I was so stupid," she blurted out with a snivel.

Kevin stood up, walked around to her side of the table, knelt down and placed his arms around her. "You were young, naïve. He took advantage of that. Come on, we're on holiday. I didn't mean to upset you," he said as he rubbed her shoulder and looked at her.

She looked back at him. Those beautiful warm eyes, she touched his face and he moved closer to her. She kissed him hard and he responded. The heat pounded down on her back, she could feel it burning into the nape of her neck but it somehow felt sensual. It was then she knew that being with Kevin felt right. If a kiss could tell then this kiss had just told. It told her that he was the one. It happened so naturally, no awkwardness, no fumbling and no nerves. Just a burning need in all ways for this wonderful man who was kneeling before her. She pulled away and hoped that he had felt the same. Kevin looked at her, confused but pleased. He moved back a little. He gazed at her as she looked at him. "I've missed you," she whispered. She held his hand and smiled. With his other hand he stroked her cheek, eyes still on hers.

"Have I missed anything?" Selina asked as she and Rachel approached. Kevin stood and walked back to his side of the table. As they joined them the waiter served their breakfasts.

"No, we were just reminiscing," Eve replied.

"Yeah right! Two coffees please. A strong one for the invalid," Rachel said to the waiter. Selina fell into the chair next to Kevin and slumped over the table, head on hands. Eve began to cut into her boiled egg.

"I can't sit here," Selina said as she stood and sat at the next table. "Urgh. What happened to me last night?"

"You had a bit too much," Eve laughed. "Sure you don't want some of my egg?" Selina pulled down her sunglasses and peered over the top of them with her glassy half closed eyes.

"Do I look like I need an egg Evie?" she said. Rachel lit up a cigarette, once again Selina moved tables. "Do you have to?"

Rachel laughed then puffed away. Their coffees arrived and Selina took a few sips before placing the cup back on the table and slumping forward once again.

"Anyway, what are we doing today?" Eve asked as she tucked into the olives and tomatoes.

"What would you like to do?" Kevin asked.

"Nothing," groaned Selina.

A wolf whistle made Selina sit up to attention despite her hung over state. Mehmet was approaching up the path behind her. His flip flops slapped onto the ground with every step. He wore khaki shorts with a white vest slung over his shoulder. "Hello, beautiful lady," he called as he approached Selina's table. She took her glasses off, revealing her squinting puffy eyes and no make-up. Without hesitation he placed his arm around her and kissed her on both cheeks. "You look beautiful."

Eve laughed at Kevin. Although she hoped that Mehmet thought something of Selina, he was more likely just after a short holiday fling with this week's woman and Selina was hot. She was having a bad morning but she scrubbed up to be one of the best and Mehmet had spotted that. "What are you lovely people doing today in this beautiful sunshine?" he asked.

"We were just talking about that weren't we?" Eve replied. The others nodded. Rachel took a large drag of her cigarette and blew circles of smoke as she fiddled with her nose ring.

"Well how about jeep safari, I can do a good deal for you."

"I don't think so. Look at her, she wouldn't last five minutes in a jeep," Rachel said.

"I can book you in for tomorrow."

"We'll let you know if that's okay with you." Rachel replied with a false smile.

"Okay, I'll leave you lovely people to it. I may see you about later," he said as he kissed Selina on the cheek and left. She stroked his hair with her shaky hand.

"Some people just don't know when to give the sales patter a rest," Rachel said as she stubbed her nub end out.

"You know, he was only being nice. You should try it some time." Selina replied as she struggled with her hoarse voice.

"He was just trying to sell. Should I be nice like you are, should I shag him?" Rachel said as she took her last cigarette out of the box.

"Now now you pair. Let's try and have a nice time," Eve interrupted.

"I'm going back to the villa my head is killing and that miserable cow is making it worse," Selina shouted as she stood and stomped off.

Rachel laughed and lit the cigarette. "I think I'll go get some more fags, have a good day all." They watched as Rachel's black shorts and vest top disappeared around a corner.

"Well that leaves me and you," Kevin said. "I'm going to take you out for a fun day you'll never forget." He placed a couple of notes on the table, put his glasses back in his breast pocket, grabbed Eve's hand and led her towards the sea front.

"Where are you taking me?" she yelled, unable to control her laughter.

"I hope you have your swim wear on under those shorts."

"I don't actually. What are you doing to me?"

"You're going to get your shorts very, very wet," he laughed as he continued to lead her to the sea front. "Two on a banana boat please," he said to a man in a beachside hut as he emptied the last of the cash in his pocket over.

"No, I can't. I'm not good at swimming," Eve shouted, her smile disappearing.

"I am, got all my badges at school, besides you get a life jacket," he said as the man led them to the front.

"Please hold my bag," Eve said as she passed the man her small bag. Kevin flung his cash and glasses into her open bag before zipping it up. The man gave it to his assistant behind the counter and nodded.

Before she knew it she was positioned on a banana boat that was being revved up. Without notice it shot from the shore and into the blue sea ahead. She felt the cool spray on her legs. Her stomach flipped with excitement, they whizzed in a circular motion, afraid she'd fall she grabbed hold of Kevin's waist and held onto him.

"I said it would be fun," he yelled. Eve couldn't stop laughing. She looked back at the beach; they had come a long way. Sun loungers were dotted along the golden coast like dolls house furniture. A corner took her by surprise; both she and Kevin were flung off the boat and into the cool sea. She fell under the water's surface and held her breath, trying hard not to inhale a mouthful of sea water. In an instant she floated to the surface. Water dripped down her face, she was met by Kevin. She smiled; she had never had so much fun.

Flinging her hands around his neck she held him close and whispered, "Thank you." He held her and nuzzled into her neck. Bobbing on the water's surface they embraced hard and long, she turned her head to kiss him, he kissed her back. Gentle salty kisses that tasted so good. He had fuelled a feeling in her she hadn't felt for such a long time. Her body felt alive, desiring his every touch. His hands caressed her back, she wanted more; she wanted his hands all over her body. She kissed him harder and pushed her body into his. He smelled so good, he felt so good and she needed him.

"You two, you need to get back on the boat. I have six minutes to get you back to the coast." The man operating the boat said. Eve looked up at him with a flushed face and smiled. Kevin still looked at her, she looked at him. He kissed her on the cheek and smiled as he helped her back onto the boat. She held onto Kevin but not out of fear, to touch him. She placed her small hand up the front of his life jacket, under his tee-shirt and felt him. His naval first; then the bottom of his chest.

The boat slowed down. As it reached the shore she laid her head on his shoulder taking in the subtle fragrance of his shampoo, she closed her eyes and hoped that this was not some holiday thing, that whatever was happening to her was more. She wanted him forever, only time would tell if that was to be. For now she was willing to open her heart to him, try again in love.

The boat reached the shore and stopped. He got off and held his hand out to her; she took his and followed him. The man passed Eve her bag as they left the beach. Two drenched bodies walking along the beach heading back to the villa. They never spoke, there were no words to say. Kevin opened the door; they held their breath and tip-toed past Ryan and Stephen who were still fast asleep on the sofa bed. He placed his index finger over his mouth "Shh," he whispered. She smiled as they tip-toed up the stairs. They crept past her and Selina's room, past Rachel's little box room and through the door into his room.

She sat on his bed feeling awkward. She had no protection and did she want to expose her post child body to him? Then she noticed a pack of condoms on top of his toiletry bag. All the water from her clothes soaked into his bed, she stood. "Sorry," she whispered.

"It's okay," he said as he kissed her. She allowed his kisses to wander, enjoying every touch, every caress. He placed his hands over her front and began to lift her tee-shirt up.

She grabbed his hands and pulled them away. "I'm so sorry," he said. "I thought, well, I hoped."

"It's not you," Eve replied. "I haven't shown this body to anyone since having Harry. Things aren't what they used to be."

"I understand Eve, you've had a child. I still think you're beautiful."

She lifted up her tee-shirt to expose the mangled caesarean scar. "I had an infection when he was born, we both came close to death," she said as she began to cry. Kevin knelt down and traced his finger along the scarred flesh and kissed it gently.

"That just adds to your beauty." She stroked his fair hair then wiped her eyes dry. He stood, pulled her tee-shirt back down and kissed her. "Shall we get changed and go out?" He turned towards the wardrobe.

She grabbed his arm. He turned and she kissed him hard, she pulled him close to her and tugged at his tee-shirt. It wouldn't move; the water had caused it to stick to his body. He stood back and lifted it over his head and dropped it to the ground. She traced her fingers through his chest hair, feeling his goose bumped skin. She took her tee-shirt off, he his shorts, she hers.

They got into his bed, dampening the sheets with their clammy wet bodies. He kissed her neck and moved down towards her breasts. He undid her bra, as he embraced her she heard it drop onto the marble floor. A warm breeze floated by and caused all her senses to come alive. She could hear the birds singing outside; she could feel the wetness of their bodies and enjoyed the smell of his masculine fragrance.

His gentle kisses now brushed her nipples and they responded immediately. She could feel him harden above her, pushing him away she took her pants off and dropped them to the floor. She wanted him now like she'd never wanted anything in her life. But he wouldn't give it. He continued to caress her, she tried to pull him close but he moved away and smiled.

His hand reached her and his fingers caressed her, he was so gentle but she needed him in her, she needed him hard. She had never felt a wanting like this. Her previous relationship had been dominated by a lie, used for his pleasure without a regard for hers. But this was different, she trusted Kevin, dare she say it but she now realised she had always loved him and now she needed him. She ached for him to be in her. Her body arched as she groaned with pleasure. She saw the condom wrapper fall to the floor.

He lay on top of her lifting his upper body up with his arms so that he could see into her eyes. She looked back at him; that look made her body tingle. His arms so strong, she hadn't realised he was so strong. She traced his muscular frame and placed her hands behind his neck. Leaning up to kiss him, he responded, this time hard and desperate. Their tongues in and out of each other's mouths. He moved on top of her, rubbing himself hard over her, increasing her desire for him. Then he went in, she felt it, like sparks building up. So furious, so desperate they clinched together, moving hard and fast. Sweating they grasped for each other not being able to touch enough of each other's bodies. He rubbed his one hand all over her body, her hair, her breasts then her buttocks and he penetrated her hard. She could not wait any longer, the sparks were now alight. He the same, they groaned not holding back and taking everything they could. It was everything she had hoped it would be.

He moved to her side and traced his fingers over her cheeks and then flopped onto his back. She curled up on her side and placed her head on his chest. They lay there in the heat, spent and happy. No words to say, no regrets and so natural. He placed his arm over her shoulder and kissed her head. She felt this overwhelming sense of belonging for the first time in her life and smiled to herself.

Chapter 6

Eve crept down the stairs then passed the kitchen. Rachel and Ryan were sat on the sofa bed, smoking with their feet up on the coffee table. She could smell the sweet air as they exhaled. Ryan turned; his dilated pupils stared into hers. "Where's lover boy?" he said before bursting into fits of laughter. "Miss Prim is the first to get some." Rachel slapped him hard on the arm. "What?" then they both laughed. Stephen then entered with a clunking bag containing beer. Eve shook her head and continued to the garden.

  She pulled her mobile out of her pocket and turned it on before selecting Justin. It rang several times but there was no answer, straight to voicemail. "I'll try again in a minute; I'd love to talk to Harry just for a couple of minutes." Throwing the phone onto the sun lounger she sat beside it. He never answered the phone on first call; it was as if he could sense her desperation to speak to Harry. She thought about the last time she had him to stay, the previous weekend. After breaking up from work for the summer she celebrated by taking him to the Safari Park. She smiled at the thought of the fun they'd had, his delight at seeing the animals, especially the tiger. She wiped her eyes and picked the phone back up and redialled.

"Hello," Justin whispered.

"Hello, it's me. Can I speak to Harry?"

"He's busy at the moment with Ellen. She's just getting him on the swings besides we're on our holiday as well. You're having him next weekend."

Eve wept silently thinking of that woman with her son and cursed herself for not fighting harder for full custody. But things had not been straight forward, after her parents rejection, the infection and the post natal depression it had been the right decision at the time. 'Justin has the good job, Justin has the good house, Justin has the car,' she could hear them all still saying these things to her. No match for the eighteen year old classroom assistant who still lived with her parents at the time. She had sat by whilst Harry was taken from her without the energy to fight. As far as Harry was concerned Ellen was also his mummy too, his Monday to Friday mummy. She burst into tears and snivelled down the phone, just one little chat would help fill the void for a while. "Please, I only want to see how he is, I miss him. You have him all the time and you don't know how hard it is for me not being with him."

He paused as if contemplating her request. "Okay, I'll call him. Harry, it's Mummy Eve."

Mummy Eve, that's what she'd been reduced to. Not Mummy, the one and only, exclusive; but Mummy Eve. In the background, she could hear his tiny feet running.

"Watch you don't fall over your lace," she heard Ellen call.

"Say hello to Mummy Eve," Justin said as he passed the phone to Harry.

"Hello Mummy Eve, what are you doing?" he asked in his child like voice. "I've been to a park and I've been to Disneyland

and I've seen a show with dolphins. We went on a boat yesterday and saw an alligator," he yelled.

"Oh that's lovely Sweetie. I'm so glad you're having a wonderful time." She smiled as she loved to hear his happy voice but deep down she wished the good times were being had with her.

"Daddy and Mummy Ellen are taking me to a fun castle later."

"Oh," replied Eve. Her eyes welled up once again and a tear trickled down her cheek. "I miss you Sweetie and next weekend when we have Mummy and Harry time, we are going to have so much fun. We'll build a den in the garden and make mud pies."

"Yay. Mud pies!" She heard him shout. Wiping her eyes she exhaled. She knew how to have fun with Harry; it wasn't all about taking him to places and buying him things but having real fun. She made it her mission to be the best Mummy Eve she could be and imprint the fondest of memories into his mind. "Can you bring me some shells home? There are no shells here."

"Of course I can Sweetie. I'll go and collect you some nice ones."

"I have to go now, Daddy wants his phone back."

"Okay. Just remember, I love you loads and I miss you always and be a good boy."

"He's back on the swing, kids ay," Justin said. "Anyway, I'll see you a week Friday at six when you collect him. Don't be late as we're going out." With that he hung up. Eve clutched the phone and held it to her chest, a week Friday was such a long time.

Eve sat back on the sun lounger and gazed into the pool. Bits of tree floated on the surface, she watched the twigs float back and forth as the breeze channelled them with every change in wind direction. They had started to gather up the one end, she watched how the leaves joined the little twig and leaf pile. Hands touched her shoulder; she flinched and turned, "Kevin."

"I wondered where you were, I woke and you were gone. You don't regret-"

"No," she interrupted. "I don't regret anything," she stood and kissed him.

"It's just, have you been crying?"

Eve looked down; all the emotions she had felt a few moments ago welled back up and burst out of her. She wept as Kevin held her. "What's happened?"

"I just spoke to Harry, that's all. I miss him."

"Look, we are going to have a good holiday. Harry wouldn't want you to be upset."

"I know. You're right. Will you come with me to collect some shells from the beach for him?" she smiled.

"I would love to. I'm the shell expert. I didn't see many shells earlier though; we'll get some from somewhere." He smiled as he held his hand out to her. She took his hand; he then kissed her as he brushed the stray hairs off her face. "There, beautiful."

Chapter 7

Looking up towards the brightness of the early afternoon sun Guz could see two turtle doves resting on a branch. They reminded him of how he and Celile used to be together. He remembered the first time he saw her several months after his divorce. He drove the pick-up van at the farm; she picked the apples. Leaning up to reach them in her ripped cropped jeans and her blue headscarf, he knew it was love. Fifteen years his junior he didn't think he stood a chance but they then spent many a hot afternoon together, engaged in meaningful conversation. Then, just like in a romance story, they became inseparable. They had reached levels of passion he never knew were possible. Her never-ending energy for making love and for pampering him made him feel like he'd been reborn. She also got on well with Sadik and Mehmet which is all he could've asked for. The three most important people in his life had all been happy together.

Guz smiled. They were some of his fondest memories; he couldn't believe how lucky he had been back then and how it was all turning sour. He mopped his brow with the bottom of his tee-shirt, forty two degrees the weather report had claimed it would be today. "Celile, can you bring me the water?" he called.

"Get it yourself, you fat fuck," she replied as she meandered towards the waterfall. Charming as always, he looked down at his belly. He had gone a bit overboard with the fast food lately, he held his stomach in but he couldn't sustain it; he exhaled.

He remembered a time when she would have done anything. 'Oblige me with a cool glass of beer Celile; a quick sandwich with the pickles arranged just the way I like them and a blow job while you're there.' These days he had to settle for insults and occasional drunken sex of which he inevitably struggled to manage. Since she'd moved out into a rented room he rarely managed to get her to stay with him but she always 'stayed' with him. Claiming they were good for each other and she couldn't live with him. He knew the truth, it was Sadik.

Why didn't she call an end to the relationship? Guz thought. It wasn't his charm, or his looks or his loving nature. Maybe it was necessity; or the business. She loved money; or was it the familiarity or the arguments? That woman certainly got off on an argument. You could see the pleasure in her eyes every time she spurned anger. In fact, he recalled some of their best sex following a row. Maybe her calling him a 'fat fuck' wasn't a bad thing. He felt his pants tighten as he became more turned on. He took his tee-shirt off and wiped his head with it again. Without warning a pine cone fell from the trees above and clipped his nose. He stamped on it then kicked the mangled cone towards Celile. She turned her head as it skimmed the ground behind her, stared at him and turned back.

In the distance, he could see her with her green sun dress hitched up to her waist and her legs dangling into the pool. "This is the spot; we'll set up here next time. I don't know why you chose to stay back there before, besides," she said as she placed her head in her hands, "we need to spread them out a bit. It doesn't feel right to use the same area twice." There it was, decision taken.

He analysed how much space there was, they would set up the barbeque to the left. There was enough room for several people in the clearing. It was a good flat strip of land; next to a beautiful pool which was just a little way down from the waterfall. Behind him, he visualised the tourists trying to make their escape but him and Sadik knew this land. They had done their homework, spent the closed season researching the area, finding all the little hiding places. They had picked this area as it was approximately six miles to the nearest village and then there were only a handful of spaced out farms. The nearest main road was at least two miles away and even then not many cars frequented it, two, maybe three a day. He was confident they could hunt anything down in this area. He was also aware that after completing three jobs already on this patch that they would have to move downstream after the next job; that was if he hadn't made his escape before then.

"I verlassen bald," he laughed.

"I leave soon" he whispered, pleased with how much German he'd picked up in the past few days.

"Is it okay?" Celile asked.

"It will do." Guz had chosen their last location as he'd preferred the coolness of the forest, it helped a bit when the temperatures were this high but Celile never got flustered with the heat and she could never understand his reasoning. He could still stand back and get under the trees. He grinned; Sadik could be in charge of the barbeque for a change. He and Celile want to be together; they can sweat like pigs and do the cooking. He would let the sun loving tourists get their fill of the intense heat, maybe that and the alcohol would make them too dopey to put up a fight which would make it easier for him. And he knew they were close to a bite, he had tasked his boy to come on board and entice some young ones. How his boy would do on his first job, he had no idea.

The Boss wanted people, attractive young people and he was getting close. Maybe at the end of it all; he could do a deal for Celile.

He laughed at the rhyme. "Deal for Celile," he whispered under his breath. The two timing cow could get what she deserved, he laughed.

He had bussed Mehmet in to help a week ago. He wasn't sure how he would take it when he found out what he really had to do; but he knew he could rely upon him. He knew Mehmet had hit upon hard times and needed the money; this operation would be perfect for him. He too could make his fortune in a season and move away, start a new life. Maybe become Gerhard's friend and come away with his Dad. Time would tell how he would react when it came to doing the 'real' job. The job he hadn't fully told him about. He'd led Mehmet to believe that they were robbing the tourists' accommodation while they were out for the day. "No old or ugly ones," Guz had warned him. He questioned why but Guz knew he could get away with giving very little away. "No reason Son, just want something pretty to look at in a bikini."

With Celile's back still facing him, she made circular shapes with her legs in the water, how he longed to just sit beside her and slip into the pool for a dip. Then he thought of Sadik with his slimy hands and tongue all over her. He would never have believed it but he had saw them kissing when they thought they were alone.

"Celile," she looked up with her chocolate brown eyes and exposed her plunging neckline. Her glossy brown hair fell to the back of her waist cascading over her velvet latte coloured skin. "You would never lie to me would you?"

"No, why would I lie to you?"

"It's just, you and Sadik. You're always together."

"Not this again," she shouted as she lifted her feet out of the water and stood before walking back towards the car. "I don't want to listen to this crap anymore. How many times have we had this conversation?"

Guz picked up the bottle of water that she had left, he took a long swig. Warm, he grimaced. What he wouldn't do for a cold drink. Barefoot, she positioned her feet so as not to prick them with fallen pine needles or cut them on rocks. "What is it you want?" he asked.

"I don't know. Why complicate things. We have a good thing going here. I don't owe you anything after the way you've been. In fact you're lucky I stick around at all. You'd treat a dog better," she yelled.

"Like hell. I do all this for you so you can have things, so you can be happy. Or do you want to work on some slave farm picking fruit for the rest of your life because that's where you came from."

"Thanks for reminding me. And what you've got me into isn't worse? You make it sound like you're my saviour, some kind of God. Look at me now, I steal, burgle, kill and I can't quit, we all know the consequences of not doing what The Boss wants. It's all your fault I'm living this miserable existence. Send me back to the fruit farm." She began to walk away getting ever closer to the car.

"You bitch," he yelled as he chased after her. He'd started doing all these 'jobs' to make a better life for them, hoped she would change her mind about marriage and children one day. But his plans to go it alone were now confirmed, he would play out this charade for his deceitful swine of a brother and his bitch of a girlfriend. When it was all over Sadik could have her, they could have each other. He grabbed her arm and swung her around to face him. "I wanted a better life for us, but now I couldn't care less you lying little bitch," he shouted.

She slapped him hard across the face. Warmth radiated from the contact point then outwards, he could feel his cheek burning red. Then he could feel himself getting turned on again. He slapped her hard and she almost fell. "You bastard, you wonder why things aren't working out," she said as she spat in his face.

He wiped his chin and stared at her. Breathing deeply, his blood began to pulsate through his body causing his veins to swell. With a clenched fist he punched the tree just missing Celile's head. All he received in return was an icy stare. Stubborn, she refused to let him see she was scared. She had never shown fear since he'd met her. Even when she met The Boss, no fear. 'That girl has balls,' he thought as he let out a laugh. He rubbed his fist, a small trickle of blood oozed down his arm.

He grabbed her and pushed her up against a tree and began to kiss her hard. She stood there allowing him to carry on but not responding. She occasionally allowed him even when she wasn't in the mood, confused he carried on kissing her neck. He looked up at her. Her steely eyed focus was directed behind him towards the car as if imagining what she would have for tea. He didn't mind that she wasn't into it; just the fact that she was letting him would be fine. He continued to nuzzle her neck and lifted up her dress and felt her soft skin. The ground was quite soft beneath them. Then he shuddered as he noticed the turned earth that had been lifted by his feet. Gerhard and Ilse. He began to shake, the heat overwhelmed him. All he could visualise were Gerhard's eyes. He needed to get away, leave, go home. "Let's go," he said as he grabbed Celile's hand and led her towards the car. "The location you picked is good, we've had a good day but I need to get out of here, it is sending me crazy."

She didn't reply. She straightened up her clothing and rubbed her cheek before following him to the car.

Chapter 8

The kettle began to boil, flecks of hot water splattered out from the spout of the overfilled machine. Eve took several cups out of the cupboard all of which were either chipped or stained. She lined them up and added the coffee. No milk, it would have to be black. Shopping and planning hadn't been a strong point of her temporary house mates. They had coffee, but no one thought of milk and sugar; the ingredients that made the coffee taste nice. She flinched as two warm arms took her by surprise from behind. Then she settled the back of her head into his warm chest allowing him to embrace her. "I was trying not to wake you," she smiled as she breathed in his familiar aroma. She felt his hands wander up past her clothed breasts before caressing her neck.

"I missed you, I had to come down and check that it wasn't all a dream and you hadn't run off with some Turkish hunk," he said as he stroked her hair. He moved her hair out of the way and brushed his lips across the back of her neck. She shuddered as goose bumps trailed up her chest. Reaching her arm behind her she stroked his hair and felt the hook on the side of his glasses. She turned to kiss him and then stopped. They both stopped, prised apart by Stephen's entrance.

"Sick, sick, between you pair and Romeo on the couch with his bird, I had no chance of any sleep. I had to bed down on a bloody sun lounger last night," Stephen shouted. Kevin loosened his embrace and they turned to see Stephen looking red eyed at them. His unshaven face stared back. The kettle clicked off.

"What happened to your ... ? Well not just your face, all of you." Eve asked as she looked Stephen up and down. Kevin began to snigger.

"It's not funny. You wouldn't be laughing if you'd been mosquito food all night." He replied as he tried to pull his sleeves down over his exposed raw arms.

"Sorry, you must be in a lot of discomfort," replied Kevin as he held back the laughter. Eve watched as Kevin looked away, trying not to laugh herself.

"Here have a coffee." Eve poured the water and passed Stephen a coffee. He took it and went through to the lounge. Kevin burst into laughter, Eve followed. Every time they went to speak, the words were usurped by fits of more laughter.

"Oh bloody hell, they're still here," Stephen shouted.

Eve poured the rest of the coffees.' She took two through to the lounge. Ryan and his one nighter were still lying there naked. The woman was about thirty five with mousy hair and fake tan with streaks. She was still asleep. Ryan was sprawled out naked without shame wearing a grin, with his drinking hat still intact. She wondered how he'd managed to remove all his clothes in the state he'd come back to the villa in but still keep the hat on. The woman stirred and prised one sticky eye open. She turned and looked at Stephen who still wore his big grin then turned once again to look at all the strangers around her.

"Coffee?" Eve offered.

The woman bolted up to a sitting position, grabbed the sheet that had slipped to the floor and ran out of the room and up the stairs.

"I think you scared her off with your psycho stares," Ryan laughed as the slight bend in his nose was lit up by a dusty sun beam. "Oh well plenty more where she came from. Stephen, I've found a MILF prime hotspot. Me and you, we're going there tonight. I'll sort you out mate. Thanks for the coffee by the way," he said as he took the cup from Eve. Stephen did not respond, he hadn't heard. He was more preoccupied with scratching his mosquito bites.

Banging travelled across the landing. Doors slammed and footsteps were heard entering every room. Then more doors slammed. Then there was a loud scream; Selina. Ryan grinned enjoying the havoc that he had created.

Within seconds Selina ran down the stairs, Rachel followed behind her. "What the .... Why has some deranged woman just ran into my bedroom and who the heck is she?" she shouted.

"That was Ryan's bird," Stephen replied as he scratched his boils. Ryan laughed, still enjoying the attention.

"You're such a knob." Selina shouted as she flung a cushion at his head knocking his drinking hat to the floor.

"Look what you've done to my hat sis."

"I'll make it your head next time."

Rachel got onto the sofa bed next to Ryan, leaned on his chest and closed her eyes. "Wake me up when something interesting happens," she mumbled as she pulled her crumpled night shirt over her pants.

"Ha ha, I lose one then gain one," Ryan shouted. Rachel slapped him with her eyes still shut.

"There's coffee in the kitchen," Eve said. She had hoped they would all start waking up and want to go out. "Shall we do something today? I mean, we can't just sit around nursing hangovers all week. It would be good to say we've done something." Eve was met with silence. She pulled out a chair that had been tucked under the dining table and placed her mug hard down.

"Do you have to make so much noise," cried Rachel. "Trying to sleep around here is hard work. With her screaming and not to mention all the other noises of the night." Eve blushed.

"Excuse me, I did have that weird woman barge into my room looking like something dredged up from the jungle," Selina shouted.

"Whatever, I wasn't referring to your noises," replied Rachel as she prised herself from Ryan and sat up. "Maybe we should do something though. I need to take some photos for my course work. What shall we do then brains?" she asked as she stared at Eve. She then took one of Ryan's cigarettes from the floor and lit it.

"Do you have to do that in here? It's gross smoking in the house." Selina said.

"I'm too knackered to move. Where's the ashtray?"

"Outside, in the garden." Selina replied.

"Ha bloody ha," Rachel said as she flicked ash into her cupped hand.

The tensions were rising. When they had booked the villa, it seemed big enough, now it felt cramped and full of bodies all wanting and needing their own space. "Let's go out for breakfast," Eve suggested.

"But it's one in the afternoon Evie, they won't serve breakfast." Selina replied as she untangled her hair with her hands.

"Okay lunch. Let's go for a bite to eat and decide what we are going to do for the last few days. Does that sound good?" No-one answered. "We could do a boat trip, or get on a bus and go to a city or .... well .... anything that isn't drinking or baking on a sun lounger. Let's go out and make some memories," Eve said. She hadn't realised she'd been standing. Sitting down she blushed, she had just delivered that speech as if she were running for a parliamentary election.

"I think that sounds good. Well are you all going to get dressed and we'll head out?" Kevin said. Everyone nodded and gestured in agreement.

"The café across the road in one hour. I need me something greasy," Ryan said as he took the cigarette from Rachel's mouth and took a drag.

"Sounds like a plan," Rachel said as she hauled herself off the sofa bed and up the stairs. "I'm first in the shower," she yelled as she began to sprint.

Eve smiled at Kevin, he smiled back. He held out his hand and she took it, then he led her upstairs. "One hour, that's loads of time," Kevin smiled. Eve followed him knowing exactly what he meant.

Chapter 9

"I'll have a chicken sandwich and a coke please," Eve said as the waiter noted down her request on his pad. With all their orders complete he went back into the cafe. Sweat already began to form around Eve's hair line. "I wonder how hot it is today."

"It reached over forty yesterday, I would say it's hotter," Kevin replied.

"Don't my bites know it? That stuff they sold me from the chemist is crap. I'm sure they've done me. Probably sold me something for nappy rash. I didn't like the way that woman grinned at me when she took my money," Stephen said as he rubbed the contents of the little tube onto his arm. All six of them were sat around the table, lounging back with sunglasses on. Around them, children ran; people gathered pace to get to places. Others laughed and were so full of energy as they headed to the beach carrying their various inflatables. Eve looked at her friends, they looked dead. Rachel's head was leaning back over the top of the chair she sat in.

With her arm hanging down, her cigarette had burned to the filter leaving an ash trail that was just about to drop to the floor.

The waiter returned with one plate of food. He handed the fried breakfast to Ryan. "Way hay, just what the doctor ordered. Who said you couldn't get breakfast this time of the day?"

Rachel stirred and the ash dropped to the floor. "What a waste," she said as she placed the nub end in the ashtray. "Have we decided what we're doing?"

"No, not yet," Eve replied.

"I should say now; I really hate boats. I get sick on a paddle boat going down the river. I'll do it if I'm out-voted but I'm warning ..." Selina paused. "Why hello," she smiled as Mehmet approached. He went over to Selina and kissed her cheek.

"You look beautiful today. I've missed you since we went up town the other night." He smiled. Ryan ignored him as he tucked into his food. Eve watched as Mehmet pulled up a chair and wedged it under the end of the table; he nodded to the waiter and ordered a coffee.

"I've made a full recovery now so maybe we could do something." She smiled as she twined her hair around her index finger. Mesmerised, Mehmet watched. "Do you want to do something?" she asked. He looked up.

"I would love to do something with you," he smiled.

"I bet you would," shouted Ryan as he spluttered out a few flecks of toast. "You watch out for my Sis."

Mehmet stared, "I will look after her, just take her out. I promise."

Ryan burst out laughing. "Seriously mate, she'll have you for breakfast. Watch out for her. It's a warning for you," he said loud and slow.

"Oh just go walk in front of a bus," Selina said as she kicked Ryan under the table. The waiter emerged with the food and handed out the plates. Moments later he came back with the rest of the drinks.

Eve tucked into her sandwich and took a swig of coke. She flinched as she felt something tickle her leg. Kevin smiled; his hands were buried under the table cloth. She placed her hand over his and weaved her fingers in and out of his.

"Do you actually go on these trips you sell?" asked Rachel.

"Sometimes, I stay here most of the times but I can help if I want. It is my father's business."

"What are they like? I need to take some photos for my photography module at uni and I'd like something special."

"My father has found a wonderful spot. We take you if you want, that is to the most splendid waterfall. It is one of the most beautiful and secluded spots around here. It takes about one hour to one hour and a half in the jeep. It is up the mountains and it's nice and cool with the roof off," he smiled.

"Did you say you could do us a good deal? Only some of us are poor students." Rachel asked.

"I can do the best deal you will get. We take you to a gold shop also, you can have watermelon on the roadside; we drive through a traditional village and take you for a wild drive for a bit of excitement."

"I like the sound of the wild," Selina said.

"Then of course you can swim by the waterfall, we also do a barbeque dinner and provide soft drinks. You can of course bring alcohol if you wish."

"That, we would do. Fifty pounds for the jeep, for only us, for the day" Rachel shouted.

"You are a hard bargain," he replied. Eve laughed at his garbled language. But less than ten pounds a head would be a good deal if he agreed. She watched as Mehmet went silent and kept looking over towards the stand outside his shop. Stood outside was a man with a short sleeved shirt and jeans on. He sat on a stool under a canopy.

"Well? Is it a deal?" Rachel asked.

"Rachel, don't you think-" Selina flinched as Rachel kicked her under the table.

"Wait one moment. I will just go and ask my Uncle Sadik as he may not be very happy with me." Mehmet left the table, Eve watched as he nearly tripped up a curb in his flip flops as he ran to his shop.

"That was a bit of a cheek, he seems a nice guy and you want to rip him off," Selina shouted as she pushed her half eaten sandwich away from her.

"It's alright for you lot, but I'm here on a budget. You'll thank me in a minute when he comes back and says yes," she smiled.

"If you sleep with him Sis he'll probably take us for free," Ryan laughed as he placed his knife and fork onto his empty plate. Selina flicked a piece of cucumber at him; he lifted it off his arm and ate it. "Throw me some more food, why don't you."

"He's coming back," said Selina as her angry face turned to a big smile. She sat up straight and flicked her hair.

"Yes, we can do for fifty. But we need it in cash now for tomorrow."

Rachel grinned. Eve looked at her; she certainly knew how to drive a bargain. "How much is that then brains?" she asked Eve.

"I don't know, about eight pounds."

"It's eight pounds and thirty three pence recurring. Two of us are going to have to pay an extra penny," Stephen said as he rubbed some more lotion into his arms. He started scratching the spots, some of them were bleeding.

"I've got no chance of fixing you up with a MILF or even a desperate, you anal," shouted Ryan.

"Oh just shut up and get your money out. If what you were to fix me up with looks anything like the monster from the deep that you brought back last night, I think I'd rather keep the appointment I already have with my right hand," he shouted.

"Can I get you another coffee Sir?" the waiter asked. Stephen began to redden.

"No, I'm fine. Here's my eight pounds and thirty three pence sterling," he said as he counted the money out of his pockets. He left it on the table before leaving.

"You're such a knob; I am so right," Selina said as she opened her purse.

"We can only take notes, sorry" Mehmet said as he looked at them. Kevin placed a twenty on the table; Eve smiled at him and squeezed his hand. The others placed their share on the pile and swapped the coins for notes.

"What time do we leave tomorrow and where do we go?" Eve asked.

"Pick up is at twelve, we leave from the shop and we will see the night in. We like to show you how beautiful it is at night. A lot of people like to swim in the evening and take lovely photos of the sun going down," he replied. Rachel smiled for the first time since they'd been on holiday.

"Sounds good," said Eve as she stroked Kevin's hand once more under the table. "I can't wait."

"Me neither," Kevin replied as he looked into her eyes. They were going on an adventure. Eve's stomach fluttered, she and Kevin could enjoy a day of being together in the woods. They could swim, caress each other, and play little touchy feely games when their friends weren't looking. Kevin could sense her excitement; he leaned over the table and kissed her. Again, the hairs on the back of her neck prickled and her senses heightened. She was sure Kevin could sense the effect he had on her. She touched his face and his kiss lingered. She knew she had the same effect on him. "Let's go and get an ice cream," he whispered.

"Yes, go. I'm about to regurgitate my fry up," Ryan shouted as he made vomit noises before bursting into fits of laughter. A couple with three children sitting at the table behind them cast disapproving looks at Ryan before continuing to eat.

Kevin and Eve placed some money in the middle of the table before leaving. He held out his hand, she took it and followed him.

Chapter 10

Selina sat on the cool plastic sun lounger and listened to the gentle waves lapping next to her. The lights of the neighboring bay in Marmaris reflected elongated forks of oranges and yellows into the blackness of the sea. Occasionally these soft tones were harshly interrupted by neon colours, purples and greens, the flashing signs from bars and restaurants. She loved to watch the lights. The lamps and fairy lights from the boats at sea and docked were like a mass of stars.

    In the background she heard music, exotic and sexy Turkish music. She had spotted the belly dancer in various hotel grounds performing to her admiring crowd but Mehmet's eyes had been on her only. She lay back, satisfied. Moments earlier they had been romping underneath an upturned boat on the edge of the beach. She smiled as she hitched her dress down; knowing from the moment she saw him on that first hot sticky day, she had to have him.

    "Shall we get a drink? My treat," Mehmet asked, sitting up on the sun lounger to her left.

"In a moment, I'm just taking all this in. It's so beautiful."

"You are beautiful," he said as he slid off the lounger, onto his knees and leaned over Selina. She could smell aniseed from the Raki they had sipped with their steak meal a couple of hours earlier. He touched her breasts over her dress.

"Maybe tomorrow; if you're lucky," she laughed as she took his hand from her breast and held it in hers. "Anyway, I bet I'm not the first and I won't be the last."

"First, last. What do you mean?" he asked.

"Lots of girls before me and a new one next week. It's okay, you don't have to answer that," she said as she dropped his hand before stroking his thick dark hair.

"Not lots before. It is my first week here. I came from the North of Turkey last week. No work for me back home. I had a girlfriend for two years but we not get on, we grew up," he replied.

"I didn't realise, I thought you'd have been here longer. You seem so confident."

"I'm just like you, a long way from home." Selina held his hand and placed it back on her breast.

"Tomorrow," she smiled. "Are you with us on the jeep?"

"I begged my Dad to let me go. I will be working of course, but at least I can look at you while I work," he said as he bent over and kissed her. In bliss she accepted, invited him in, his kisses, his touch. She was on holiday after all. It was early, another hour and she would head back, get some sleep, ready for the day to come.

Chapter 11

Opening her bag for the third time, Eve went through her check list in her head. Water – check; sun cream – check; phone – check; emergency money – check and her sun hat. She took the floppy cream coloured hat from the beach bag and placed it on her head.

Kevin laughed, "You look like a big flower." Eve peered over her sunglasses and gave him a stern look before breaking into a smile. He leaned forward and kissed her. "A beautiful flower."

"That's okay then," smiled Eve.

"What time is it?" Rachel asked.

"Just gone twelve," replied Selina as she looked up and down the road. Every time a car came around the bend she tensed up only to be disappointed.

"They've got our money and now they're not coming and what can we do about it? A big, fat nothing," said Rachel.

"They'll be here. Mehmet said he was looking forward to taking us," Selina said as she paced up and down the curb.

"Let's hope your boyfriend wasn't just saying that to get into your pants."

"Firstly, he's not my boyfriend. Secondly, he already said it after he'd been in my pants." Selina shouted as she turned away.

"That's my Sis," laughed Ryan.

"And you can shut the hell up. At least I don't pick up men that are old enough to be our father."

"I don't pick up men," he laughed.

"Women. You know what I mean."

A loud rumbling vehicle came around the bend. It was a large green jeep with a turned down canopy and metal frame. Mehmet was sitting in the driver's seat with his sunglasses on, hair slicked down and his toned torso bursting out of a khaki vest top.

"I told you he would be here," Selina smiled. The jeep pulled up against the curb next to where they were all waiting. Mehmet stepped out of the jeep and opened the back door so that they could get in. Inside it was basic, two benches were all they had to sit on. "Can I ride in the front with you?" Selina asked.

"I was hoping you would ask," he replied as he lead Selina to the passenger side and opened the door for her.

Eve slid along to the front of the jeep with Kevin tailing close behind. Everyone else clambered on after.

"Way hay, here goes. I have the beer," shouted Ryan.

"Great, can we have one now?" asked Stephen.

"Why not?" Ryan replied as he handed his cans out. Rachel took one and began sipping. Eve turned down a beer and pulled out her first bottle of water, the last thing she needed was a tea time hangover when they had all evening to go.

It was now gone midday and the heat was relentless. She was sure all the bickering had partly been down to the heat. Sweat gathered down the back of Eve's back, she could feel the wetness begin to seep through her thin white tee-shirt. Kevin placed his clammy hand over her shoulder and stroked her. There was a loud bang as Mehmet slammed the back door. It was time to go; Eve smiled at Kevin still disbelieving how good things were.

The engine began to rumble as the vehicle started up. As soon as they got round the bend the air thrashed through the jeep cooling everyone down. They passed the town, they passed Marmaris, and then they headed off, up into the hills. Snaking around the bay, Eve looked down at the view. The boats now looked like Harry's toys. As they climbed higher, her hearing was subdued, she swallowed and it returned. They were now high up on the road, signs pointed to Mügla, a city she'd heard of. The cool air blasted through the jeep and she instantly felt energised.

Slowing down, the jeep took a succession of tedious bends. Eve grabbed hold of Kevin as they swung close to the edge of a killer drop. Behind the jeep, a bus full of hot passengers looked on at them. They chugged up the hill until the bay of Marmaris could no longer be seen. Veering off up a bumpy gravel path they headed inland. To her left were a row of detached white houses. Old looking, with vines growing up them, rows and rows of fruit on trees and farmed land. An old man walked a donkey along the roadside. Mehmet beeped as they passed and the old man waved. A group of children moved out of the road as they trundled on.

"You want a beer?" Ryan shouted as he pulled a can out of his backpack and held it over towards Kevin.

"No, I'm good" he replied as he took a sip of his water. Eve shook her head also. It was going to be a long hot day. All of a sudden the jeep veered off-road.

"I'm going to take you on a short cut my father told me about," Mehmet shouted. Without warning they then trundled down a steep bumpy mud hill. The jeep jumped and tilted.

"Stand up," Kevin shouted. Eve stood and held onto the bars and screamed as they fell. Exhilarated and wind swept she laughed and kissed Kevin. He looked at her and smiled. She fumbled for her phone and after a few moments fiddling with the buttons she managed to access her camera function. She took a picture of Kevin. A picture she would treasure, one of him smiling, with his hair blown back and him looking at her in a way that made her melt. A look she wanted to enjoy for many years to come.

Chapter 12

The temperature crept to thirty five degrees. Guz began to set up the fold out chairs by opening them out and facing them towards the waterfall. The last one was jammed, he pulled it hard. It flew open, sending him off balance, stumbling backwards towards the hard ground. He fell to the floor and the chair landed on his stomach.

"Shit," he cried as he held onto a tree and dragged his sweaty body up.

"Shit! Fuck! Shit!" he yelled as he whacked the chair onto the floor several times. He then grabbed the frail canvas frame and flung it at the tree before falling to the ground and sitting on the dried mud below. Leaves and grit stuck to his legs and hands, he grabbed a handful of earth and threw it into the water. "Stuff you too," he yelled. He looked at his watch; he had so much to do and not much time. He had to sort the food, prepare the barbeque, make it all "look pretty" he said aloud as he pulled a sour face. He stood and walked over to the water's edge. Kneeling down, he scooped up the icy water and splashed it over his face and body. He shook his head and focused on what was around him.

They would approach from the back and park up close to where his car was. They would have to walk for a few minutes battling the shrubs and the rocky surface before they arrived at the clearing.

Guz walked back to the car, taking the route he was thinking about so intensely. Arriving at the car he opened the boot. He lifted the car blanket up, beneath it sat his real helpers. The gun, the syringes and the knives. He smiled as he pulled the blanket back over them. "Later," he said.

He grabbed the cool box and the barbeque bag and began to walk back. Already the heat was making him clumsy. He tripped up a rock propelling the food box forward as he landed face down on a row of ants. The box flew open and the food at the top of the box spewed out and landed in a pile of mud dust. Swearing he sat up. The food was destroyed. Several pieces of chicken had been thrown out of the bag and were now finely coated with debris. There was no more food; Celile had only packed the bare minimum.

He cursed Celile. She was meant to be with him, helping. "I'm not feeling well," she had proclaimed earlier that day. "But I'll definitely be there later." But here he was, doing all the hard work alone.

He knew better though. Sadik had said he had some errands to run, that he was still getting over the night they met up with The Boss. Excuse after excuse is all he'd had from both of them. He was under no illusion that they were sitting round the pool drinking beer knowing that they had him out the way for a while. He would watch them later and he would watch them closely. His original dream was that he would get a new identity and move. Gerhard had become that identity. If only Celile had been a good girl, she could've been Ilse. The passport would need some work but they could do it with their contacts. Sadik, he was beyond caring about. Blood had always bonded them but he questioned how thick blood was now. That very blood was so diluted, he felt he had flushed Sadik down the toilet and was trying to spot what was left of him in the sea.

Standing, he regained his balance and took a long swig of cold water from a bottle before pouring the rest over his head. His thin black hair flopped forward over his brow as the water cascaded over his face and down his tee-shirt. Taking a deep breath he knelt and picked up the chicken before placing it back in the bag. He carried the luggage over to the water and knelt down, with the bag of chicken in hand he began to rinse it off. He watched the dust soak off the sticky meat and disperse into the water. He then dried it out on his tee-shirt and placed it back into the bag. "Looks okay to me," he laughed. "Time to light the barbie." He decided there and then that he would not be eating any chicken that day. He couldn't care less about the tourists and he certainly didn't care about Celile. They could all have the chicken.

He pulled out the two disposable barbeques and set them up on a tree stump. Lovely, he thought. He put up the small fold out table for the salad and bread and closed up the food bag. It was all getting warm but he may as well keep it as cool as he could. He would inevitably pick at some of it also and he didn't want to give himself an upset stomach.

It was odd he hadn't heard from anyone whilst he'd been there. He delved into his pocket and felt for his phone. It wasn't there. He searched his other pocket and the floor around him. Had he dropped it when he was leaning over into the water? Grabbing his hair he pulled it outwards as he paced the clearing. He looked in the food box then in the barbeque bag checking all the pockets. No phone. He leaped over the rocks and pushed his way through the spiny shrubs before reaching the car. It wasn't on the front seats; he opened the door and checked the glove box. It wasn't there either. His heart beat fast and his breath quickened; it was his only way of communicating with The Boss. If he had gone off radar they would send someone to find him. Things could get bad; no one ever ignored a call from The Boss. He took a deep breath. What were the chances of The Boss calling? The boot, he had leaned into the boot. Running around the back of the car he opened the boot. No phone.

There was a beep, it came from close by. He knelt down on the floor and he saw it tucked up against the back wheel. He must have dropped it while he was struggling with the bags. The screen lit up, his battery was low. That's why it had beeped. He laughed loud, then louder. The battery was half down. "Stupid phone. You can't hold a charge for long," he said as he laughed. Allowing himself to sit and recuperate in the car's shadow he enjoyed the sound of the water, he felt the cool earth. He looked at his watch, still lots to do he thought as he dragged himself up. He opened the passenger door, turned the engine and plugged his phone in to charge. The phone flashed again, no signal. It then flashed once more, the signal had come back. Then he noticed it. There was a missed call from The Boss.

Chapter 13

Deeper inland they went. The jeep swerved round a bend and jerked sideways onto a main road. Selina screamed as she grabbed Mehmet's leg. The young man looked at her hand and smiled.

On the roadside, a bony man wearing an open shirt sat under a large yellow parasol in front of a stall. The old man placed his newspaper down on the floor and put a rock on top of it to stop it blowing away. He stood and smiled as he walked around to the front of the stall. Eve spotted the large refreshing watermelons.

"This is free for you, to stop you getting thirsty," Mehmet said as he pulled on the hand brake and opened the jeep door. "Please do get out and have a walk for a few minutes." He walked round the back and opened the hatch.

"Stuff that, I never came all the way to Turkey to eat fruit. Want another beer Stephen?" Ryan shouted as he remained in his seat.

"No, I think I'll give it a rest for a bit," he said with his eyes scrunched together as he tried to find the tube of bite cream in his bag. "And do you know watermelon isn't a fruit? It's part of the same family as cucumbers and things like that."

"That's a really exciting fact Stephen. I think you should have another beer. If you're going to start with your usual talking shit to me I'd rather us both be smashed when you do it." He replied as he opened a beer and forced it into Stephen's hand.

Selina ran around the jeep and stood by Rachel, Kevin and Eve. "I told you all he would come," she said as she watched Mehmet approach the stall.

Now they were out of the moving jeep Eve felt the heat hit her. They were in the open, during the hottest part of the day standing still on a stony road. "I've got to make a quick phone call," she said as she let go of Kevin's hand and smiled as she walked away. He smiled back at her.

She walked over towards the stall. The watermelons were arranged in a tidy pile, some were cut into half, some into slices. She felt saliva build up in her mouth as she craved the melon's juice. A car sped past and left a dusty gust behind it. Eve almost enjoyed the moment even though the coolness had only lasted a second.

Standing to the side of the stall, Eve pulled out her phone and dialled, she needed a few words from her little boy's mouth. Straight to answer phone. After a few seconds she tried again, it rang. Her heart quickened and she smiled, then the call was cut off. "What?" she said as she looked down and saw that her phone signal had gone. Placing her mobile phone back into the pocket of her shorts she began to walk back towards the stall and the jeep.

Eve watched as Mehmet walked over to the stallholder and pointed to the cut melon as he spoke in Turkish. The bony man stared at Mehmet. His expression went from welcoming to fearful in a moment. "Alti Lutfen," Mehmet said. The man held six fingers up and Mehmet nodded. At no point did the man take his eyes off Mehmet. He placed his hands in front of his face and took a step back. Mehmet smiled and went to touch the man's arm. The man flinched and stepped back once more. Mehmet then took a step back and held both of his hands up in the air and smiled at the distressed man. From beneath the wooden table the bony man pulled out a carrier bag and placed five slices of cut melon into the bag and held it out to Mehmet before sitting back on his plastic chair under his parasol. Shaking, he pulled out a towel and wiped his head, his eyes still fixed on Mehmet.

"What was all that about?" Eve asked.

"Oh nothing. I think he is nervous of strangers," Mehmet replied as he handed Eve a piece of watermelon and walked towards the others. Eve looked back at the man and walked over to him. She pulled out a couple of lira from her pocket, "thank you," she said as she handed him the coins. Again the man flinched and put his hands up. She left the money on the table and stepped back, he looked towards Mehmet who had his back turned before grabbing the coins and placing them in his pocket. Mehmet looked back and the man looked away. Eve began to walk back to the others. Why had the man been so nervous? He obviously met strangers all day long selling on a roadside. She shuddered as she watched Mehmet handing out the fruit. The others laughed, ate and drank. Selina shared her slice with Mehmet and Rachel had joined Ryan and Stephen back on the jeep.

"Are you alright?" Kevin asked.

"Yes," she paused. "I don't know," Eve replied.

"You'll be able to speak to Harry later. Was it engaged?"

"I got cut off, my signal went," she said with her eyes still transfixed on Mehmet.

"Is there anybody there?" Kevin said with a smile as he stroked the ends of her hair that had stuck to her neck.

"Sorry. Something odd just happened."

"Odd, in what way?"

"See that man over there? See how he is watching Mehmet's every move?" she said as she pointed to the stallholder. He was sitting still as she had described, watching them. He began to rock back and forth in his plastic chair. "There's something not right. He's scared."

"It's probably just the heat doing-"

"It wasn't the heat. I watched him hand over the melon and I saw him trembling. He is scared of Mehmet. Why, I don't know. But he is scared. Something's not right, I have to warn Selina."

"Wait, Eve." Kevin shouted as she jogged towards Mehmet and Selina.

"Can I just have a word?" she said.

"Go on then Evie," she said.

"In private," she replied as she dragged Selina by the arm.

Mehmet smiled and got back in the jeep. "We will leave in two minutes," he shouted.

"Eve, this isn't funny. What's so important that you have to drag me away from Mehmet? You came across as rude just then," she said.

"Something's not right with that man over there, the one with the melons. He was scared of Mehmet. I don't know why but he was. I'm worried about you Selina."

Selina pulled her sunglasses down to reveal a stare. "Evie, you must be joking. Try to lighten up. Please, for me. I'm having a good time. He is just selling watermelon and there's nothing wrong with Mehmet. Look at him, he's fine," she said as she pointed over towards the melon seller. Eve looked over; the man was now sitting down, leaning back on his chair reading his paper.

"I didn't make this up, I swear, there was something wrong."

"Eve, please. I don't want to hear any more. Are you jealous that I'm having such a good time?" she shouted.

"Shush, there's no need to raise your voice and no I'm not jealous just concerned," Eve replied as Kevin approached her from behind.

"I don't know what's going on with Eve. I suggest you have some of your melon, you're probably dehydrated. I'm getting back in the jeep." Selina said as she left the couple and got into the front of the jeep.

"We're leaving now, can you get back in," Mehmet shouted.

"I'm not sure," Eve whispered to Kevin.

"Come on Eve, it was nothing and you can't stay here," he smiled. "I'll look after you," he said as he kissed her. She looked around; there was nothing, no buses, taxes or shops. He was right, she couldn't stay. She didn't even know where they were anymore. There were mountains all around, pines everywhere and a relentless heat that was beginning to drown her.

"Maybe it is the heat," she smiled as she pulled out her melon and took a bite. As the jeep door slammed she looked back at the melon stand. The man looked over his paper, watching as the engine started up and the jeep pulled away. As they did he placed his paper down and wiped his head with shaking hands. Eve waved at him, just a subtle wave and the man held his hand up. She could see that he was trembling as his hand wavered. She continued to watch until they headed back the way they came, off road. Kevin placed his hand over hers and stroked the insides of her fingers.

"Come on, let's have fun. It'll all be over before we know it," he said as he kissed her cheek. She clenched his hand and forced a smile back knowing she would be much happier once the trip was over and they returned back to the villa.

Chapter 14

The skin on his knuckle began to peel. Whacking the rocky floor had seemed like a good idea at the time, a way of releasing all his tension but now, all he felt was a burning pain around the torn skin. Guz tried to call The Boss again; it rang twice before he got cut off. The Boss was cutting the call off on purpose. Was the deal off? Were they all in danger? He tried to call Celile to warn her of what had happened. No answer. It was mid-afternoon, she was due to arrive soon with Sadik but neither were picking up. He left a message. "When you can pull yourself away from my dick of a brother, answer your phone." Then he hung up. Selecting re-dial he tried The Boss again and like before the call was cut off.

For several minutes he sat against the car, there was no point moving as he didn't know how the whole scenario would pan out. Tarkan sang and the phone lit up. Grabbing it, he placed the phone against his ear.

"Hard man to get hold of. I don't know, we play a game and you don't follow the rules. Rule number one; I call, you answer immediately. Even if you are taking a piss and it's running down your pants, you piss and talk at the same time. Do you hear me?"

"I'm sorry. Please forgive me. I lost my phone and when I-" Guz said as his throat dried up. His hands shook as he held the phone to his ear. The trees started blurring as his head lightened with the heat. He scratched the rising heat that was crawling up his neck. The sun had now crept over; he flinched at the light that reflected off his silver car. He cleared his throat. "It won't happen again."

"If it does happen again there will be a forfeit. Your little flat will turn into a big barbeque and you will be its prize meat. Do we understand each other? Pass the message on to your stupid brother. Not only will I barbeque you all, I will then feed you all to my dog," he said before erupting into laughter.

"Your dog eat them for dinner. That's a good one," he heard one of The Boss's henchmen repeat before joining in with the laughter. It sounded like Scrawny. For a moment he was transported back to the basement office. Claustrophobic, alone, trapped. All this land surrounding him and he felt trapped.

He took a deep breath and croaked. "We have something coming in today, something good. Six of them. Goods, passports, money and I am assured that there are women. Young women."

"Make sure they are good enough to sell, the better quality, the higher the price. I have an order for the passports already. We'll collect them from the farm house," he ordered. "I will collect the girls before sun up; they have to go as soon as possible."

"Yeah. We enjoy these visits," the other voice shouted and jeered.

He heard someone humming down the line, a woman. "Anyway, my massage has arrived. Rule number two, get me the goods. If you win the game; you live, I get the goods and I even pay you well and then we play the game all over again. In this game, we are all winners." He hung up. Guz allowed the phone to slip from his fingers onto the ground. He closed his eyes and took a deep breath. The sun was stalking him. He needed to get up, set the weapons.

"Next time, this is the last time. There won't be a next time," he whispered with a smile. Scooping the phone back up he placed it in his pocket, stood and opened the boot. He took out the gun, the knives, the full syringes, some tape and the rope. With his sharpest knife he cut the rope into several lengths, these would be used to bind the cargo. He took out a large sports bag and placed everything into it. He then topped it off with some rags to gag them with, a packet of boiled sweets for himself, two large bottles of cola and an old green blanket to sit on.

He closed the boot and headed over towards the picnic area. From the cool box he took some bread and cheese and a few bags of crisps. It was going to be a long evening. He felt his shoulder twinge; he placed the bag down for a moment and rubbed the affected area. Walking closer to the water's edge he felt the spray from the waterfall. He sat and dangled his feet in the water. His phone sang.

He grabbed the mobile from his pocket and juggled it, almost dropping it in the water. His heart throbbed as he took a deep breath and gripped the phone in his hand. He held it to his ear, it was Sadik.

"Why the hell haven't you been answering? All sorts of shit has been happening here. I lost the phone," he cried.

"We, I mean I have been busy. Out doing things,"

"Doing things, really?"

"Yeah really. I just thought I'd call to say we're on our way. Celile is driving."

"Yeah, yeah, whatever. I've done all the work as usual and you and Celile get to have a nice little day and a nice little drive. Had a nice day?"

"What the hell is in you? Remember it was you that got us all into this," Sadik shouted as he cut the call.

"Well fuck you too," Guz shouted as he threw the phone behind him, onto the ground, into a trail of ants. He watched as the ants crawled over it. They carried bits of leaf and followed a little trail that had just been interrupted by his phone. Ants crawling, his skin crawled. He scratched his arms hard until they were tender to touch.

For a while he would move over to the chairs and have a rest. He predicted that Celile and Sadik would be half an hour yet. Whilst they'd had an easy morning of lying about and screwing, he'd had another day from hell and he deserved a rest. He lifted his cold, wet legs from the water and staggered over to the nearest chair. He pulled his cap over his eyes and sat with his feet splayed out under the trees.

Chapter 15

Eve watched Selina twiddle the gold bracelet she had just bought from the gold store. They had been jumping about in the back of the jeep for several minutes and were now heading down a dirt track. Ryan had fallen asleep on the jeep floor and was bent over with his head in Stephen's lap. "I don't know how he can sleep through this. I wish he'd move. He's started to dribble on my leg." Stephen said.

"Wait," Rachel shouted. "Stop the jeep."

Mehmet slammed on the brakes and the jeep carried on skidding down the dusty slide. It came to a stop next to a tortoise that ambled in front of them. "Are you alright?" he asked as he unbuckled his seat belt and walked around the jeep.

"I'm doing good." Rachel shouted as she opened the back door and stepped out with a big smile on her face.

"I thought there was some emergency," he said.

"There is. Have you seen how beautiful this waterfall is?" Her nose piercing glistened in the sun's ray that shone between the trees causing Mehmet to squint. "I really need some photos of this." Out of the small case she pulled out her digital SLR and held it into position before beginning to focus and snap. Wandering off she was now almost out of view.

Eve stood and looked down as she stepped off the jeep. "I think I'm going to stretch my legs."

"We have to get back for food. My father will be waiting," he said as he checked his watch.

"Well I'm sure he can put it on hold for a few minutes," Selina said as she held his hand.

"Well, just a few minutes." He held her hand and began to walk off towards the water. "Ten minutes, then we have to go," he shouted.

"I think I'll stay here and chill. It's too hot to move. Is it morning yet?" Ryan asked as he pulled up his cap revealing crumpled skin on the one side of his cheek.

"No, we're still in the jeep," Stephen replied. "Don't worry, I'll stay with him," he signalled to Eve.

Kevin stepped off and walked over to Eve. "It's beautiful. I'm glad we stopped," he said as he stroked her hair. "Shall we walk down to see the waterfall?" Eve smiled and took his hand. They walked over the lumpy earth and through a thin dusty pathway that led to the fall. The water fell and crashed about fifty feet below. Eve's legs buckled as she looked down, she held onto Kevin tighter.

White spray crashed onto the rocks that lined the fall and sprinkled them with cold water. Eve held out her hands and enjoyed the feeling of being closer to its coolness. Kevin joined her. A large splash landed on the side of his head, catching him in the eye. He removed his glasses and dried them on his tee-shirt then smiled as Eve wiped away the wetness. She looked into his eyes; the sun was positioned behind him like a halo. She touched his fresh shaven face and he moved towards her and kissed her. She responded back, feeling his soft face against hers. He had this way with her, every touch, every breath and every look provoked a response. Lust and more. She thought back to the night before and their love making and enjoyed the moment of closeness with him. "I can't wait to get back," he whispered as he pushed his fingers up through the back of her damp hair knocking her hat off. She left the hat on the floor and enjoyed the feel of his hands and the little tickles that massaged her head.

"Smile," Rachel shouted as she snapped away. Eve moved back from Kevin and picked up her hat. He placed his glasses back on.

"She knows how to ruin a moment," Eve said.

"She certainly does," he replied.

"That one's going on Facebook as soon as I get the opportunity," Rachel shouted as she passed them and headed downwards.

"Are you feeling a bit better now after earlier?" Kevin asked as he straightened her hat up.

"I think so," she replied as she thought about the watermelon seller's face. Maybe there was a reasonable explanation as to why he seemed scared. "I worry. I mean he just worried me; I was probably being silly. Anyway, I must try to call Harry again," she said as she leant forward and kissed Kevin before heading back up the dirt path. He followed closely, she held her hand behind her and they linked their fingers together. In her other hand, she held out her mobile phone in front of her. "I can't seem to get a signal. I'm just going to have a quick walk around, see if I can find one." She let go of Kevin's hand and carried on ahead without him. She watched as Mehmet's phone went off, he had a signal where he was. Selina had walked back to the jeep and was sitting in the passenger seat ready to go.

Eve hurried over to where Mehmet was standing next to a little stone recess. He shouted down the phone in Turkish and she heard someone shout back. He began to pace the floor and move his arms violently as he spoke. As she approached he looked at her and then turned his whole body one hundred and eighty degrees so that all she could see was his back. He scrunched his fist up as he replied. Tension caused the veins on his neck to protrude.

She had a signal. It was only one bar but it was all she had. She selected Harry's number and it rang. Answer phone. Infuriated, Eve tried again and again until eventually it rang. "Hello, it's early," Ellen said. It was her, his wife.

"Can I speak to Harry?" Eve knew full well they would be up early and out as Justin had always been an early riser when they had been in a relationship.

"I'll find out for you," was the frosty reply. Eve waited; she could hear muttering in the background. Wishing they would hurry up, she looked up at Mehmet. He shouted one last time and hung up.

"We've got to go." Mehmet shouted.

"Just a few more pictures," Rachel called back.

"We haven't got time," he snapped.

"Hang on, we're paying you for your time," Rachel yelled back as she neared Mehmet.

"I'm sorry. What I meant is your dinner is ready and it will be spoiled," he replied.

Selina got out of the jeep and walked over. "You can be so self-centred sometimes Rachel. It's not fair to keep the chef waiting," she said as she stared at Rachel.

"Whatever. He can wait another minute or two," she snapped back as she wandered over to a flowering bush and took another photo.

Eve began to pick her nail, worried she may not be granted permission to speak with her son. "Mummy," Harry shouted. "I've just had pancakes for breakfast and now we're at the fair. I can go on the roundabout. I'm going to ride on the horse, it's really big." She smiled as a small tear fell from the corner of her eye. She wiped it away.

"That's good Baby. Mummy misses you lots," she replied as the signal dropped. There was a crackle on the line. She could no longer hear her son. "Harry. Harry," she shouted. The signal came back.

"Mummy, Daddy said can you call me tonight about nine?" he said with his little voice. She imagined him smiling and happy to be going on the ride and only wished she was there to share his experience.

"Of course I will. I'll call you later. Mummy loves you lots. Mummy loves you big mountains," she said as another tear rolled down her face.

"We have to go," Mehmet shouted. Eve held her hand up to dismiss his comment.

"I love you big mountains too Mummy. Bye," he said as the call ended. She felt a warm touch on her arm. Kevin held her. He knew how it hurt her to be apart from Harry. He rubbed her arm as he held her tight.

"Please, we have to go," Mehmet shouted.

"Alright, we're coming" replied Eve as they both stepped over the undergrowth to take a short cut back to the jeep.

Chapter 16

Guz jumped away from his fold up chair as he slapped his arm. His heart pounded hard and his mouth was dry. He cowered into the shade, the sun had blinded him. After taking a few deep breaths, he pulled a crumpled tissue from his pocket and mopped his drizzling brow. He checked his watch. Sadik had been over an hour and the tourists were late. What was taking them all so long? He knew the answer to that question only too well. He pulled the phone from his pocket, no signal. As he walked back towards the car the signal came back. He rubbed the bite on his arm. A livid red hive had appeared. "Shitty forest."

He called Sadik, no answer. They were half an hour away an hour ago. Had they stopped to have a sexual rendezvous or had something happened? Maybe a break down. He had told Sadik on several occasions to get his crappy little car serviced. He imagined it to have chugged to a standstill in the middle of nowhere. Him and Celile calling one of their friends and panicking that they couldn't get hold of him. He looked at his phone, there were no missed calls, no texts; not his preferred choice of communication but he checked his e-mail. There were no e-mails from Sadik. Did he want a penis extension or some black market Viagra? "Not today," he said as he closed his e-mails and tried to call Sadik again. It rang.

"We're five minutes away. Are they there yet?"

"No. They are not here yet. And neither are you," Guz shouted. He heard Celile whisper and the phone get muffled.

Sadik cleared his throat. "We stopped to get a drink, it's really hot."

"No shit." Guz shouted, shaking as he clasped the phone to his ear. "Do you think I'm sat here under a fan drinking beer? I've been humping 'happy day out' crap for these bloody tourists through shit and bushes all day and you stop for a fucking drink. Just hurry the hell up. More than five minutes and The Boss will be the least of your problems." He hung up and placed the phone back in his pocket.

Shaking with rage, his red face began to sweat even more. He took the tissue from his pocket and wiped his face again. The tissue fibres rolled up and stuck to his neck and became entwined in his coarse stubble. "Fuck this, fuck it all." He would 'do today,' one last job and he would go. Tomorrow he would be Gerhard and he had decided Celile would come; he wouldn't give her a choice. Stuff blood, Sadik was no more than water. He would get rid of him. His betrayal was too much to take. Stuff family, stuff them all. Celile would be punished, she would come and she would learn to love him, she would have to love him. He yelled and his legs buckled. He sat on the dusty ground next to his car and stared at the trees as he contemplated the big night ahead, the biggest yet.

He had eight thousand Euros saved and an I.D. He had enough to go, to start a new life. He closed his eyes and visualised him and Celile in an apartment somewhere nice. She was making bread and cutting up tomatoes. His breathing deepened, he shuffled back and lay his head against his car in the shade and closed his eyes. He felt wet mucous drip down his nose; he left it there. He was far too relaxed to remove it.

In his thoughts, she was making coffee and chopping hard. How could she make coffee and chop at the same time. The chopping became more rhythmic and he realised he was in bed. She on top of him, thrusting her naked body hard into him. Then he flashed back to the kitchen, tomatoes. Then back, flesh. He allowed his hands to cup her breasts, his breathing quickened and as he was about to find a release: Slam. A hard slam. Beneath him, he saw Celile holding the knife and laughing. In her hand she held his penis, dripping with blood. Small and fleshy and bloody. He gasped and opened his eyes. Once again he had dozed off. What had it all meant? "What does it all mean Celile?" he whispered as he took a deep breath. And, what was happening to him? That was twice he had fallen asleep within the hour. It was almost as if reality was mixing with fantasy. He dry heaved. Trembling, he stood and took a warm bottle of cola off the passenger seat and drank for what seemed like ages. He couldn't allow himself to become any more dehydrated than he already was. He shook his head and checked his watch. Several minutes had passed.

In the distance he heard an engine humming. It was too far away to know if it was the jeep or Sadik and Celile. He threw the cola onto the back seat, locked the car and ran. If it was the jeep, they couldn't see him. He held his breath, ran fast and threw himself down behind a tree and some dense foliage. The vehicle got closer. He exhaled, it was Sadik and Celile. Relieved, he panted as he staggered back towards the car.

"We're here Brother. What do you want me to start with?" Sadik called. Guz stared at Celile. One sign, one give-away. Her hair was neatly pinned into a bun; her aviator glasses concealed any truths that her eyes would've revealed. Her denim shorts, zipped up to the top were all clean and tidy and her body looked freshly moisturised. No evidence of tampering. He held out his hand and took off her sunglasses.

She grabbed them back off him, "I can't see without them," she said as she placed them back on.

"The barbeque is set up. You need to wait here, greet them and feed them. Encourage them to relax, wander, and drink. When it gets darker, that is when I will have them." Guz grabbed the sports bag from the floor, grabbed his sunglasses and cap and left them. "I will see you later when we are done. Make it good. Remember, there is a lot at stake here. I'm going to be here all the time, in the background, watching, waiting, watching," he realised he was rambling on. He turned his back and began to walk. In the distance he heard the jeep hopping over the lumpy ground. They were coming. "A lot at stake," he shouted as he hurried until he could no longer be seen where he sat in his spot. In his spot is where he would remain until he could take them out or bind them up. The last job and then he would be a free man. He smiled.

Chapter 17

"Do you have any water?" asked Selina.

"Not much, we're here now so we'll all get drinks. Just behind these trees we reach the most beautiful clearing in the forest," he shouted as the jeep trundled up next to the parked cars.

Rachel stood and began to film, "Wow, this place is amazing." Through the trees ahead she could see the glistening pool. Surrounding them were thousands of pine trees that seemed to reach into the clouds.

The early afternoon heat had turned into a late afternoon scorcher. Eve watched as a petite woman weaved in and out of the bony shrubs. The woman waved as she approached. "Welcome. I'm Celile. We have food for you. You must come with me," she called.

"Where's my Dad?" Mehmet called. Celile replied in Turkish. Eve watched as their conversation turned from jovial to bordering angry within a few moments. He slammed the jeep door and wiped his brow. Walking over to the woman he guided her towards a tree where their conversation continued.

Eve shuddered. She was allowing her doubts about the day to creep back in. She was transformed back to the old woman on their first day, 'people are not always good, trust what you think.' Then she thought of White Suit and his icy glare outside the shop, then the melon seller showing fear with every gesture. Maybe this was their way, something cultural that she didn't understand. She looked at Kevin and he kissed her, she smiled. They were on holiday, it was fun, and there was nothing wrong she told herself.

"I don't know what they're so peeved about." Selina shouted, "Mehmet, when's this party starting?" He waved back but still his eyes remained focused on Celile. He stomped back over to the jeep and opened the back door. They all got out except Ryan and Stephen. "Can someone get him off me?" Ryan yelled.

Rachel put her camera back into the case and stepped back onto the jeep. She shoved Ryan; his head dropped to the floor and landed with a light thud. "What? Who?" He cried as he stared at her, squinting to focus.

"We're here," Rachel said. Ryan flinched as the sun caught his eye. Stephen moved out of the seat where he'd been trapped for the whole journey and jumped out of the jeep before Ryan could position his head back in his lap.

"Oh. Here," Ryan yawned as he stretched his arms out and grabbed his bag of beers. "Great, let's start partying," he said as he stumbled off the jeep, still yawning. A small lizard scurried off under the parked car.

"I can't believe he's drank so much already," Eve whispered to Kevin as they followed Celile to the pool. Eve laughed and looked up at Kevin as Ryan tripped over a rock. She felt him squeeze her hand twice; he looked back at her and laughed. She planted a quick kiss on the side of his head. It had only been a few days but they already had the code, the hand squeeze code. Above her the trees rustled with the movement of many birds that nested and landed on the branches. It was so alive with nature. She inhaled; the pine aroma cleaned her airways.

Ryan stumbled again but this time he crashed into the back of Stephen, grabbed his shorts and pulled him backwards. "Sorry mate." Eve squeezed Kevin's hand again just to make sure it was their code. He squeezed back. She looked at him and laughed. Eve watched as Stephen straightened his shorts and stormed off ahead. "You could've helped me," Ryan shouted as he pulled himself back to a vertical position.

Moments later, they arrived at the clearing. Eve flinched as a loud squawking sound came from above. She looked up, a bird of prey. "It's an eagle," Stephen shouted.

"So what. Can we get a drink?" Ryan replied.

"I think you've had enough for now," Eve said. "You're struggling to walk."

"Oh little Miss Party Pooper. We're on ho-li-day," he replied.

"Here," the woman called as she tossed a bottle of water across to Ryan. He automatically held out his hands to catch it but he missed and it landed on the gritty earth below. He gave her a long confused look and with his mouth wide open he squinted. "Drink it. It will stop you getting ill." He stooped down, picked up the water and began to guzzle it down.

"Who's the Party Pooper now?" Eve laughed as she brushed past Ryan. The party had barely started and he was already hammered. "Mmm, food looks good."

The air was now filled with a savoury smell from the barbeque. A man wearing a crisp white apron stood up from behind the table. "This is Sadik, he's the chef," Celile said. Eve watched as the man looked up and forced a smile back.

Eve dragged Kevin to the water's edge and watched. The clearness of the water showed how deep it was. A school of small fish swam away from her shadow. She bent down and felt the temperature. Icy cold, she shivered. She flicked some of the water at Kevin's face. He grabbed her and kissed her. Sweat poured down her forehead, icy cold water would help to cool them down. Pulling away from his kiss she said, "This is so beautiful, we should go in."

"Please do go in. You will love it," Celile called over to her. Eve waved back at the woman.

"We should do as we're told." Eve removed her tee-shirt, then her shorts before kicking off her sandals to reveal her orange swimsuit. The pool was calm, she could do this, she could swim in a pool. She positioned herself on the water's edge. "There's only one way to do this," she shouted as she jumped into the pool feet first. As she broke through the surface, she felt the water's icy fingers caress her whole body. Opening her eyes she could see the fish in the distance. To her right the water was cloudier, the waterfall she thought. She swam towards it and allowed the water to pull her up to the surface. She came up from the ice gasping and trod water under the best view she'd had that day. The water cascaded over the rocks above; as it landed it splashed cool flecks across her face. "Come in, it's great," she yelled.

"I'm on my way," Kevin yelled as he dived into the pool and met her over by the waterfall. Within minutes the rest of the group were stripping down and entering the pool. They yelled, they screamed at the cold shock, they laughed and played. "I'm having the best time ever," Kevin said as he swam up to Eve. Her heart skipped a beat as they kissed.

*****

Hours had passed; they'd eaten, drank a lot and danced a lot. A light was positioned behind the table and Turkish music played in the background. Selina and Mehmet gyrated in the clearing, arms entwined, her grabbing at his hair, him holding her bottom. Ryan sat under a tree next to Rachel. Eve smelt the sweet smoke that came from their direction. He looked better than he did earlier that day. When they first arrived he had been almost comatose but now he seemed relaxed. She watched as Rachel took a drag of the roll up and passed it back to Ryan. Her dilated pupils stared at him, her mouth laughed at the joke that never was. All of them were either drunk or stoned.

Stephen was splayed out on a fold up chair with a spilt can of lager beside him, his snoring body was being silently attacked by more mosquitoes. Eve pulled out some repellent from her bag and sprayed it over his flesh. "I love you Eve," Kevin whispered as she came back over to him.

Eve gazed deep in to the eyes behind the glasses, he loved her, she could tell. Her heartbeat became erratic and a shiver ran through her body. For years she had known him, for years he had been in her life. Both of them too shy to ever make a move. He had been a dependable best friend through her teen years. She knew there was always something special between them, but she never predicted how strong or quick those feelings would develop once they had spent a few years apart after leaving high school. She smiled and touched his hand, he was always the one. Looking back she knew that now, at least she hoped that he was.

When she had met Justin and fell for his charms, then suffered the wrath of everyone over their relationship and had Harry; she had always speculated at the 'what ifs' when it came to Kevin. He was the one she let slip away during her journey into adulthood. During her depressed year she had thought of him often but could never have made the first move back into his life. She was young with a child, trying to make her way into some sort of respectful existence. Even her new job and evening classes hadn't pushed away the haters, she had too much to prove back then and felt that any contact with Kevin would've been littered with 'I told you so.' She should've known better, he wasn't like that, she had been stupid again. Eve rubbed the back of her neck while still looking at Kevin. "I'm getting worried now Eve," he said as he smiled back.

"I love you too, I've always loved you," she whispered as she leaned forward and kissed him. He played with the back of her sun dried hair and stroked her face. The light around them flickered as insects fluttered in front of it. She grabbed him and held him tight. She had never felt so much love for someone except Harry. Harry! She pulled away from Kevin and grabbed her phone, it was just gone nine. "I've got to call Harry," she said as she stood and walked off leaving him sat alone.

No signal, everywhere she walked it was the same. A little circle with a line through it. She trudged across to the cars. She had a flicker, one bar. Quickly she dialled the number but before the call had connected, the signal dropped again. She walked farther away. Scurrying back up the dirt track they had come down, she was soon in darkness. The only light that she had was that from her phone. It had plenty of light but still no signal. She leaned against a tree and wept. She had let Harry down. She saw in her mind his little face waiting for her call. She then saw in her mind his little upset face when his father told him that Mummy Eve hadn't called even though she'd promised. Would he hate her for it? She placed the phone in her pocket and allowed her eyes to adjust to the darkness. The clear night sky twinkled with a few stars. She could see the light by the pool flickering in the distance.

There was a rustle behind her. "Who's there?" Silence. "Is that you Kevin?" Again silence. There was another rustle. Her heart beat hard and fast. Rooted to the spot, she tried once again to latch on to the rustling sound. A branch snapped. She ran fast, back towards the light. As she tried to look back she stumbled and fell into some warm arms. Screaming, she hit the body hard.

"Eve, it's me. You've been gone a while. I was worried," Kevin said as he comforted her.

"I heard something in the bushes," she replied weeping.

"And I'm sure we're not alone out here, animals, birds," he smiled.

She looked up at him; her heart was now running at normal speed. "I got spooked. It was so dark. I couldn't get through to

Harry. He's going to think I don't care," she yelled as she burst into tears.

"Of course he's not. Look at me," he said as he placed his hand on her chin and looked her in the eye. "You are a wonderful mother and he loves you." She fell into his embrace and enjoyed being comforted. She would call Harry first thing. Tell him how much she loved him and explain that she couldn't call him even though it had hurt her heart not to. He would understand, at least she hoped he would.

*****

That was close. Guz's hands shook as he placed the knife down. She would be the hardest one to control. Why had she not drunk as much as the others? Why was she so alert? Mehmet was right. Some of them looked good. The one who came close would be worth a bit and the drunken one with Mehmet. He stared over and saw Sadik stroke a loose strand of hair that had fallen from Celile's bun. She removed the clip and allowed her hair to cascade over her shoulders and down her back. Sadik stroked her mane again. Grabbing the knife he stabbed it violently into the earth below. He panted hard and spittle escaped from his mouth and dribbled down his chin. He wiped it off with his arm.

He slouched back down, watching, waiting for the right time. He had to be there as soon as they broke the crowd and some of them began to move alone. They were now ready for easy picking.

Chapter 18

"Hey. Is it time to go yet?" Eve shouted as she sat up from the floor.

Ignored by them all except Kevin, he replied. "I don't think anyone's listening."

"It's gone eleven, I've had enough of being here now. I want to go back."

To her right, Mehmet and Selina lay on a rug laughing and kissing. Behind her, Ryan and Rachel still giggled at nothing as they ate crisps. Stephen had turned his bag into a pillow and lay on the floor snoring.

"Here, why don't you have a drink and enjoy yourself," Celile said as she approached from behind and held a bottle of beer in front of Eve's face.

"No, I mean no thank you. I've had enough and I'm a bit tired."

"Anyone would think you were older than your friends," Celile said without smiling.

Eve turned her head and looked at the small woman. "No, thank you. I don't want a drink. It may seem old to you for me not to want a drink, but I've had enough and I'd rather go."

Celile went back to the table that her and Sadik had been sat behind and pulled out a full bottle of Vodka. "Your friend here wants to go. Do you all want to go or shall we crack this open and it's on us?" She shouted as she pointed at Eve.

Ryan, Rachel and Selina looked up. "Like hell we're going anywhere," shouted Ryan. "Crack it open and turn up the music," he yelled.

Celile broke the seal on the bottle and took a swig, all the time she kept her eyes focused on Eve. "Have some Honey. You'll feel much better," she said as she thrust the bottle into Eve's hand.

"She said no," Kevin said as he grabbed the bottle from Eve and handed it back at Celile. The woman was then beckoned over by Selina; she headed over to her, glancing back at Eve as she did. "Let them have their fun, this can't go on forever," he said with a smile. She felt his delicate fingers tease her hair as she snuggled into his chest on the floor.

There was something wrong. Why couldn't anyone else see it? They had fed them a feast, given them watermelon, given them drinks, opened up a bottle of exported vodka. Was it generosity or was there something else going on? They can't have made any money on the excursion and the way that woman had tried to force the drink on her wasn't right but no one else could see. Eve lay down, put her head on her elbow and gazed around. The light flickered as insects fluttered in front of it. The whole night seemed surreal creating an uneasiness in her stomach.

Needing to pass the time, she closed her eyes and imagined she was at home watching Disney films with Harry. His most recent obsession was with Pinocchio. She smiled as she remembered their last weekend together. They had been sitting on the sofa, his little body snuggled up to hers under his favorite blue blanket. They ate chocolate buttons and laughed as the wooden boy's nose had grown. She had stroked his soft hair until he'd fallen asleep in her arms. She would do that again as soon as she could except this time Kevin would be there. She pictured Kevin with them having a movie night; they could order pizza or even go out for pizza.

"Smoke?" A voice whispered in her ear. Eve looked up. Celile now had a roll up, the same type that Ryan and Rachel were smoking earlier that evening. "It's good stuff, we've got more if you need it," she smiled. "Let us treat you while you are here." She looked around, Kevin slept next to her.

"I really don't want any," Eve replied.

"You should have a bit; it will make you enjoy yourself. All your friends are enjoying themselves."

Maybe she was a bit tense. Eve had never smoked before, let alone smoked drugs. She thought of Harry and how she'd let him down if she took it. She watched everyone else, all so serene and having so much fun. She took the roll up and held it in her hand.

"Celile? I need help putting this table down," Sadik called.

"Okay, I'm coming," she said as she looked back.

Eve forced herself to cough hard and fast. She rubbed her eyes, smudging what was left of her eyeliner into her face.

"See, it is nice isn't it? Celile said as she turned back to Eve. "Keep it and have the rest."

"Thanks," Eve replied as the woman walked back. She pushed the lit end into the earth and extinguished it. Her pretending to smoke the spliff had at least got Celile to leave her alone. She stretched her legs and yawned. What she wouldn't do to be back at the villa. She looked around, Rachel was now rubbing Ryan's crotch over the top of his shorts. Selina was giggling and drinking from the vodka bottle. They would have so many regrets the next day, Eve thought. Celile and Sadik were putting down the fold up tables and filling up a bag with rubbish. Maybe they were getting ready to go Eve hoped as she stared at the dark pool in front of her. She took a swig from the bottle of water beside her and placed the empty bottle back down.

Fidgeting, she could no longer get comfortable with her full bladder. She looked around, aiming to seek out a quiet spot to relieve the aching. She opened her beach bag and took out a bit of tissue, there was no way she could wait until they got back to the villa and the journey would be horrendous with a full bladder. She looked up at the stars, they were twinkling brightly, at least there would be a little bit of light to help her navigate the shrubs.

She stood carefully so that Kevin could stay at rest. So tired from the day, he was now sleeping peacefully. Not being able to resist she knelt and gently kissed him on the cheek, he stirred but then went back to sleep. To her side were her pumps, she put them on. She stood and walked to her left along the water's edge. The dirt pathway became thinner the farther away she walked. Using her phone to light up the earth beneath her, she trod onwards. The music became distant, she was far enough away to have a wee without being disturbed. She turned behind a clump of shrubs. First she took off her tee-shirt, then pulled down her swimsuit and shorts. She stooped as she listened intently to the laughter and music. She heard Selina scream playfully in the distance. As she stood she heard that familiar crack in the bushes. Similar to the noise she'd heard earlier that evening. Animals, she said to herself. In the distance, she could see that everyone was still at the party, no one was missing. It was her imagination. She pulled her swimsuit and her shorts back up.

Another crack. This time louder, closer. It was a well-defined crack, one that would have been made by a large animal. Shaking, she turned to see the outline of a figure. Lit up by starlight only, she couldn't make out any features. Her stomach tightened as her heart raced. The figure took another step closer and vanished behind the tree that was right beside her. She turned and ran, screaming as she reached the dirt path and screaming as she reached the clearing. The music had been turned up. Why had the music been turned up?

She looked across at Sadik and Celile. Sadik nodded at her. Celile then turned away and whispered into his ear. Her screaming had barely registered with the others. She threw herself on her knees beside Kevin and shook him until he woke up. Startled, he sat up, grabbed his glasses and looked all around him. "What's happening?"

Eve flung herself down beside him and held him tight. Wrapping her arms around his neck she sobbed, blood pumped around her body. "Eve, tell me. Why are you shaking?"

"There was someone. I needed the loo. There was someone back there in the bushes."

Celile came over with a bottle of water. "Are you okay? Can I help?"

"No. You know what this is all about don't you? It's all a set up. This, here."

"I'm sorry?" Celile replied with a confused look on her face.

"They're fucking with us Kevin. Something's going on around here."

"Look, calm down and tell us what you saw." Kevin replied. Celile sat next to them and lay her hand on Eve's shoulder. Eve shrugged it off.

"I needed the loo. There was a man back there. I saw his outline. He was coming at me and I ran. I ran," she sobbed. "I was so scared Kevin."

"There's no one else here. We're miles away from any houses," Celile said.

"Really? Well who did I see then? I'm the only one sober here and I saw a man," she yelled back.

"It's my fault," Celile laughed as she looked at Kevin. "I gave her a spliff, thought she might enjoy herself more. It's just a side effect Honey. A bit of paranoia."

"I didn't smoke your fucking spliff," Eve yelled as she pulled it from the earth and threw it at Celile.

"Right Honey. I saw you take a puff. But for you and to reassure you both, I will get Sadik to go and check. Happy?" Celile snapped. Eve stared at Celile, Celile stared back. She couldn't trust that woman one bit. The woman grinned then stood. "Sadik," she called. "Go and check down river. The lady says she saw a man in the bushes. It might be the Bogeyman." Celile shrugged, pointed her finger to her head and pulled a face.

"I'm not crazy," Eve whispered in Kevin's ear.

"I know you're not. Are you sure you didn't have any of that smoke? It wouldn't take a lot you know?"

"Don't you believe me either? This is insane." Eve yelled. "Why can't anyone see what's happening here apart from me?"

"What's happening? Tell me," Kevin asked as he took her shaking hand.

"I don't know. It's just something. We're not safe."

"What can they do to us? There are three of them and six of us. We're safe," he said as he kissed her on the head.

"And the one in the bushes, that makes four. We're all drunk, helpless and that's what they want," she cried.

"Come here. It'll all be over soon." Kevin said. She snuggled into Kevin's chest. He didn't believe her, no one did. How had she become such an uncredible witness in a few short hours? She saw a man, there was a man. She kept repeating the sentence in her head. She wouldn't be convinced otherwise. She saw him, she heard him and she smelt him. Her heart quickened as she flashed back to a brief smell of sickly sweets and rotten sweat that flashed by her nose from the bushes.

"There's nothing there," Sadik called as he trampled back along the mud path. "I found this tee-shirt though," he said as he placed it next to Eve on the floor. She had forgotten about her top, she must have left it hanging on the bush.

"Well, thank you for checking," called Celile. She came back over to Eve. "See, there's no one there. Can I get you a drink?" she smiled. Eve ignored her and closed her eyes. They would have to go soon, they couldn't stay forever. She sniffed and wiped her eyes. There was a man; there was a man; there was a man. She kept repeating the sentence in her head as she stayed in the safety of Kevin's arms. There was a man.

Chapter 19

"Find out what's happening back there," Celile whispered to Sadik.

"It'll look odd. Anyway, they are Guz's problem. I'd rather stay here and look at you," he replied as he stroked her cheek. He looked into the distant darkness and couldn't see any movement. Sure that Guz had retreated farther away he stroked Celile's neck and released her hair from the clip. It fell down her back releasing the fragrance from her shampoo. Roses, he smiled. She always smelled of rose. The smell transformed him to earlier when they'd made love, taking their time in the knowledge that Guz would definitely not be back. His stomach flipped and he smiled as he replayed the memory to himself. She was the only woman who'd ever made his stomach flip.

She pushed him away and stepped back. "We can't let him see us like this. Soon my love. For now, you have to go and find out what went wrong. He should've taken her out and then we'd all be a step closer to going home tonight."

Eve stared at them, Sadik nodded and smiled. "She's a problem," he whispered as he maintained his smile for Eve.

"Don't I know it?" Celile replied.

"Well, I need a bush myself," Sadik shouted as he stood trying to make himself heard over the music. He watched as Eve looked away and snuggled into Kevin's chest. He was safe to go.

He scurried off along the mud path searching for his brother. The music was now a distant sound. He stepped over the wild undergrowth heading in the direction that Eve had ran from. Farther he travelled through the bushes but his brother was nowhere to be seen.

"Guz, Guz," he whispered. His eyes darted in all directions following the various sounds of the forest but he couldn't see Guz. He looked around then stepped forward again, "Guz?"

"Boo." Sadik gasped as he stepped back and fell into a tree stump. "Got you," Guz said.

"What the hell was that for?"

"Just passing the time brother, just passing the time."

Sadik's heart beat at an uncomfortable speed. He stood, then bent over and took some deep breaths.

"Did I make you piss yourself," Guz said as he laughed.

"Fuck you," replied Sadik. "We're here to do a job, not mess about."

"Except you're taking too long getting them hammered and I'm getting bored."

"You had a chance. Why did you let the girl go? You're getting slack old man." Sadik laughed.

Guz stared at his brother. Sadik's laughter subsided. He gulped. Guz grabbed him by his tee-shirt and shoved him to the ground. Sadik coughed, winded by the impact of being hauled onto his back. "You think you can do better, young man? You think you can butcher them, and then bury them?"

"I was just joking. What the hell is up with you?" Sadik stood and dusted his clothes off. Guz stepped forward, his nose touched Sadik's. His eyes were full of rage, his sweat dripped onto Sadik's nose.

"I can see you brother, I can see everything you do from here. Everything."

Sadik gulped again. His nose twitched as he inhaled Guz's stale breath. Unpleasant but he couldn't move, fixed until Guz gave him permission to leave; the same as it always had been. His mind raced with fear. Had Guz seen the way he looked at Celile? He probably had. He shouldn't have touched her. She'd said he was becoming too complacent with his open affections but he thought Guz may have mistaken it for a sister-in-law type love.

"If I see you touch her again, it will be you buried in the woods, alone. Do you understand?"

Knees shaking he forced his head to nod in a slow up and down motion. Guz drew his head back a few inches. Sadik closed his eyes and waited for the impact of Guz's head on his. Breathing in and out, in and out. Faster and faster. He waited until Guz burst out laughing.

"Old man, you make me laugh. You need to grow some hair on your balls," he said as he burst into a bout of mocking laughter. Sadik opened his eyes. "She wouldn't go for a mouse like you. That woman back there needs a man. That's why she's with me brother. Just don't keep drooling over her, you're an embarrassment."

Relieved, Sadik exhaled as he tried to gain his composure back. Maybe their relationship wasn't exposed but he knew from this that they had to be more careful.

"You should get back to the party, they may get suspicious and come looking for you," Guz said as he leaned against the tree, took out a cigarette and lit it. He inhaled and blew the smoke into

Sadik's face. Sadik coughed. "Market baccy," Guz laughed. "Maybe this lot have something better tucked in their bags." He took another drag. Sadik moved back not wanting to get in the path of the toxic smoke that would inevitably come his way if he remained rooted to his current spot. "Go on. Move it." Guz waved him away and turned to face the crowd. Sadik walked backwards until he was out of Guz's view. He turned and scurried off back to the mud path. The music became louder as he got nearer.

"You took your time. I was getting worried," Celile said as she went to touch his face.

He grabbed her hand and stood away from her. "He's been watching us, he suspects." Both of them stood together, not touching or looking at each other. Sadik scanned the clearing; Eve was once again looking up at him. He could see her mind working quickly to piece the puzzle together. He knew the rules of the game. The Boss was the game maker. Guz and he were the players. A game you had to play, no option given. But, they could all win; it was a game of winners. He stared at Eve and forced a smile once again. He swallowed hard, it wasn't a game of winners for them; he looked away from Eve's direct stare. She knew; what she knew he couldn't fathom out, but she knew. She was on her guard. This game was a challenge bigger than the previous games.

Rachel giggled and stood. She and Ryan began to kiss hard, fast and passionately. She held out her hand and drew him towards the mud path. He saw Eve stand and shout. Too quiet for him to hear the details, he knew she was trying to stop them from going off. Rachel shouted back and Eve threw herself to the floor and shuffled along the ground to be by Kevin. Kevin hugged her and stroked her hair.

Past him they went. He watched as they stumbled along the uneven path until they disappeared into the distance. His heart skipped a beat, let the game begin.

Chapter 20

As she stumbled over the dirt track Rachel stopped causing Ryan to slam into her. She began to laugh as she turned to face him. "Are you sure you want this?"

He looked into her dilated pupils, "Yes-" she placed her finger over his mouth silencing his next words as she laughed. She grabbed his hand and led him unsteadily over the mounds of moss and rocks until they were far away from the crowd. The only noise she heard was the distant thumping of the music. Close by, water trickled; they were alone.

Rachel dragged him deep into the bushes. She turned back and smiled as she made eye contact with Ryan. Barely able to see him in the dark, she hoped that he could see enough to read her expressions. She wanted someone, he was here, now and willing to be with her. Pulling her tee-shirt over her head, she revealed the khaki bikini top that she'd displayed earlier. Her large cherry blossom tattoo snaked around her abdomen and up her back.

Laughing again, she unclipped her bikini top and dropped it to the floor revealing the dimly lit outline of her small pale breasts.

Ryan stood there motionless, waiting to be directed. She stepped over to him, grabbed his hand and placed it on her breast. He stroked her, she kissed him, trying to draw him in further but his responses were restrained. "What's wrong?"

"It feels weird. We've never-"

"Don't you like me? I thought, all night you've been over me like a rash and-"

"Shh," he replied as he held his finger to her mouth. "I never thought you liked me. We've known each other for a long time. I just-"

"You just what Ryan?"

"I want you here, now," he said as he leaned on her slightly to maintain his balance.

"Well I want you too, so take me," she grinned. He stared at her, a devilish smile emerging from his lips. Without hesitation, he grappled with the button on her shorts as she tried to drag his top over his head. With each moment that passed their lips locked hard, she felt the blood pumping through her body, she needed him now. Her shorts down, bikini bottoms next, she stepped back and stood against a tree dragging him with her. Hot and sweaty she lead him close, directed his movement, they were ready. Enjoying his rhythm, she tried to tap out of the surroundings. She thought it would be exciting but the woods were so dark, so dense. The music sounded distorted and she felt light headed. The sickly sweet smoke smell that lingered in her hair kept coming back to haunt her.

"Ahh," Ryan yelled as he came to an end. His hands grappled with her breasts. He leaned into her, keeping himself upright by placing his hands palm outwards on the tree with Rachel locked inside his arms. "That was good, you are good," he said as he slumped to the floor. Disappointed, she slumped beside him as she rubbed her splintered lower back.

She grabbed her tee-shirt and pulled it over her head. A few seconds of what? she thought. It was as if it never happened. The blood that pumped through her body was beginning to calm down. As her breath returned to normal, she analysed her thoughts. Hollow, unsatisfied feelings and thoughts. "Have you got a cigarette?"

"In the pocket of my shorts," he replied, eyes closed.

She stood, put on her bikini bottoms, then her shorts and fumbled in his pocket. Cigarettes and a lighter. Two left. "Do you want one?" No reply. He was sitting up against the tree, now flaccid and snoring. Rachel grabbed his top off the ground and placed it over his groin area. The whole scenario now felt awkward. Grabbing her bikini top she turned to leave, he would wake up and join them once he'd rested. The music still sounded distorted and her vision was laboured, she vowed to quit smoking pot once she returned home. Stepping carefully, she negotiated every bump on the ground and every tree root that protruded through the hard soil.

Crunch, then again. A snapped twig. A smell of sweat, not her smell. Then, in a moment she found herself on the floor face first, hands behind her back, then thud. Pain struck the back of her head. She tried to scream but only a gentle yelp emerged. She heard the sound of tape being peeled off a roll. "Please don't hurt me," she whimpered. The tape was placed across her mouth and around her head, wrapped around twice. Her senses began to come back after the blow to the head. Struggling, she tried to free her arms but they were bound; rope, tape, she couldn't tell. The perpetrator rolled her onto her back before binding her feet with rope. His outline lit up, all she could see was an average height man who was whispering to himself in Turkish. Shaking, she tried to wriggle free but the bindings were so tight. Her stomach turned, she closed her eyes and concentrated hard trying to suppress the nausea. Her legs trembled and her body felt clammy. She felt bits of the ground stick to her hair and body as she wriggled in the dry mud and pine needles. He straddled her as he held a large hunting knife in one hand. Through the darkness she could see the chips on his white teeth as he grinned at her. Tears rolled down her cheeks and her nose began to fill with mucous. Stop, she thought. Stop or you will die.

Looking away, she tried to think of happier times. She thought of her nanna who she might never see again, her lovely nanna who had sold things to buy her the wonderful camera that she'd been snapping away with. The nanna who had brought her up. She hadn't made her that proud; she might die without making her nanna proud. More tears rolled. Then she stopped. Who was he? What was happening? She had to remain calm, remember everything; survive.

The man stood and walked away. Ryan. She wriggled, trying hard to find a trail of rope or something near her hands that she could grip. There was nothing. She was helpless. All she could do was listen with the one ear that wasn't covered by tape.

"What?" Ryan murmured. She heard a loud thud and a wheeze coming from Ryan. Then scuffling, earth being strewn around. Grunting. Moaning. Running. Ryan almost fell as he darted from behind the tree, shouting as he emerged. He stared at Rachel and stopped.

Her mind and eyes shouted, 'get these binds off me, help me,' but her body lay there, helplessly bound. Wiggling around on her back, she hoped that Ryan would bend down to help her but he turned to run and was followed by the man who had attacked her. Behind her she heard Ryan yelp followed by a thud. Her heart beat fast, Ryan was her only hope. He had to get away, get help, and get the others. There was shouting and struggling but the details were lost by the dominant sound of the pumping music. She struggled and managed to loosen the rope on her hands. Desperate, she rubbed the binds hard on a stone, so hard it began to miss the binds and cut into her wrist. Flinching with every scrape, she continued until she heard footsteps behind her.

The man had returned. A dark liquid dripped from the side of his knife. "It was all over quick, he didn't suffer. That's what happens when you fight me," said the man. Clouds passed and they were plunged into darkness. Tears welled up once more and were harder to suppress this time. Her nose filled up with mucous. She blew hard, expelling it down the side of her cheek. Inside she was screaming. In her mind she was smashing up the furniture and kicking anyone who came near her. She wanted the bindings off so she could lash out, break down. Ryan had gone, she knew it. He had shared his last moment with her. Who would she spend her last moments with? Again she blew her nose hard. Two ants crawled across her face; she closed her mouth and then her eyes. "If you want to live, you will play by the rules. Shut up and keep still. Do you understand me?"

Rachel nodded. She wanted to live more than anything. Without warning she felt a needle prick in her arm. Within seconds the blackness took over and she was in another world. Home with Nanna.

Chapter 21

"They've been gone ages. I told you something was wrong." Eve shouted as she twiddled a strand of hair, weaving it between her fingers before releasing it. The music pounded through her head.

"They've been gone a few minutes that's all. I can't exactly chase after them and demand they come back now. At least, I don't think Ryan would thank me." Kevin said as he sat back down. "I think you should sit next to me, let me massage your neck and relax."

The light twinkled off his blue eyes, he looked at her convincingly, she wished she could let herself sit, relax and enjoy the party but her stomach fluttered and not in a love struck way. It nagged her, telling her that things were strange, that she needed to do something. "We should go and check on them. It'll only take a minute. If you don't want to come, I'll go alone."

"You can't do that to them. We both know why they've headed off into the bushes. They don't want anyone else around."

"They won't know I'm there. I just want to see that they are okay." Eve stood and walked towards the path, gazing out into the darkness she couldn't see a thing. She looked back. Celile watched her and grinned as Sadik whispered in her ear. Eve wandered down the dark path, just a few steps into the darkness that had scared her so much a few minutes before. Trembling, she stepped forward while trying to look for movement ahead. She couldn't see anything. The music blared out, hearing them wouldn't be possible.

She flinched, a warm hand brushed across her side. "Kevin? You decided to come and help me look for them."

"No, I've come to tell you to leave them be. They don't want you sneaking up on them in the middle of whatever they're doing and scaring them to death. They will be back soon, let's just go back and wait." Kevin said. She took his hand and allowed him to lead her back into the clearing.

Eve picked her nails, not feeling at all reassured. She watched as Kevin walked over to Celile and came back with a bottle of water. Selina fell over while trying to dance and wearing only one sandal. Mehmet lifted her back up and helped her over to Eve. She flopped to the floor and giggled as she rolled aimlessly on the ground. Stephen coughed and sat up. "What time is it?"

"Why do we care? Time is time and is time and we have it don't we Mehmet?" Selina shouted.

"Yes, a lot of time." Mehmet said as he smiled back and walked over to Celile. Eve observed his mannerisms as he reached his uncle. This young, happy, drunken man tensed up. His shoulders straightened, he ran his fingers with precision through his dark greasy hair as he leaned up against a tree.

"Turn around," Eve whispered. She wanted to see his face, read his expression, wait for him to give something away but he remained in the same position with his back to her.

"Evie, can I have a cigarette?" Selina said as she rolled into Eve and yanked her tee-shirt.

"You know I don't smoke Sel. Wait until Rachel gets back, she'll give you a ciggie." Eve replied. Selina continued tugging on her tee-shirt and laughing. "Selina, you're being annoying now. Why did you have to drink so much?" Eve shouted.

"Evie's fed up with me. Evie won't help me. Sel wants a ciggie."

"Selina, can't you just have a nap or something? Oh why me?" Eve yelled as she stood and grabbed her hair with her hands. Selina lay on her back looking up at the stars, pretending to grab them out the sky.

"Look, she's just had a few too many," Kevin said with a laugh.

"You and me both," Stephen interjected as he scratched the bites on his legs. "Pissing nature. I'm all natured out."

"I know. Everyone seems to have had a few too many, that's what I'm worried about. He," she said as she pointed at Mehmet, "has been over there talking for ages. He doesn't look as drunk as he should be. I haven't seen his face, if I could see it I'd know. I'd read it. Rachel and Ryan. Where are they? You tell me that. It's been about twenty minutes now." Eve yelled.

"At least she stands a chance of enjoying it then," Stephen smirked.

"It's not funny. They could be in danger. They could need our help and all we're doing is sitting here, drinking."

"And wanting a ciggie," Selina yelled as she pretended to catch a star and place it in her pocket.

Eve felt her neck redden, why wouldn't any one take notice of what she was saying? "Do any of you hear what I'm saying?"

Kevin placed his hand on her shoulder. "Look, when Ryan and Rachel return, I'll kick up a stink with you and we can all go back."

"We don't want to go back, it's exciting here." Selina replied.

"You're not in a position to exercise any rational form of decision making being as pissed as you are," Eve shouted.

"I maybe pissed but at least I know how to have a good time," Selina grinned as she stared at Eve before bursting into a full fit of laughter. "Have a good time, have a good time," she sang to the music as she howled with laughter. Stephen shrugged his shoulders and joined in.

"You've got no chance of getting any sense out of them," Kevin said as he opened his bottle of water and took a swig before sitting back down on the floor.

"I've had enough of all this, I've had enough of you all." Eve bent down and grabbed her water.

"Eve-" Kevin said.

"I need a moment to myself. I need to think."

"Evie needs to think," Selina sang, "Rhymes with, Evie needs to stink, Evie's looking for a bush," she once again rolled on the floor in fits of laughter.

Kevin stood and ran after her. "Eve wait."

"I just need a moment alone. Okay?" She looked away; her eyes were welling up with tears. What she wouldn't give to be back home with Harry. She glanced over her shoulder and saw Kevin standing there.

"Okay, don't wander too far," he called back. She walked off uphill towards the jeep and took her mobile phone out of her pocket. Still no signal and the battery was running low.

Away from the music, she could hear herself think. Taking a deep breath, she used the light from her phone to illuminate the undergrowth. A tree stump. She sat with the light off in silence, thinking, dreaming about leaving this night behind. In the distance, she could see Celile leaning against the tree talking to Sadik and

Mehmet. They seemed engrossed in conversation. Mehmet shook his head as Celile stared at him before holding her hands up. She needed to get farther around, closer to them. She wanted to see their features and find out what was going on. "I will see your face," she whispered as she stood.

Chapter 22

Mehmet stared hard into his uncle's eyes, then back at Celile. She looked away. "How can you be doing this? This is wrong."

"We're in too deep. We have to complete this job or we're all going to end up being drowned in the concrete foundations of The Boss's next villa," Sadik replied as he stared at the ground.

"I can't hurt her. You can't hurt them." Mehmet grabbed his own hair and pulled; he released a roar and began to weep. "I thought it was robbery. We were stealing a few Euros', maybe a passport or even a handbag. This is murder. I haven't travelled half way across this country for this. How can you do this to me?" he shouted.

"Shut up. You're going to draw attention to us," Celile said.

"What the hell does it matter, they can't understand us." Mehmet shouted as he waved his arms and held the side of his head.

Celile grabbed his arms and forced them back down by his sides. He stared at her, simmering anger waiting to be released through his chattering teeth. "But they can see your arms waving about. They can see him," she pointed at Sadik, "arguing with you. Just grow up; this is the way it has to be. It's us or them, only good thing is we end up richer too."

"It's not too late. We could pack up, go, leave."

"It is too late. Firstly, no one packs up on The Boss. Secondly, I think we've already eliminated two of them. There's no going back."

"Eliminated? Rachel and the other one?"

"That's right. And you know who's out there doing the work we can't do?"

"No. How could he?"

"Your father's doing this for you, for us." Celile looked across at Sadik and winked. Mehmet looked at her confused, spittle dripping out the side of his mouth as he inhaled and exhaled fast and hard. "He only wants what's best for you. You are all he ever talks about. His boy, his wonderful boy." She smiled at him and stroked his cheek. Mehmet grabbed her hand hard and squeezed maintaining eye contact. He squeezed her harder; she showed no pain, just a stark look of defiance. Letting her shaking hand go, he looked away.

"Now have some gratitude and help him. Besides you are one of us. If this doesn't go smoothly, you will be boss bait or end up in jail if you're lucky. You're in it with us. You protect us and we'll protect you." Celile placed her hand under his chin and lifted it up so that his eyes were once again at her level. "Do you understand?"

"You hurt Selina; I'll break your scrawny neck," he whispered.

"You hurt her, I'll break you." Sadik said as he glared at Mehmet.

"What was that? I just saw a light, behind you." Celile said, her eyes focusing on the spot. Mehmet scanned the scenario in front of them. Stephen was still sitting on the ground; he was gazing at the trickling water. Selina, his beautiful Selina was lying on her back singing something, maybe humming along with the music. Her long soft hair splayed all around her gathering dust. Kevin was standing and gazing into the bushes while swigging water. Eve? She was gone. The light in the bushes. It had to be Eve.

*****

Had they seen her, she couldn't tell. She hopped away as she rubbed the sting on her foot, gathering speed as the pain calmed down. She'd only wanted to see what was biting her which is why she'd used the light on her phone, that woman saw the light. Her heart pounded, she felt bile rising up her throat. She had seen his face and in it, she had seen a look of fear. Celile was a predator, showing no fear in the face of threat. She ran and ran, the music got louder as she approached her friends. She had to warn them.

Chapter 23

"Kevin, I saw him. I saw his face. They were arguing about something. I couldn't understand but it's not right." Eve shouted while still trying to compete with the music. She took a deep breath; sweat dripped over her brow and her face glowed red.

"Calm down, you saw what?" Kevin took her hand and led her aside.

"Look at them." As they turned to look Sadik pushed Mehmet who stumbled into Celile. "Now tell me all is good. We have to get the others and go." Behind her Stephen lay on a blanket, with his eyes shut. Eve gave him a gentle kick. "Wake up, we've got to go."

"Is it time?" He mumbled as he lifted his head and rubbed his eyes.

"It's way past time," she replied. She edged over to her rucksack and began packing her water and bug spray away. She looked in her bag, there was nothing sharp that could be used as a weapon. Selina lay on the floor, still humming to herself with her eyes closed. She smiled, parted her lips and licked her teeth before having a spurt of the giggles.

"Wait. Rachel and Ryan. We have to find them."

Stephen stirred and stretched his arms out. "I'll look for them. You can keep an eye on Selina. It's not like a few more bites will kill me anyway," he said as he laughed and took a swig from the can beside him. "Empty, damn." He laughed once more as he crushed the can.

"It's not funny. Go now," Eve insisted as she bent down to help Stephen up. Kevin leaned over to help her. Stephen sighed.

"Okay, I can stand on my own," he said as he shook Kevin off and got to a standing position. He took a step back and hiccupped. "I best get a move on. Where should I look first?"

"Down the dirt path that runs alongside the river." Eve pointed. "They went that way. Wait," she pulled Stephen back. "I saw a man back there. There is someone out there. Go quietly." Eve looked across at their hosts who were still arguing. "Don't let them see you go, be quiet and stay hidden. Do you understand?"

"Don't you think you're being just a little bit paranoid?" he asked with a mocking smile.

"No, just do it," she said as she gently tapped him on the arm.

"Okay, okay. I'm going." He saluted her and turned to go.

Kevin hugged Eve. "It will all be okay. We'll get the others and go. I'm sure that lot over there are having some family problems or something."

"That doesn't explain the man in the bushes," Eve replied as she pulled away from his embrace.

"Eve, did you smoke any of that weed?"

"No, not a single drag. That woman kept trying to force it on me so I pretended to inhale some to get rid of her. I stubbed the rest out. You saw it." He looked her in the eye. She watched as his features softened and his breath deepened as he tried to process what she was saying.

"And, how sure were you when you said you saw someone in the bushes."

"As sure as I can be. I saw him, I could smell him and I felt his body heat. I can't be more sure." She shuddered at the realisation of what she'd just sent Stephen off to do. "What if Stephen gets hurt?"

"He's a grown man, he'll be fine. Someone has to go and check on our friends and someone has to stay and keep an eye on you and Selina. I got the best job," he said as he smiled.

"He's going to get hurt. They've been gone so long, something's happened to them," Eve burst into tears. Kevin embraced her and stroked her hair. She felt his warm fingers massage her head. Over his shoulder through teary eyes she saw Celile shout back at Mehmet. Arms flailing, faces irately sweating, pointing fingers shaking with tension, veins bulging on Sadik's head. Celile caught a glance at her weeping eyes and looked back, she shouted at the other two, they stopped and looked across at her. Then, as if instructed, they all looked away at once.

"Another drink?" Celile shouted with a fake smile plastered across her face.

Eve buried her head into Kevin's chest. "Don't turn around. They've stopped arguing and now they're looking at us."

"I'm going over. It's time we turned this music off and called an end to this party. We're going home." Kevin prised himself from their embrace, cleared his throat and began to walk over.

Eve turned, "Kevin," she beckoned him back. Celile smiled, holding up the bottle of vodka. Eve shook her head and smiled back hoping that her red watery eyes wouldn't give her fear away. "We can't let them know we're on to them."

"I think they already know you are."

"Probably, but I'll feel better when Stephen comes back. We get the others and go."

"Shall I go and look for Stephen?" Kevin said.

"No, don't leave me."

"He might have got hurt or something. You have Selina here with you." Selina turned around on the hard floor trying to get comfortable. Still open mouthed she had started breathing gently as she drifted off to sleep. A detached honey coloured hair extension lay next to her head.

"I somehow think I can't defend the two of us while she's like this." Eve said.

"Okay, we'll give it a few more minutes. You should wake her though. Tell her we're getting ready to leave."

Crouching, Eve shook Selina. "It's time to wake up." Selina shook off her hand, curled up into the foetal position and continued to sleep. "Selina," Eve called. Her friend began to rub her eyes and wake up. Her glassy half closed stare looked straight through Eve. Selina hiccupped hard and held one hand over her mouth and the other out as if to keep Eve out of the way. "We're going soon Sel; I need you to wake up."

Selina removed her hand from her mouth and smiled. "I'm good Evie, am I not good? I'm going to be alright but I'm tired. Can we go to bed?" she droned.

Eve smiled, sat next to her and stroked her hair. Selina placed her head onto Eve's shoulders and rubbed her eyes. "We're going back to the villa. As soon as Stephen gets back with the others," Eve whispered into her friend's ear. Selina reached out and held Eve's hand. Kevin cleared his throat again as he paced. Staring at the entrance to the dirt path, Eve shuddered at the thought of what was happening and could only hope that the others would hurry so that they could go.

Chapter 24

As he scratched his head, his shaggy hair got tangled in his fingers. "Ryan. Put Rachel down for five, we need you back here." There was no answer. He'd walked far enough for his flip flops to gather grit around his feet. He took the left one off and tipped out the grit before dropping the flip flop to the floor and sliding his foot back into it.

For the first time that evening, he could hear the water flowing past. "Hey, Ryan. You tosser. Give me a shout." He continued to stagger forward. "Ryan. You're a dick," he laughed. He pulled his shorts away from his swelling belly. Desperate to urinate, he stepped over to the river and laughed; he heard his urine splash with force as it pierced the water's skin. Hiccupping, he rearranged his shorts and carried on through the clearing.

In the distance he saw something white lay on the floor under a tree. Ryan's tee-shirt. He stumbled over and picked it up. Next to it lay his shorts. Feeling around in the pockets, Stephen found some cigarettes. Pulling the last one out, he placed it in his mouth and felt once again, this time for the lighter. No lighter. "Damn, where the hell are you?" He shivered, directly above him; something rustled then cooed and cawed. "Ryan?"

A branch snapped. Stephen laughed. "I see, you two are having a little game. You've finished playing games of your own and now you're bored." Walking over towards the direction of the noise, he stared at the spot. "I'm getting close." He took another step, grabbed the foliage and shifted it to the side with his arm. The light from the moon illuminated the edges of the leaves, edges of twigs but no edges of Ryan or Rachel. Running his fingers through his hair, he laughed. "Maybe it's Eve's bogeyman. Ryan the bogeyman, she wouldn't be far wrong." No response, no noise, no movement. "How about a fact?" He looked up towards the moon. "The surface area of the moon is about nine point four billion acres. You can tell me how anal I am again now. I'm waiting." No response.

"This isn't funny anymore. I've come to get you guys. We're leaving in a minute." He stood there and put the unlit cigarette in his mouth and pretended to take a drag before taking it out and putting it behind his ear. "I've got your clothes here Ryan. Seriously Dude, I don't want to come any further and catch sight of your incredibly white arse. Or even worse, I don't want to catch sight of yours Rachel."

After standing for a minute with no response or noise his feet led the way. Was it him or had the volume of the music been turned down a bit? Firmly grabbing the bush he prised it apart and proceeded on. He passed a group of smaller trees in a spiny bush lined clearing. His feet were getting sore from treading on pine cones through such thin soles. "Rachel," he called as he bashed his toe into a rock and fell to the ground. "Oh shit," he cursed as he struggled to achieve a sitting position before nursing his stubbed toe. He felt around the dark floor and picked up a stone. He dropped it down before feeling around again. His touch met something long, cool and soft. He lifted it up, it was attached. Dropping it he got to his feet. Snakes, maybe it was a snake. Trying hard to focus, he squinted and tried to stare at the dark snake, there was no movement. He prodded it, it remained. As he tried once more to lift it from the centre of its body he fell forward towards it. "You're a heavy snake," he whispered. The clouds parted and the moon shone again to reveal a mass. "Sausages," his drink addled mind struggled to process what lay before him. On his knees he took the mass and felt it more intricately. His fingers slid between the snakes fingers and the fit was near perfect. He dropped it and gasped for breath. "What the hell. Ryan, is that your hand?" He slapped the arm and pulled at the hand. "Ryan?" He parted the leafy mass and the only thing he saw was the moon's reflection in Ryan's open lifeless eyes. His breathing quickened as he let go of the arm and stood. Shaking he stepped back. Gasping for air he leaned to the side and heaved hard, vomiting up everything he had in him; a sobering reality setting in. Rubbing his eyes he turned in disbelief at what lay before him.

"Think Stephen, think," once again, he kneeled down. His reluctant hand touched Ryan's wrist. He tried to feel for a pulse but there was nothing. He tried to remember how to do CPR. An advert, he pictured Vinnie Jones in the CPR advert. Focusing on Vinnie Jones and not the body that lay before him, he stood, took the arm and with his weight behind him, dragged Ryan from under the bush. Kneeling again he began to thump hard and rhythmically at his chest, "Come on Ryan." His hands were wet, sweat maybe. As he pumped he heard a squelch and the wetness flowed harder. His hands were soaking, his shirt was soaking. Opening his mouth no words would escape him, a metallic stale smell hung in the air. He lifted his arms up towards the light. Blackness covered them and continued to trickle up his sleeve. Glaring down at his splattered front he began to cry silently but violently, no noise escaping. He felt along Ryan's naked body, first his chest, his arms and then his stomach. It was pierced. Shuffling backwards he curled up in a ball and sobbed, his silent sobs now turning into cries.

He'd done all he could, he now knew that he was covered in Ryan's blood and was sat next to Ryan's wounded dead body. Sobbing, he thought of Rachel. Had she done it? What had been happening back here while he'd been sat there drinking and sleeping all night? In the distance he heard another twig crack. He shuffled into the leafy recess where he had only seconds ago dragged Ryan's body from and he closed his eyes. If something was out there, it wasn't going to get him. His body trembled and his teeth chattered and he realised he was making a rustling noise himself.

    Trying hard not to think about the reality he tried to picture being home at work in the pet supply store. He thought of Mrs. Jenkins who came by once a week for her Collie Stanley's dog meat and Angie, his favourite yummy mummy. Even Angie couldn't make him smile after what he'd seen. His future; he was going to University in September to do the engineering degree he'd deferred and decided now was the time to do it. He wanted that, he wanted a girlfriend one day, he wanted a family. Just normal things. "I don't want much," he whispered in a controlled sobbing way. He heard another crack; whatever was out there was near. Maybe Eve had been right, maybe there was someone out in the mountains, a man. He shook his head, maybe it was Rachel. Maybe Ryan had come on too strong, he was wrecked. Maybe he hurt her and she had defended herself. He rocked back and forth in attempt not to cry out. So many scenarios running through his head. Rachel, the man, Ryan's body, Ryan's blood, Rachel, cracking twigs, creatures hooting, rustling. Even with his eyes closed he couldn't escape the one thing that haunted him now, the images of Ryan and thoughts of death were etched into his mind.

    Hyperventilating, he began to shake and panic, he had to get help. He forced himself to stand before turning to run. As he stood he caught a glimpse of a figure emerging beside him. Too stout for Rachel. Eve had been right, there was a man. The tremors ran through his knees, his arms felt like jelly as he stumbled back the way he'd come. Was it the way he came? All he could see was darkness. Disorientated, he stopped and turned around. Where's the music coming from? He couldn't hear it, maybe it was turned off. Maybe they had all gone and he had been left behind. In the distance he saw a light flicker; that was the way. He heard rustling behind him, he needed to run faster, the flip flops were slowing him down. He kicked them off to the side and carried on running. His whole body weight pushed his feet onto the solid curvy pine cones. Pine splinters stuck in his foot. Stumbling off track he emerged in a clearing and was faced by Rachel's body. She lay still, tape around her mouth, her wrists bound with rope. He stumbled towards her, dropped to his knees and began to pull at the binds on her wrists. He felt a shallow pulse. "Rachel, wake up," he shook her. She did not wake up.

    Thwack. His head spun before he fell back on to the hard ground. Above him stood a man, the whites of his eyes shone in the moonlight. He was holding up something long that caught the light. Metal; shiny. As the moon lit up the clearing he saw no fear or regret in the man's eyes. Was this his end? He grabbed hold of a handful of grit and threw it upwards, half of it falling back down into his gaping mouth. The beast that stood above him growled. Stephen attempted to turn onto his front so that he could stand and run. He had to warn the others, he kneeled then stood. Beside him he saw the man struggling and rubbing his eyes. As Stephen stood, the world was spinning. He closed his eyes and rubbed his head. Blood, his head was cracked. He dropped to his knees, the vertigo was too much to fight against. The man beast roared with anger and he felt a sharp pain in his upper back. He coughed and spluttered before falling face down onto the floor. He felt his ear get brushed and the click of a lighter as a smell of smoke filled the air. "I'm sorry Rachel," he said in his mind as his thoughts turned to blackness.

Chapter 25

Selina lay on her back gazing at the stars, everything spun for a moment. She closed her eyes and tried to divert her attention from the unpleasant wooziness that was kicking in. Throat dry, she swallowed with difficulty. Water, she needed water. In order to get water she needed to open her eyes, sit up and ask for some. She pushed herself up to a sitting position and opened one eye. "Even my hair's falling out." She grabbed the hair extension, screwed it up in her hand and threw it to her side. She part opened the other eye. The world wasn't spinning which was good. Then, pound; pound. The blood pumped through her body in time with her thumping head. "Evie, I'm getting a hangover already," she said. There was no answer.

Confused, Selina forced her head to turn. She spotted Eve with Kevin standing by the water's edge. He had his arm around her; she pulled away and looked over towards the light. She was saying something, speaking fast, erratically. Selina couldn't hear her, all she could see was their moving lips. She watched as Kevin stroked her face and kissed her once on the lips. "Evie," she called in a croaky voice that was barely able to escape. The need for water was becoming urgent, she needed it now.

Turning her head she spotted Mehmet, why did he look so angry? Were they arguing? It looks as though we've all had too much, she thought. Maybe Mehmet could get her some water. She placed her hands on the floor and tried to push herself up. Spinning again, she dropped back to the floor. Flat on her back she closed her eyes and rolled over onto her front. She placed her elbows down on the ground and leaned her head in her hands. It was best that she stayed floor bound for a while until she'd awoken properly. She coughed to try and alleviate the dryness in her throat before opening her eyes once again. The world was now the right way up. She watched as Celile shouted and Sadik pushed her aside. In one swift motion he grabbed Mehmet and punched him hard. The young man stepped back, shaking, aghast. He used his arm to wipe his bloody nose. "Mehmet." She pushed herself up and forced her unwilling body onto its feet. She swayed for a moment and the world was spinning again. Blood pumped hard through her body. Head throbbing harder, she took a step. "What are they doing to you? Stop it."

He looked back at her and a tear was falling down his face, blood trickled onto the floor. She had to get to him, shield him from his attackers. Both Celile and Sadik had left him behind and injured while they stood to one side talking. Concentrating hard, she placed one foot in front of the other and staggered to where Mehmet was standing.

"I'm so sorry," he wailed as he battled with the mucous and blood that fell from his nose. "I'm so sorry, I can't take this anymore."

Once again, the trees began to sway; Selina fell to the floor by Mehmet and grabbed his hand on the way down. He slid down the tree and sat next to her, grabbing her hand back.

"They hit you," she said slurring each word. Mehmet cried harder before taking Selina's head in his hands and holding her tightly. She felt his warm grip, breathed in his musky sweaty smell and allowed herself to be comforted in his arms. Whatever was happening would sort itself out. Tomorrow would be another day, although she'd never drink this much again. Tomorrow was a new start.

Chapter 26

"We've got to do something now," Eve said. "The jeep isn't far. If the keys are in it, we can take it and get help. We will get the cops then come back for the others."

"We can't leave them. Stephen, Rachel and Ryan are out there somewhere," Kevin replied.

"I know, but have you noticed that anyone who goes down that path doesn't come back? We have to go. I'm going to get Selina."

Eve walked over to where Selina and Mehmet sat embracing under a tree. She kneeled down and shook Selina. "Sel, we're going for a walk, come with us. It will help you sober up."

Mehmet looked up at her with his sad, blood smeared face. He lifted Selina's chin. "Selina, please go with your friends." He gave Eve a knowing look, almost pleading with her to take Selina to safety.

"Let go of me, I'm not going anywhere Evie," Selina replied as she half looked up. "If I move I'm going to be sick."

"It doesn't matter Sel. Be sick and we can walk. Please try." Eve pleaded.

Selina stayed buried in Mehmet's arms and placed her hand out before turning away.

"No, go for a walk on your own. I'm not coming," she said from Mehmet's muffled underarm.

Mehmet began to sob, his eyes red as he threw his head back against the tree trunk in despair. "But Selina, you need to go."

"Shut up," she said as she began to snore. Eve watched as Mehmet held her tight and sobbed harder. His desperate hands became tangled in her hair as he stroked her.

A tear emerged from the corner of Eve's eye. "Please keep her safe." She kneeled down and kissed Selina on the head and walked back towards Kevin. She watched as Celile and Sadik continued their bickering to one side, too engaged to even notice her as she passed them. On reaching Kevin, she threw her arms around him and held him tight.

"I don't know what's going on here; I just know I have to get out of this with you. I have to be with you Eve," he said as he grabbed her and embraced her back, hard.

She felt his stubbly chin press on her forehead and enjoyed the moment, wrapped safely in his arms. She pictured what they had seen. Sadik whacked Mehmet hard in the face, his bloody nose. It had been hard convincing Kevin that their situation was urgent but now she'd succeeded, she shivered at the prospect of what the next few minutes held. Eve knew that they needed to sneak off inconspicuously, get in the jeep and drive to the nearest police station. She was sure they passed a small village with a police station and police check area but she couldn't remember in which direction. They had taken so many twists and turns it was doubtful that they would even find a main road but they had to try. It was stay here and get embroiled in whatever was going down or make a run for it. It was survival. She held onto Kevin and tears began to flow down her face and land on Kevin's arms soaking part of his cotton shirt.

"There's something I have to tell you, that can't wait. I was waiting for a better moment."

Eve pulled away from his embrace and looked tearfully into his eyes. "Am I going to like it," she forced a smile and cried at the same time.

"I hope so." He paused and looked away towards the water. Frowning, he opened his mouth and then closed it again.

"Are you okay?"

"When I said I love you. I meant I really love you and I want us to make it out of here and be together. I've always loved you Eve. I should've listened to you earlier, I should-" she watched as he looked away, his hair fluttered as the gentle breeze caught it.

She grabbed him and kissed him hard. "Let's do this. I love you and we're going to get out of this hell."

Kevin took his glasses out of his shirt pocket and placed them on before holding her hand. Eve led Kevin towards the edge of the clearing. Sadik looked up at her. "I've left my mosquito lotion in the jeep," she said as she passed him. He stared at her; they stood there as if they were waiting to be dismissed. Sadik nodded and looked away. As they got out of sight, they began to hurry, they parted shrubs; kicked pine cones out the way; stepped over branches. It wasn't too far, just a couple of minutes away.

Eventually they reached the jeep and two cars. "There has to be keys in one of these vehicles. Get looking." Kevin called as they parted. Eve started with the car farthest away as Kevin tried the jeep. The door was locked, she looked through the windows and tried to focus under the moonlight, there were no keys in the ignition. The back seat contained an empty bottle of cola and a bag, not much use.

"There's nothing in this car," she called as she hurried over to the other car.

"Nor this jeep. Just Ryan's empty beer cans from earlier and a bag with water in it."

"I'll have the water, we might need it. We may be on foot if we can't get out of here by car."

"What? Everything's miles away." Kevin replied.

"I'll take it. You just never know," she said as she took the bottle out of his hand. They both scrambled to the next car, again it was locked. She pulled her phone out of her pocket, there was no signal but a message had come through earlier. She waved it about hoping for just one bar. "Please, come on," she yelled as she shook it. One bar would solve all their problems, she could call for help. Her phone beeped, the battery was running low. She looked down at the message.

'He was waiting for your call!!!!'

The phone went blank, the signal had gone.

"What was that?"

"I had a message earlier from Harry's Dad. I did try to call him, you know I tried to call him and I couldn't get a signal," she said as she began to sob hard. "Harry hates me."

Kevin ran over and lifted up her chin. "He doesn't hate you Eve. He loves you. We have to get out of here and then you can call him," Kevin said as he kissed her on the head. "And I love you too and we're all going to be fine. It has to be fine, I haven't met Harry yet," he smiled. "But we have to go."

"Hello, you two. Did you find what you were looking for?" Celile said.

Eve stepped away from Kevin. There was a crackling noise in the bushes. "Yes, we're just heading back now. I wanted my water," she said as she pointed to the bottle.

"I thought you said bug spray." She paused as she stared at Eve. "Never mind, it doesn't matter. You can stay here as long as you like. I'm going in a second, you can make out then," Celile smiled.

"It's okay, we want to go back, don't we Kevin," she said as she squeezed his hand.

He squeezed back. "Yes, we'll follow you."

"Great, I just need to get something from the car," she said as she turned away.

Eve and Kevin walked back towards the clearing. "We should get the keys off her and take the car." Eve said. They both stopped, Kevin looked at Eve and she looked at him both knowing what it was they had to do. She bent down and picked up a rock from the floor, Kevin took it off her. Eve walked behind Kevin back towards the car, trying not to make a sound. Celile was bent over fumbling for something on the floor of the back seat. "I thought you were both heading back," she said without turning.

Eve stepped back and frowned at Kevin, he held the rock down by his side, gripping it.

He shuddered; he heard Sadik talking as he emerged through the trees in the dark. He held the rock by his side. Celile turned around and smiled and passed Sadik the bag she was holding. Sadik stared at them.

"I've just got my water. Thought we'd wait for Celile." Eve smiled as she turned with Kevin to go back. The two of them started walking, not looking back. All Eve could hear was Celile and Sadik's footsteps close behind them. They began uttering words in Turkish and rummaging through Celile's bag. They were being marched back. Eve turned and was sure she saw a glint of metal mixed up with all Celile's clutter in the bag. Her heart sank as she shouted, "Race you back Kevin."

"What," he shouted.

"Race." She grabbed his hand and ran through the trees until they reached the clearing. She pulled Kevin to the other side nearest to the dirt path and gasped for breath. "I think they have a gun," she blurted out.

"Are you sure?"

Her heart raced as she struggled for breath. She watched as Celile and Sadik went back to their post by the tree that Mehmet and Selina were slumped under. "I saw something metal in her bag. Only for a second, but I saw metal."

"Don't panic, it could've been a cigarette lighter or something."

"Maybe. I hope so. We have no chance against a gun," she said as her eyes welled up again. Kevin held her tight, she hoped that this would all be over soon and they would be back at the villa. She could call Harry, tell him Mummy Eve was sorry and she wanted to call him earlier but couldn't because of the silly phone. She knew he would be upset with her. She needed a chance to speak to Harry again, just once to tell him she loved him. Her life was beginning to fall into place. She thought of her job assisting in the classroom and hoped she would see the children again, she thought of Kevin and the life he was promising her. What she had now was all she'd ever wanted. She squeezed his arm and knew she would fight until the end to keep all the things that she had worked so hard for.

Chapter 27

Mehmet fidgeted, "I need to find my father and put an end to this." he prised Selina's sleeping head off his shoulder and leaned her up against the tree.

"You think you can stop this?" Celile asked.

Without answering, he stood, turned and walked off towards the dirt path.

"Spoiled brat," she whispered. Celile watched as he left in his search.

"He'll calm down. It's a lot for him to take in," Sadik said. Near the water's edge, Eve and Kevin watched and whispered as Mehmet walked past them.

There was no time like the present to start clearing away; it wouldn't be long with only two of them to take down. Celile wedged all the rubbish bags into one large waste bag. As she bent down to pick up a can, she saw Sadik kneel down to Selina's level. She watched as he placed his hand on her hair and touched her cheek. This is what she was risking everything for. A man who, as soon as she turns her back, flirts with another woman. Selina moved and smiled before her head and body slipped down the tree and onto the floor where she lay curled up open mouthed. Sadik folded up his over shirt and placed it under her head. Shaking and gasping, Celile couldn't believe what she was seeing. He stroked her shoulders, then her arms before cowering over her and running his hands down her waist and legs over her clothes. What had that little bitch done to deserve such affection?

For months she had worked hard on pushing Guz away and proving to Sadik that he was the one she wanted. All the lies, the sneaking around. All the times Guz had still taken her as his property because Sadik wouldn't stand up to him. Feeling filthy, she rubbed her arm until it burned as she thought of the times that Guz's sweaty body had lay over hers. All that, to keep up a pretence that Sadik was meant to be fixing. She now knew he was too gutless, it was all empty promises to fulfil a desire to be better than his brother. Promises, promises, take her away, start a new life. Couple of kids. All empty, void of sincerity. Her white knuckles shook with anguish. Gasping for breath, she grabbed the cutlery pot, selected the paring knife and stomped over to where Sadik now lay, alongside Selina.

"I was just making sure she was okay and checking her out. She's good stock, The Boss will be happy with this one," he said as he held his finger to his mouth and sprung up to a sitting position. "She's still sleeping. It's easier if we can keep her that way."

Celile stood above him, tears now sliding down her cheek. "Really?"

"What's that supposed to mean?"

"That's not what I saw from back there. I saw you touch her."

"I didn't touch her, not like that anyway."

"I thought you were different. I thought I was all you wanted," she said with tears streaming down her face. She turned around; Kevin and Eve were still staring down the dirt path.

"You are all I've ever wanted," Sadik said.

"Do you know what I've been through to be with you? What I've had to endure. No you don't." She paused. "Prove I'm all you've ever wanted. It's time you endured some of the pain," she spat as she waved the knife towards his face.

"I love you. We'll talk about this later when this is over." Sadik flinched and shuffled back almost positioning himself behind the tree.

"Stab her." Celile held out the knife to Sadik, point first. "Do something, then we will both have a memory to endure for the rest of our lives." Once again, she flicked the knife in his direction, he held his hand up to protect his face and she caught his palm.

"Are you fucking crazy," he said as he stepped back.

"Not crazy, just hurt, scared," she said, still shaking while gripping the knife. "Go on then, prove you'll endure something for me. Stab her."

"What do I tell Guz?"

"You tell him, she knew what we were up to and was going to tell the others. She lunged at you so you stabbed her. See, an accident," she smiled as she wiped her wet eyes.

Sadik took the knife from her shaking hand and stared at it for a moment. "Gutless," Celile spat as she snatched the knife back and directed the sharp point at Selina.

"Look, you're being stupid. We need to keep the girls. You're being irrational, give me back the knife," he said as he held out his hand. She flicked the blade again to warn him away. He stood, hands raised in front of his body. As he stepped back he raised his hands above his head. "What are you playing at?"

"I saw the way you looked at her and the way you touched her. Oh, I'm only helping her out by making her comfortable," she mimicked. "If you won't do it I will." With a trembling hand, Celile flung herself to the floor and plunged the knife into Selina's chest. As she plunged the weapon, she twisted it and turned it almost breaking her fingers with the force she used.

"What the hell have you done?" Sadik stuttered as he held his head with both hands. He fell to the floor beside her and snatched the knife. He watched helplessly as blood pumped out of Selina's wound. Her smiley expression, changed to a frown before all her facial muscles went limp. She coughed and a few flecks of blood splattered over Celile's chest. Selina inhaled, and then exhaled. That was her last movement.

Celile stared at the lifeless girl, her shakes turned to deep uncontrollable breaths until she wheezed, unable to catch her breath. She'd never killed before, not directly. Falling to the floor, she sat and cried hysterically. Sadik placed his shaking hand on her shoulder, reached across and turned the music back up.

*****

Eve stared into the darkness. "I can see movement, he must be coming back or maybe it's the others."

"I hope so." Kevin replied as he stood beside her, gripping her hand. "And I wish they'd turn this music off, it's the fourth time I've heard this one. It's beginning to drive me insane."

A lean figure emerged into the low flickering light. Mehmet appeared and brushed past them as he marched towards Sadik. Eve watched as he approached the recess of trees where they had sat, she couldn't see Selina but there seemed to be a crowd over the one spot. Mehmet held his hands up and fell to the floor yelling and crying. Then he screamed in Turkish before dragging his limp body off the floor. From a walk to a staggering run, Eve saw how he grabbed Celile by the hair and spun her round. Sadik grabbed his neck, the young man threw him off then a stout moustached man came from behind the tree and planted a solid punch onto Mehmet's face "Kevin, look. It's him, the man."

"Oh God, we need to get Selina." they watched as their hosts fought and argued. As they approached, Eve spotted the flecks of blood on Celile's neck. She looked down as the crowd dispersed and through the gaps and flickering light she spotted Selina's blood soaked chest.

"No, what have they done to her? They've killed her," she yelled as tears spurted down her face. She thought of her friend and the trust she had given Mehmet. Poor Selina, so trusting and now this had happened to her.

Kevin grabbed her. "We have to go. Go now. Run," she looked in his eyes and saw the panic. She followed his lead; he turned her around and pulled her to the dirt path. As they passed where they had been sitting she grabbed her rucksack and placed it on her back. Her head pounded with adrenalin. Inside she was hysterical but to survive she had to remain calm and in control. She looked back and met the gaze of the man she had seen earlier that night in the bushes. He pulled out a gun from Celile's bag and pointed at them. "Go," Kevin yelled as he pushed Eve onto the path. "I'm right behind you," he shouted as he followed.

Their pursuer began to charge towards them. Over branches, through spiny bushes; they dragged their bodies through everything they had to. Close behind, she heard shouting. She glanced back over her shoulder and saw Kevin frantically keeping up with her. Darkness made it impossible to follow any direction, all she knew was that the water was on her right and it was close by. The moon was almost covered by cloud and they were in denser woodland. The man's shouting got farther away, maybe they were losing him.

A loud bang filled the air and she heard a thud behind her. "Kevin," she yelled as she stopped dead and turned. He lay there holding his leg.

"You have to go Eve. Go now or we both die. You've got Harry to think of," he said between clenched teeth.

"But I can't leave you," she kneeled down beside him.

"I'm coming for you," a voice shouted as it howled with laughter; their pursuer was close by.

She dragged Kevin off the track, into some thorny foliage and held him tight. "We can stay here until he passes, he won't find us," she whispered. As she looked down she spotted a small blood trail that led to the bush they were hiding in. She grabbed a handful of dirt, scattered it over the trail and kept silent.

"You can't hide forever and when you come out, I be here, waiting," the voice yelled as its owner cocked the gun. The footsteps got closer. Eve's heart beat loud and fast. Kevin gripped her hand and looked into her eyes before closing them and holding his breath. The footsteps passed and then they came back. Their pursuer was now standing firm in front of them. Eve inhaled and was taken back to when she first saw the man and breathed in his smell. Silent tears fell as she gripped Kevin's hand harder with her own trembling hand.

'Please go,' she thought as she swallowed. It was as if he had heard her plea. He stepped a few meters away, undid his flies and urinated up a tree. Eve heard Kevin exhale, she watched him under the moonlight as he clenched his teeth and held his leg, cracking a twig as he moved. The man turned sharply and faced them, was he looking at her? The moon's light began to shine brighter as the cloud passed. He was looking above them, and then he turned and walked back in the direction he came from. Eve grabbed Kevin and hugged him hard, stroking his hair and kissing his head. He gasped in pain as he reached for his glasses in his top pocket and put them back on.

"You need to go and get help, I can't come with you. I can't walk any further. Just keep running downstream, follow the river. Keep going. Did you say you had water?" he asked.

"Yes," she cried. "I can't do this, I can't leave you and I can't do this on my own."

"You can do this," he said as he looked her in the eye. "You are all we have; we are all counting on you."

Eve nodded; she pulled her hand towel from her rucksack and wrapped it once around Kevin's calf before tying it tightly.

"I love you Eve and we are going to get out of this one and things are going to be great. They are going to be really good, I promise," he whispered as he kissed her.

"I love you too, I love you so much Kevin. I'm going to sort this, I'll bring help back. I promise," she whispered as she stroked his head. "You stay hidden and be quiet." She took out the bottle of water and offered it to Kevin; he took a swig and passed it back to her.

"You've got to go now. You know he'll be back to look for us." Eve eased herself out of the tangled branches and stood up on the path.

Bang. Gunshot fired in the distance, he was trying to scare them into the open. She smiled one last time at Kevin, turned and ran.

Chapter 28

"You," Guz pointed to Sadik. "Find them. And you stay and help him."

"I can't do this Dad, please I want to go," Mehmet cried. Guz pulled his hand back and slapped his son hard on the cheek.

"You can and you will do this. Do you know what trouble we're in? You're in? If this fails we all go down." Mehmet rubbed his cheek and wiped his eyes. He took Celile's wrap that stuck out of the top of her bag and placed it carefully over Selina.

Celile grabbed it back. "You'll get blood on it."

"I don't care," he said as he snatched it back off her. "She deserves some dignity and how will she get that if we leave her bleeding body splayed out like that on show?" Celile went to grab the wrap again; Sadik placed his hand firmly over hers preventing her from reaching over. Mehmet kneeled down before placing the wrap over Selina's body. He leaned over and kissed her on the cheek.

"That'll do, don't get too attached to the corpse," Guz shouted as he pulled Mehmet back up. The lad refused to oblige and fell back down to the floor.

"Now. Who's going to tell me how this happened? Do you know how much money we've lost by losing her? After all, she was the pretty one or shall I put it bluntly, the pay out."

Sadik looked at Celile, Celile looked back. Guz watched how they interacted in their unspoken language.

"I-," Celile began.

"It was an accident," Sadik blurted out interrupting her. "We thought she was asleep, she saw us arguing and tried to run off. She became hysterical then attacked Celile. It was me; I didn't know what to do. I grabbed the knife and .... I tried to get her arm, just to slow her down so that we could get her under control. But I missed and it was too late."

"You have cost us dearly. The Boss will make us pay for this. I promised him three girls. I have one heavily sedated in the woodland and the one that you're going to catch," Guz said as he looked into Sadik's eye. "She ran in that direction," he pointed towards the dirt track. "She won't get far. You can do what you like with the boyfriend. I'm sure I shot him so we can leave him out here to rot. Here's a gun," he said as he passed the weighty metal weapon to his brother. "Use it if you need to and for heaven's sake, don't kill the last girl. I'll come back for the other one later; she won't come around for at least four hours. I've given her enough stuff to knock out a horse."

"How could you have done this to her?" Mehmet cried as he rocked back and forth by Selina's side and stroked her hair.

"She's nothing. Get her out of your head. There's plenty more where she came from. In fact there will be another plane load tomorrow." Guz spat.

Mehmet placed his hand on the tree and stood. Tears washed over his face. "She'd never done anything to you. How dare you?"

He yelled as he lunged at his father. He attacked him with his powerless fists. Within seconds Guz had thrown him to the floor and straddled the young man's body.

"How dare I? How dare I you ask. How about I dare for you, for her even, for him," he said as he pointed to all of them in turn. He grabbed Mehmet's sweat soaked tee-shirt with clenched fists and shook him hard. "We all want a better life. These people they are nothing. They come from their privileged backgrounds, flashing their cash then knocking us down on prices. They've forced us into this. I don't feel even a bit sorry for them and you shouldn't either. Now get up and find the others. Have some guts like a son of mine should."

"I don't want to be your son," Mehmet replied as he took a deep breath and stared back at his father. Guz clenched his fists harder almost ripping the tee-shirt, then he let go and stood. Turning away, he shook his head.

"After tonight, you won't have to be. I'll give you your share and you can leave. I never want to see you again."

"I don't want a share of this blood money and I'll still go and I never want to see you again either."

Guz's phone beeped, he looked down. A message from The Boss. "He needs us to get a move on; he's collecting the girls as soon as the sun rises. Right Celile, we'll go to the villa now, get that done, get back here for the clean-up after that pair have caught the runaways."

"I can stay here and help, it's too much for them. I'm quicker than them and Mehmet's not fit for much given he's upset," Celile said. Guz watched as Celile looked at Sadik. That look, a fleeting moment. Was she angry with him? He noticed the slight tremor in her hands. She was usually so calm and collected.

"No, you come with me. Mehmet will do this, it's better than spending the rest of his long life in prison. If he doesn't I'll make sure it's all pinned on him." He stared down at his boy, disappointed that he had no courage to see this through. "We need to go to the villa, get the passports and whatever else we can find. Mehmet? It's the run down one opposite the shop, is that right?" Mehmet held his hand up and turned away. "Whatever. Let's go," he said as he grabbed Celile's arm and led her away towards his car.

Chapter 29

After several minutes of sprinting along the lumpy ground and crashing through spiny shrubs, Eve stopped and leaned against a tree trunk. Gasping for breath she doubled over then put her open hands on her thighs before falling to the floor and sobbing. Her eyes filled up as she pictured Kevin's vulnerable face beneath the bush where she'd left him. Breathing in and out, she began to hyperventilate. In a panic she clenched her fists and hit the solid ground hoping that the pain would divert her attention away from the panic. A red heat crept up her neck and spread across her face. Breathe in; breathe out; she regained control. In, out, in, out. The hotness across her face subsided and she felt a weakness wash over her. Her legs shook; she placed her hands palm down on the floor and tried to push her body up to a standing position. Her legs then buckled and she fell to the floor and sobbed hard, letting all the pain and shock spill abundantly down her face. Her nose filled up and began to drip.

As she cried, she hugged her battered body and thought of Kevin, left alone suffering a gunshot wound to his leg. She hoped he could be quiet and stay still. Then she thought of Harry and felt doubtful that she would see him again, he may never know where Mummy Eve went. Then, her last memory of Selina covered in blood latched onto her thoughts and wouldn't go away. Her best friend Selina; together since primary school; friends until the end. Was this their end? Would anyone ever find them?

Sobbing open mouthed she hit the ground again and again. Hopelessness set in at the thought that it was her alone who could help Kevin but she didn't know how. She gazed in all directions and all she could see was darkness enshrouded in a spooky denseness. A claustrophobic layered curtain that was pressing hard on her chest forcing her down, keeping her on the ground. She wiped her wet face with her hands and then scratched her arm. It burned and itched like crazy. She rubbed hard. She felt the same sensation brush over her hand then creep further over her bicep. It wasn't an itching sensation, it was crawling. Masses of little feet were crawling up her arm and into the sides of her tee-shirt, across her swimsuit.

Standing, she brushed her body and hit her arm against the tree stump. She flinched at the pain as she rubbed the affected area. A slight parting of the clouds revealed the little black insects creeping all over her body. She continued to brush, hop and jiggle around until the sensation subsided. She shook out her hair and stood looking at her front, they were gone. Shaking, she wiped her face once again. On her right, she could still hear the river; she had done as Kevin asked. She gazed around and the stars lit up a steep hill that had to go on for miles. She could see no lights of any towns, no sign of movement, it was a hopeless venture. The terrain was also getting lumpier and denser. Her arms felt tender after being brushed against twigs and spines. She took her rucksack off her back and opened the zip. Bug spray and sun tan lotion. She sprayed on the bug deterrent and plastered some of the cream over her tender arms, flinching as she rubbed it in the scratches.

What if the answer was not downstream? From what she could deduce, she would have to battle this terrain for days to reach any sign of civilised life and by then Kevin could either be dead by their hands or from his wound becoming infected. She brushed the large scar on her stomach over her clothes, the reminder of the infection that had nearly claimed her life after giving birth to Harry. She remembered the throbbing pain, the fever, the seeping pus and the smell of rot and death that she faced and she shivered at the thought of Kevin suffering in that way, especially outside and alone. He needed her, she had to go back, outwit them and get the keys to a vehicle. It was their only way. Running would kill her and Kevin would then have no chance. She allowed another tear to trickle down her face. She couldn't leave him in their hands. It was him and her together as one. Now focused, she placed her bag on her back and crept back upstream.

For about twenty minutes she crept in her thin soled pumps over the lumps and stones. This time she was careful not to further injure herself. She could feel each stone digging in through the soles of her pumps and into her foot. There was a break in the rubber and dust began to fill the gap and stick to her toes. Ignoring it she pressed on until she heard shouting, she was close to them. She looked around, sure that she had left Kevin in the spot where she now stood, she trembled; he was no longer there. Her heart raced. Had they got him? Had he managed to get away? The shouting became louder. She heard Mehmet yelling and sobbing at Sadik. Sadik shouted back at him in an aggressive tone. There were only two voices. She turned around and looked behind her for the others; they were nowhere to be seen.

Feeling too close for safety, she took a few steps back. She stood on her tip toes to try and get a view of the two men but she was too far away. Grabbing a branch on the tree beside her, she pulled and hoisted herself up. She could just see the top of Mehmet's head. Higher, she needed to get higher. She reached for the next branch up, it was too high. She jumped on the left branch and managed to grab it. She ignored the splinter that pierced the delicate skin between her thumb and index finger and used her rubber soles to climb her way up the tree until she managed to make a successful grab for another branch with her right hand. After a struggle she managed to hoist herself into a sitting position on the higher branch. Now she could see the two men clearly. A tear slid down her cheek as she saw Selina's body covered in a floral scarf. Her poor, defenceless friend.

Sadik was waving the gun around; Mehmet was sobbing and shouting back at him. She watched as Sadik grabbed the young man with his free hand and slapped him across the head. Still they continued shouting in Turkish. Sadik headed off towards the dirt trail that Eve had just came from. She exhaled. "Well timed," she whispered under her breath. Now with ease she pulled herself up onto the next branch, then the next until she felt safe and high enough to avoid their detection. Scanning the ground below, she still couldn't see Kevin. Her only hope was to get the keys to one of the vehicles. From the height of the tree, all she could see in the distance was the glint of a car and the jeep. One of the cars was gone. Maybe, she hoped, Celile and the man from the bushes had gone. This was her chance. She would spend a while watching, recouping her strength, ready for the fight of her life. The fight for her friends and to see her son again. She would fight them to the end. If she didn't, what was the alternative? Would their bodies remain hidden in the forest forever, rotting away? Their disappearance etched up to an unfortunate unexplainable incident. No one knew they had booked a jeep safari.

They had paid in cash, there was no trace; they had no flyers, no receipts and no leads for anyone wishing to investigate their disappearances. Then she thought back to the old women trying to sell her sunglasses on the first day. 'Trust your instincts.' That day as she watched out of the villa window, she should've trusted her instincts. Who was scrawny and who was the large man in the white suit that they were all so intimidated by? What had they all got themselves into?

She closed her eyes and saw the chequers pieces hit the window and the man stand. Was this a game? One where their objective is to outwit the game maker. This was their game; she had no ideas what the rules were except they wanted to kill. What else could they want? Money? Were they just sadistic killers? Fun? She looked at Mehmet sobbing and knew that this wasn't all a psychopaths power trip.

If only the others had listened. She'd felt it; she knew from the outset that they were part of something that she didn't want to be part of. From now, she would trust her instincts. They were all she had in this case and they had served her well from the beginning. Right now, they were telling her to stay put, observe their movements. Make sure that there were only two of them. Know your enemy. They told her to look out for Kevin, he had to be somewhere. She swallowed the lump in her throat down in an attempt to swallow the fear away. It was now her or no one. This was it.

Chapter 30

After a twisty rural forty five minute drive, Guz pulled up around the back of the Villa. In the distance he heard singing coming from a nearby karaoke bar. He handed Celile a pair of tight fitting gloves. "Just in case," he whispered. She twisted her hair up in a bun and wrapped her headscarf around her hair before putting the gloves on.

They both went through the back gate, passing the swimming pool before reaching the patio doors. Guz tried to slide the door open but it wouldn't budge. "Locked," he whispered.

"There's a window open, just there," she pointed as she replied. The small window above the sink in the kitchen was pushed open. He looked at Celile's thin frame and grinned with delight. "I'll never fit through there," she said.

"You will." He looked at the opening and back at Celile; he knew she would fit through the window. He held his hands together and placed them towards Celile's feet. "Climb on," he said.

For a moment she stared at him in disbelief before stepping on to his hands. He lifted her up until her head reached the window. "Get your head in," he said. He watched as her headscarf got tangled in the window catch and fell to the ground beside him. She held both arms in front of her body and placed them through the little window. Her head followed next. She wriggled around to get her shoulders in and eventually they slid through. Guz smiled, that was the worst bit done. Her weight shifted as her body edged through the gap. With a crash she landed shoulder first onto the draining board. He watched as she steadied herself and got to her feet.

"Go round the back and unlock the door," he said. She looked back at him; the whites of her eyes reflected the red light from the cooker clock. She left the kitchen as instructed. Guz scurried back round to the patio door and met Celile as she slid it open. Glancing back, he was reassured that no one had spotted them. He grinned at the young woman standing before him. She looked away. "You're getting good at this," he said. She ignored him, turned and walked into the room. Guz turned on a wall light.

"What the hell are you doing?" Celile said in a hushed voice.

"I couldn't see."

"Someone will see the light."

"No one will care," he replied as he closed the curtains.

*****

Celile fished through the bag on the floor and pulled out a hat with cups attached to it. She threw it aside and dug deeper to the bottom until she came across what felt like a familiar little book. One down, five more to go. She delved into the crevices of the bag and felt along the inside pocket. Unzipping it, she delved deeper and pulled out a wallet. She looked up at Guz, he grinned at her. She looked away. "Right, next room," she said as she zipped the bag back up and threw it by the patio doors.

She followed Guz into a small room with a stairway leading off it. They crept up the stairs until they reached the landing. He turned on the hall light. "What if there's someone here?" Celile whispered.

"There's no one here. We know that." He stomped across the wooden floor and flung all the doors open in turn. "See, we are all alone. I'll start in here; you start at the far room. Grab anything of value and bag up their stuff. You know how it goes."

In the distance Celile heard Guz rummaging through drawers and bags, she heard items being flung into his bag as he stomped across the room. She reached across to the bedside table and opened the draw. Hair extensions, a clogged up brush and some tweezers. She felt the hair and twisted it around her gloved finger. So Sadik liked fake hair. She thought back to the knife and how she had plunged into the girl's skin, straight through her top. Swallowing hard she felt sick and dizzy. Thoughts of her thumb twisting as she plunged the knife, thoughts of Sadik's gutless face that had forced her to do it, thoughts of him touching Selina's leg and stroking her hair. She wiped the sweat off her brow before taking a deep breath. She rummaged at the back of the drawer and presto, she felt the passport and an envelope full of cash. She opened it and looked inside; there must have been about five hundred British Pounds. Behind the notes was a much smaller wad of Turkish Lira. She kneeled down and felt under the bed, an iPad.

She crept over to the dressing table. Placed neatly on the top was a small pouch. She opened it. Two gold necklaces and a dress ring. Underneath the table sat a pair of shoes. She lifted them up and looked at the label. Jimmy Choo's in her size in an opulent purple colour. She sat on the edge of the bed, placed her feet beside them and pictured herself wearing them.

"You would look really sexy in those," Guz said as he walked through the door. Startled she dropped the shoe and stood. "Try it on."

"No, I'll take them and try them on later. We need to get out of here."

"I'm not in a rush," he grinned.

"No, I don't want to try them on now," she said as she started rummaging with trinkets on the other bedside table. Her hand dragged up a thin gold necklace with a pendant attached, the pendant spelled out 'Mum.' Celile placed it back down and swallowed.

Lay flat was a photo of a little boy, a tiny child with a large grin and a cartoon covered sun hat. Next to the child stood a young woman, she picked up the photo and stared hard, the woman was Eve. The one who'd been eyeing her up all that evening. "She has a child."

Guz stomped over to Celile and grabbed the photo off her before ripping it up.

"What did you do that for?"

"Well, she won't need it now, will she?" He replied with a grin. "Oh look, a box of fags," he said as he opened the dressing table drawer. "You haven't searched the room well."

"I hadn't finished."

"Too busy playing with those shoes."

"I'll get on with it now then shall I?" she replied.

He paused, stared at his watch and looked back up at her. "Try the shoes on."

She turned and looked at him, a grin spread across his face and she knew what he wanted. She thought of Sadik and his fickle male behaviour and decided maybe she would allow this idiot that she had once loved to get his way. After all it would be an easy feat and just the punishment Sadik deserved. And if she didn't give it, he would just take it and become angry, the rest of the evening would be unbearable. It was easier to get it over with and quickly on her terms. She thought back to Sadik earlier that evening. She wanted him to prove his love, prove that he would do anything for her and he'd let her down. Guz would've killed for her. Guz would do anything for her. The fact that Guz had quite often beaten her when she stayed at his was neither here nor there at this precise moment in this surreal situation. In the past, when she had given him what he wanted he was easy to control and his level of trust in her had diminished over the past week; she needed to simmer down his violent tendencies and regain that control. She slipped off her sandals and stepped over to the shoes. She would close her eyes and think of it as regaining that control.

Minutes later, she lay there as he climbed off her, off the bed. Straightforward, easy as she'd thought it would be. He stood and zipped up his fly. Sadik had not done as she'd asked to prove himself but he had taken the blame for her crime. Her stomach fluttered, he had told his brother he had committed murder to protect her. She thought of the risk he was taking and the fluttering in her stomach turned to a burning twang of guilt. Maybe he had proven his love in another way. She loved Sadik, had become obsessed with him and now she was lay on a strange bed with Guz's sweat all over her body. She thought back to when her life was less complicated, when she had met Guz, ran away with him and drunk up all his promises without any doubt and she compared that to the now. The present hell that had turned her into a murderess, a liar, a thief and deceiver of both sides. She no longer knew where her loyalties lay; the lines were now so blurred they were smudged into one confusing mess.

Her stomach turned as she inhaled the sweaty smell that now filled the air. The stale smell of Guz's breath that still hung above her as if suspended in her memories long after the smell was really gone. His wetness that crept down her thigh made her squirm. Bile rose up her throat, she jolted up and made a run for the en-suite and vomited violently into the toilet.

"Are you alright?" Guz shouted as he ran back into the room and turned the light on to the en-suite.

She held up her hand and looked up at him with her watery eyes. "I just need for this night to be over." He stared at her for a moment, turned, then left her to it; alone with her feelings of disgust. She placed the loo seat down, flushed, cleaned herself up and left the bathroom. She had to hurry, she walked over to Eve's bedside, put her sandals back on and continued where she left off, rummaging through Eve's drawer. Another photo of the boy. She took it out, folded it and placed it deep into her pocket.

Chapter 31

Hands on head Eve massaged her temples, her head was beginning to throb and her mouth was dry. Even though the music no longer played, the repetitive tunes that had played on a loop all evening now plagued her mind. She pulled the bottle of water out of her bag and took a large swig before dropping it back in. What if they had killed Kevin? She asked him to stay where she left him but he was gone. She shivered at the thought. While she had been running hard and fast to get nowhere they must've found him. A tear traced her cheek and passed her mouth before falling off her chin and onto her dusty neck.

It had taken a long time for her to find someone she loved who loved her back so sincerely and now it was all gone as quickly as it had started. All the, 'if onlys' crossed her mind in a confusing muddle. If only she'd stayed with Kevin and fought; if only she had feigned illness on the day so that they wouldn't have gone; if only they'd gone on a boat trip instead; if only she'd spoken louder and forced them all to listen to her. All she had was a list of pointless thoughts that dredged up more tears. Tears for a hopeless situation and for the grief of her lost love. As they fell, she mourned the life she had visualised, the happy family days that her and Kevin were going to share. The wedding she had already imagined, her parents acceptance. Everything that had happened over the past few days had given her hope that her life was going to change for the better. Then the worst of the tears fell for Mummy Eve's memory being nothing more than a blur to her young son in years to come. Would he remember the mud pies and the dens and the Disney films? Or, would it simply all be gone?

She sat rigid and wiped her eyes and nose with her hand. In the distance she heard a rustling sound, she could see all around the area from the height she had climbed up to. Sadik walked down the dirt track; Mehmet stood guard by Selina's body. She looked up and saw the stars; all the clouds had dispersed and Mehmet was visible to her. She watched as his shaking hands rubbed his eyes.

A rustling sound to her right caught her attention, just behind the tree where Selina was laid. Kevin. Her heart hammered hard against her chest as a jolt of adrenalin circulated her body. She watched as the man she loved hobbled beyond the clearing out of Mehmet's line of sight. Crack, a branch. She watched as Kevin panicked and tried to stoop behind a tree. "Hide Kevin," she whispered.

"Sadik?" Mehmet called. No answer. Eve watched as the young man stepped behind the tree and gazed around at his eye level. As he walked closer to Kevin, she held her breath as she watched.

Heart beating twice as fast, her mouth was once again dry. Eve stared, unsure what to do. If she shouted he would know where she was and Sadik hadn't ventured that far as yet. She closed her eyes and held her breath in the hope that Mehmet would not spot Kevin but all she could see behind her closed lids was the metal piece that she knew Sadik still carried.

Bang. The gun went off, turning her head she saw Sadik heading back laughing as he shouted in Turkish. Mehmet started to run towards the gunshot. Relieved, Eve exhaled and allowed her body to relax a little. She smiled, knowing Kevin's location had reassured her. He was safe for the moment.

The two men were shouting. Mehmet cowered down to Sadik as he wielded the gun in all directions whilst laughing hysterically. Out of his pocket he pulled some more bullets and reloaded the gun. Eve leaned over and checked Kevin's position. He was gone. She looked behind her, he wasn't there. To her right, he wasn't there, to her left; the two men were now nearing Selina's body once more. In the distance by the cars, she couldn't see him there either. Confused as to where he could've disappeared to, she sat still and continued to look. A branch rustled. Her hands shook as she watched Kevin hobble towards Selina whilst the two men looked away. He stood behind the tree and held out his hand in an attempt to grab the bag that Celile had left there earlier. He was trying for the car keys, she knew in her heart that's what he was doing. She held her breath, hoping that the two men wouldn't hear him and turn around. He successfully grabbed the bag handle and lifted it up. Sweat beads formed at the edge of Eve's hairline as she watched him. He pulled then a crack noise broke the silence. The bag had been caught on a lower branch.

In unison, the two men turned their heads. Sadik held up the gun and paced towards where the noise had come from. Mehmet shouted, Sadik turned towards him and hit him hard across the face with his other hand and pointed towards the tree. She watched as Mehmet reluctantly walked towards the bag. Panicking, Eve grappled for something in her bag, the bug spray. She flung it as hard as she could towards the dirt track before hearing it crash to the floor. Both men turned and ran to where the noise had come from. She watched as Kevin hobbled off into the distance towards the cars without the bag. Their plan had failed but at least she knew Kevin was still alive. She watched as the men came back, Sadik held half of the broken plastic bottle in his hand as he stared in the direction in which he'd picked it up.

She climbed down the tree. They were onto her; they knew that she and Kevin were close. She had to pull back, think of a plan. Try and get to the cars. Instead of rushing, she crept across the ground until she was far enough away from them. Moments later she reached a small clearing just a little way down from where she had peed earlier that night. On the ground, poking out the bottom of a bush was something dark. She crept towards the mass and lifted up the bush, a bare leg, a man's leg. She pulled the bush back further and saw a body almost curled in the foetal position. Ryan. Her head throbbed hard. She leaned over his bloody body and felt for his pulse, no pulse. She placed his arm by his side and allowed the bush to cover his body back up as she felt warm tears trickle down her cheek. She wanted to hold him and cry for him but they would hear; they would come and do the same to her.

In the distance she heard shouting. No time to panic, no time to break down, she sobbed silently as she backed away from their shouting, determined that they would not locate her.

She grabbed a tree stump and felt her way round it as she walked backwards. Once again out of sight she breathed hard and slid to the ground before taking a few deep breaths. She trembled as she thought of all the annoyance she'd expressed towards Ryan and now he was gone. Both Selina and Ryan gone; just like that. Was it a matter of time before Selina and Ryan became herself and Kevin? That couldn't happen. Determined, she forced herself to stand and continue to step backwards until she stood on something knobbly. A lump of tape rolled up. Next to the tape was a cigarette butt. She scanned the lumpy ground below and saw a pair of feet. 'Please no, please not another one,' she thought. Eve's hands shook as she paced towards the bound feet and forced herself to continue looking. Rachel lay face down with her hands tied behind her body. She ran to her friend and fell to the ground. There was a faint pulse under Rachel's cool clammy skin. Eve's hands trembled as she fought to undo her binds. She pulled the rope off her feet and rolled her over. Her black hair stuck to her face and was caught under the tape over her mouth. Eve ripped the tape off her mouth and slapped her across the cheek.

"Rachel? It's me Eve. You have to wake up. We have to go now." Her friend didn't move. She continued to breathe but didn't respond to Eve's voice.

The shouting in the distance got closer. They were coming; they would come back for Rachel if she left her exposed. With all her strength she grabbed Rachel's flaccid arms and dragged her dead weight out of the clearing and into a thorny growth before placing her in the recovery position. She grabbed an armful of branches and twigs and built them in a light mound over her friend. She couldn't lose another one. When Rachel came around, Eve knew she stood a chance if nothing else.

The voices were now almost upon her. She spotted Sadik in the distance between two parted trees. He smirked as he shouted and held up two sets of keys in front of his grin. With them close to her and Kevin back there alone, she had felt hopeful. But now, seeing the keys; all hope was gone. She darted into the darkness away from their path and slid to the floor, hiding out quietly; playing the game the only way she could.

Chapter 32

What seemed like ages had passed without her having any opportunity to come out of the shrubs. In the distance Eve heard the revving of an engine getting closer. She remained sitting still, wedged between a thorny shrub and a tree trunk. She trembled as Sadik passed her, his body was that close at one point she heard him breathe. She flinched as she heard a rustling, then footsteps followed, crunching the undergrowth with each step. Sadik ran back towards the cars. The others must have arrived back. She and Kevin had failed to get any further out of this hellish situation and now there were four of them again. She stretched her neck, rested the back of her head on the tree trunk and sobbed. Dragging her aching body to a standing position, she crept towards their attackers, close to where she had last seen Kevin. She had to know that Kevin was safe.

   The car door slammed and yelling filled the air. A loud, shrill ranting came from Celile before the men joined in. The yelling got louder, she heard Mehmet start and then a loud whacking noise followed. Mehmet hushed. Eve crept even closer, trying hard not to disturb the dry twigs that were plentiful beneath her. As she got closer, she peered around the bush and could only just see the back end of Celile. Mehmet pushed his way through the centre of the commotion and left, heading off in Selina's direction muttering something as he went. The man who she'd encountered in the bushes clipped Mehmet on the back of his head as he passed him. Aggression and so much anger shone in the man's eyes. The three of them continued to bicker before finally becoming silent. Then a grin, the man beamed a dirty smile before grabbing Celile by the bottom, pulling her closer to him and kissing her hard. She attempted to push him away but he continued to hold her in place. Sadik placed his hand on the man's shoulder in an attempt to pull him off her before yelling as a loud punch hit him on the cheek. Eve watched as Celile backed away, the woman looked frail and wiped her hand across her mouth. The man walked off towards Mehmet, Celile and Sadik remained there alone, leaning against the car.

From what Eve could gather, the man and Sadik both had something going on with Celile. They also had a resemblance, maybe they were brothers. Knowing them and their weaknesses was her key out of this, she had to know more, learn more because who knows how all this was going to end up, she thought. She felt her pulse quicken as she watched on. Convinced they would hear her she inhaled deeply in an attempt to calm her breathing down. She watched as Sadik turned to see if the other man had gone. When he was satisfied, Celile fell into his arms and stared into space. He held her and stroked her hair. She shook her head from side to side before trying to push him away. He looked into her eyes; there was a pause, a moment before their lips gently brushed. Eve took another deep breath, she was now in control. Inhale; exhale; inhale; exhale. She had to find Kevin; they had to plan a way out, together.

She flinched as she heard loud footsteps and the cocking of a gun. The man stepped out from between two of the vehicles and held a gun up towards Sadik's chest. Celile screamed and stood there frozen to the spot, muttering to the man with the gun. Sadik ducked behind the back of the car. As his head popped back up, he swung his arm over and pointed another gun at the man. Aiming at each other, eyes fixed on each other, they remained focused and still. This time there was no shouting, both of them knew how the other was deceiving him. Alert and upright they all stood.

Eve trembled; her chance was getting closer. They had guns, how good would their shots be from a distance? Would their anger keep them pressed on each other? Would she make it? Or more importantly, would they make it? Her, Kevin and Rachel.

Silence was upon the three, their eyes darting amongst each other, none of them making a sound. All three came away from the car and into the clearing where the two men still pointed the two guns at each other. Sadik's arm trembled; the determination in his steely expression was now watering down. It was becoming obvious to the other two that Sadik had no intention of pulling the trigger. Sadik lowered his gun and put his hand up in submission towards the other man. Celile shouted as the other man grabbed Sadik's shoulder and flung him towards her. Eve dived to the ground and rolled into a small dip in the earth and remained still in the shadows. They were that close she could smell their sweat. Shaking, she closed her eyes so that what she was observing could not distract her from hiding quietly. In the shadows she remained until Sadik eventually got to his feet and was shoved even closer to her. All that stood between them was a stubby row of spiny shrubs. One more shove would see Sadik falling onto her. She remained still as the ants walked over her body, as the urge to flick and scratch became overwhelming and as the light of the moon was about to shine directly onto her. Tears welled up. It was her time, three of them, angry with at least two loaded guns. What chance did she have?

Something thudded against the car bonnet. Distracted by this bang, all three turned around. The older man stopped shoving Sadik and held out his hand to help him up. Whatever their differences were, they always seemed willing to put them aside when something threatened their plan.

"Mehmet," the older man shouted.

There was no answer. Eve lifted her chin up and peered over the ditch that she was wedged in. They were moving away from her, she sat up, placed her hands on the earth and began to push herself up. The moon shone brightly above her, if they were to turn their heads, she would be fully exposed by the light. She stood and turned, as she stepped forwards there was a loud cracking noise, her rucksack had got caught on a bush and snapped a twig. She stooped back down as all three of them began to walk towards her one step at a time. The older man held the gun out in front of him; the other two stepped behind him.

"Mehmet," he called.

Eve's heart hammered hard against her ribs, so hard, she could feel it blocking her throat. She tried to breathe in but she hyperventilated instead. Feeling light-headed, she allowed her stooping body to fall to its knees. If she lifted her head any higher they would be looking at her with a clear view and a gun pointing at her head. Little black dots began to prickle her vision, please don't pass out, please, she thought. Her breathing was now even further laboured and her vision was dotty and distorted, it was her time. Would they treat her worse because she'd given them the run around all evening? Or would they kill her quickly? If quickly, then it's game over. If slowly; whilst you are alive and however bad, there's always chance of escape. Her fate was in their hands. So close, so warm. Eve could now smell sweat once again; she could almost feel their body heat. Heat, more heat. Prickly warmth spread up her neck and chin, she felt her face burning. Without hesitation, she dug her fingernail into her leg; she needed a jolt of reality. Maybe a short sharp pain would bring her back and it worked. She swallowed. She was sure they had heard her gulp then another bang came from the cars, saving her. She listened as all three of them ran back in the direction that they'd come from. On her hands and knees she scurried out of the moonlight and back into the shadows before peering through a gap in the shrubs. Out of the corner of her eye, she caught a glimpse of Kevin staggering behind the trees ahead. She smiled as her breathing returned to normal. Relief flooded through her body temporarily weakening her, she allowed the tears to flow. She had never experienced tears of such joy in tragic circumstances but the tears that were flowing were of pure joy. She looked up again and noticed Kevin staring at her. He smiled and placed his hand on his heart, she smiled back as she did the same.

She heard the chattering of the four perpetrators getting louder. Kevin mouthed a word over and over again, she stared hard. Run, he was telling her to run. With that he disappeared into the dense growth and she did the same. She would stay in their circle but on the outside watching in, watching and waiting for that opportunity to arise. Now she had Kevin watching her back, she knew they could do it, they could get out together and be together; be happy, go home and do normal things that couples in love do.

Chapter 33

"They're playing us, keep vigilant," Guz whispered as he brushed Sadik off. "We need to get them alive, the girl at least. We get the girl, then deal with the boy and get out of here."

Celile nodded as she half listened to what Guz had said. Her mind was still on the stand-off between Guz and Sadik and how close the two brothers had come to pulling the trigger. She had watched Guz grin with the gun in his hand and shuddered at how much pleasure he had taken in seeing Sadik back down. She looked at Sadik before staring into the bushes ahead.

Guz's smell still lingered on her and she wondered if Sadik could tell. She had always told Sadik that until he did what he had to do and stood up to his brother that things would still happen between her and Guz but he had chosen to block out her words. The fact that he was aware wouldn't make it any easier for him to stomach if he knew it had just happened. She could've prevented it; she could've tried at least. Her efforts trying would have been better understood if Sadik had found out. If Guz had forced himself on her it wouldn't have been her fault. He could've blamed his brother, could've even pushed him to whisk her away to another life.

"So, do you know what you're all doing?" Guz asked. Celile looked at him blank. What had he just said? "Celile? Do you know what you have to do next?"

"Yes, I mean no. I didn't catch what you said."

"Sometimes I think you never listen to a word I say you stupid Bitch," Guz said as he stepped forward and allowed his nose to touch hers. She swallowed hard and looked away. "Maybe we should put her in with the deal whilst we're at it." Guz turned to Sadik and howled with laughter.

She allowed a tear to escape as she swallowed. When would the time come for Sadik to prove to her that she was more than just his occasional fling? She needed some confirmation that his promises were genuine. She thought back to the bland life on the farm that she'd left behind. Everyday was the same, her family was normal, but she had craved adventure and Guz had swept her off into the unknown. At this very moment she craved nothing more than being back at home with her mother, father and three brothers. Her nieces were growing up fast. She wanted children, a husband, someone dependable. At first she thought that might be Guz and then she thought it might be Sadik but now she didn't know. She needed Sadik to step up and defend her, she needed him to be a man and protect her from his bullying brother and the misery that she was always enduring at his hand. Her emotional needs had pushed her to another level, one she had not contemplated before. Her jealousy had taken Selina's life, she began to weep.

"I think we could get a few thousand Euros for this one. A scrawny little girl, could ship Celile off to Russia or somewhere. Oh shut up with the blubbing," he laughed.

"There's no need for that. We're all doing what we've got to do," Sadik interrupted."Are you alright Celile?" he asked as he placed his hand on her shoulder.

Guz grabbed Sadik by the tee-shirt and pulled him away from Celile, close towards him. "It was a joke, she knows me don't you Honey?" Guz said as his smile dropped without even looking at Celile.

"Please don't start now. I know you don't mean it Guz. Just leave Sadik alone," Celile said. Guz released Sadik and his grin returned.

"She must like you a lot," he said as he looked at both of them in turn. Both Celile and Sadik looked away. "You two, we need to get the woman. If she dies, you die too. We need her, understand? And shut that damn music off, if I have to listen to any more of that shit, I'm going to throttle someone."

They nodded and walked off towards the clearing by the river.

*****

Guz pulled out his mobile phone, adjusted the gun in his waistband and began to seek a spot where he could get a signal.

Chapter 34

After scurrying through the undergrowth and entangled shrubbery, Eve reached a clearing. The music went off. To her right she heard the sound of the trickling mountain water, in the distance she heard the gushing of the waterfall. Her eyes darted back and forth as the shuffling of nocturnal creatures disturbed the bushes. She stooped to the floor and panted as she sat still. Brushing back the strands of loose hair that had stuck to her sweaty face, she gazed ahead. Hanging above her nose was a flailing branch, thick and mossy with smaller stubbier branches emerging from its knobbly arm. In the distance she heard Mehmet call. The others called back; they were closing in on her. She grabbed hold of the branch and pulled herself up, she had to defend herself. Kevin and Rachel's survival depended on her strength. She thought of Kevin and how he came out of hiding to try and divert their attackers away from her hiding place. He had risked his life for her; she smiled. Out of it all she had found a man that she could only describe as being in love with, a man who had risked his own life and safety to help her. Now, she was going to do the same, maybe her next idea was incredibly stupid or would reward her generously. Which she did not know but there was no way she was going to die then lose both Harry and Kevin without a fight.

She wrenched at the knobbly branch, it remained in place. She tugged and twisted, splinters bedded into her clammy hands as she hauled it with all her weight. She felt the tiny warm prickles pierce her dirty skin. She closed her eyes and willed the branch to snap. She could see in the darkness of her mind, the little prickly openings in her skin, the sweat and dirt running into them and the sting that came with the continuation of the tugging. She pulled hard, then the branch snapped away from the tree. Stumbling back, branch in hand, Eve fell onto the small of her back. Her body creased in reaction to the jolt of pain, she reached around and rubbed the affected area as tears slid down her cheek. Close by, she saw torch light flashing through the dark leafy collage ahead, reflecting long rays of light over her dusty legs. She shuffled back, leaned against the tree and firmly held the branch. She slid up the rough bark and grabbed the knobbly branch hard and remained as still as she could.

The torchlight became brighter. Any second now, someone would pass the tree she was leaning against. Her pulse quickened, her veins throbbed with every heartbeat, and her hands began to tremble. A voice called back and the others replied. It was Mehmet, the easiest one to take out first in her opinion. She knew he had at least cared for Selina, she had seen the way he'd reacted when he'd learned of her death but he was one of them. Whether it be under duress or not, he would defend their attackers and preserve himself to the end and that's exactly what she was going to do.

Eve gripped the branch with both hands and poised herself as if she were having a game of rounders with the kids by her house as she often had. Bat in hand, ball coming towards her, she had the target in sight. This was a much easier target, the ball was bigger and she knew exactly how it was going to hit her bat. With a swift whack, she slapped the branch into the face of the oncomer hitting him square on. He yelped and stepped back dropping the torch onto the mossy ground by his feet. His hands drew up to his eyes; she could see what she'd done. An open piece of skin flapped just below his eye. Before he had any chance to react, she struck again, first his shoulder then his back. The young man buckled and fell to the floor; she bent down, grabbed his torch and turned it off before stepping backwards and darting off into the woodland. As she passed Rachel she threw her rucksack down, and kicked it under a shrub. She couldn't allow herself to be slowed down by luggage anymore and she was sure she wouldn't forget where Rachel was. She had to take them out and come back for Rachel and Kevin.

She heard a yell coming from ahead. Celile, she saw the moon's light glinting off the whites of her eyes. Turning, she ran back towards Mehmet. They were closing in on her. Thrashing the branch in front of her to part the foliage she kept running until she reached the pool that they had swam in earlier that night. In darkness the water crashed below, she felt the icy speckles tickle her face. The water now resembled a dark mass surrounded by hazardous rocks, rocks she couldn't clearly see.

Behind her she heard Celile running. To her left, the older man was approaching and all she could focus on was the shiny gun barrel pointing in her direction. "Nowhere to go now. Drop that branch or I'll drop it straight down your throat when I get to you," he said, spittle ejecting from his mouth as he spoke. Behind him Sadik approached and to her left Mehmet was staggering in her direction. She dropped the branch and held her hands up, if she got shot what chance did she and her friends have?

"Please don't shoot me, I have a son," she mumbled as a tear rolled down her cheek.

"I don't think you'll be seeing him again," the man said as he turned to Sadik and laughed.

"No, we have, what is it?" Sadik said looking to Guz for the answer.

"We have plans for you. Kiss your old life goodbye Lady," Guz said as he spat on the floor.

Plans? Eve's mind went into overdrive, maybe they didn't want to kill her but they would if they had too. She wasn't going to see her son again or go home. What plans?

Confused, Eve took a step closer to the water's edge. She was not going to adhere to their plans. She gripped the torch hard and plunged into the cold, dark water below. Her grasp loosened and the torch was gone. She felt the force of something dart past her body and a loud vibration. They were firing at her. As best she could she swum under the water; desperate to inhale she had to come to the surface soon. She aimed for the waterfall; she could at least try to lose them in the fall. As she emerged to the surface she felt a tug at her shoulder and a whack to the side of the face.

"You should've just sat back and enjoyed the party like the rest of them," Celile said as she spat a mouthful of water out.

Eve brought her arms out in front of her and grabbed at the woman's face, the woman grabbed back twisting her fingers in Eve's tangled hair. Celile grabbed Eve's head and pushed her under the water. Bearings completely lost, Eve tried to look around but there was nothing but darkness. She needed to breathe; she had no choice but to swallow a mouth full of river water. She floated to the top of the water in Celile's grasp and realised that she was being dragged back towards the waterside. She coughed hard and expelled a spurt of water from her lungs as she gasped for breath. The three men were calling Celile across. Eve clung onto a rock forcing Celile to stop in her tracks. With her feet now touching the ground Eve threw her hand out and grabbed Celile's hair and with one swift movement she slammed the woman's head into the rock.

She felt Celile's strength dissolve and her hands loosened their grip on her hair. Eve wrenched the last strands from Celile and felt a clump of her hair rip away as she pulled. She had released herself. She took a deep breath, pushed the front of her body back under the water and moved as far and as fast as she could.

Disorientated, she came back up to the surface, she was nearly at the other side; it was just a short swim away. She looked back and saw Sadik screaming over Celile's limp body. The older man pushed him away, Sadik shoved him back. Again they were bickering over Celile, now it was her time to get away from them so that she could at least recoup her energy and plan what to do next.

She waded with her arms under the water, hoping not to cause any rippling or splashing. Carefully treading water and steering her movement under the surface, she continued. A phone went off; what she would do for a working phone right this second. The older man stood and faced away from her. Sadik was still poring over Celile. Eve watched, she saw the woman thrash as she coughed. She then sat up and vomited a pool of what Eve imagined to be river water. Mehmet staggered in their direction. She had disabled no one. Her tears mixed with the icy water and her teeth began to chatter. She felt her joints become heavy and knew she had to get out of the pool.

She swam to the side and dragged her shivering body onto the earth in front of her. Grit stuck to her face, her arms and around her eyes. Shaking, she crawled over to a mound made up of rock and moss and stooped behind it.

Sadik spoke to Celile. She could still hear them, keep an eye on them and even look out for Kevin. For now she had to gain her senses back. She fumbled with her tee-shirt and dragged it over her head before pulling off her shorts. She was now sitting in her swimsuit, the one she'd been swimming in earlier that day. Her hands fumbled to grasp her wet clothing, as she did she squeezed them hard and drained as much water from them as she could before lying them on the mound to dry off a little. There was a gentle breeze and the humid air was quickly warming her up. In the distance she heard shouting, coughing and scurrying. It wouldn't be long before they came for her. For a moment she had to rest, she had to stop and she had to warm up. In her current shaken state she knew there was no way she could defend herself against anything, but she also knew Celile felt the same if not worse. She had smashed the young woman's head into the rock with a mighty slam. With that thought Eve allowed her head to sink back into the soft moss and she closed her eyes.

She listened to the blood pumping through her body and her thoughts darted from Harry being told that Mummy Eve was dead to her parents telling her they were proud of her. She fantasised about them being proud of her, in her fantasies she wasn't that young mum who worked as a classroom assistant. She was a teacher; she wanted to be a teacher. She wanted her parents to be able to tell their friends that their daughter was a teacher. Then, her thoughts darted back to when she told them she was pregnant, the birth, her infection, them going through the motions but not sympathising. She felt her mangled scar and thought of their shame, a married friend of the family, the harlot she had been. Her fault, her parents blamed her. His wife blamed her, even the neighbours blamed her. The only person who never got the blame was him. They never saw how he played her vulnerability and manipulated it for his own amusement. How he used and humiliated her and then her thoughts darted back to Kevin, always there in the background. So many regrets. She had been stupid. What would it take to make her parents accept her? mistakes and all. That's all she ever wanted when she rebelled heavily through her teens. Never did they tell her they loved her. The pictures she drew as a child never went up on the fridge, the bedtime stories her friends got were a mystery to her and they never hugged her.

Eve shuddered and opened her eyes, she had been weeping. Her thoughts were a jumbled mess. She grabbed her damp clothes and began to put them back on. Now she had warmed up, she could withstand the dampness. Her senses sharpened and she focused on her surroundings. She rolled onto her front and tried to stand, she stumbled. The pain in her back from her earlier fall bolted up to her underarm. That short rest had seized her up, rather than woken her up. She flexed her muscles and bent her legs working her body through the aches and stiffness. It was time to stake out. She leaned against the mound and looked on across the stream. She had to get up higher, maybe climb alongside the fall, and see what was going on. She would in a moment, just a couple more minutes.

Chapter 35

Guz grabbed the phone and held it to his ear. "Hello," a long silence followed. The sound of the lid being flicked open on a cigarette lighter travelled through his ear and lodged itself in his brain. "Hello." Once again no answer. "Boss," it was The Boss's number that had called him. To his left he could see Celile coughing hard, Sadik had ripped off a piece of his tee-shirt and compressed it against her bleeding head.

"You got them?" The Boss whispered as he once again played with the cigarette lighter.

"I got two, two good ones," Guz replied.

"I've got an order for three, you said three," The Boss said.

"Something happened, she was on to us and fought," he paused, "she's gone." Guz rubbed his temple with his free hand, this wasn't going to go down well with The Boss and it wasn't going to go down well for their payment.

"You idiot. How could you let one of them escape? Dopey here could've done a better job than you lot. Anything happens to the last two, I hold you solely responsible. I'll feed your balls to my dog."

"Escape? She didn't escape." Guz paused not knowing how to explain that she was dead. He thought back to Selina, he dare not tell The Boss that she was the most valuable one out of the three. "She had an accident whilst trying to escape and the consequences were fatal." Fatal, the word dead seemed so unusable when it came to Selina. All he saw was a waste. When this was over he was going to make Sadik pay for his carelessness. If his balls were on the line then he would make sure Sadik's were too.

"Nothing will happen, you have my word. You will have the other two by dawn as arranged. I have the passports too for all of them."

"Good, I have all the shipping arranged ready for them to start their new whore lives. When this is over we need to talk, I need more and quick, business is booming, orders are coming in by the minute. You are going to have to work harder my friend."

He shuddered. After this it was over, the end, finished. He was out and gone. "I always work hard. We will talk after the job is done."

"I will talk, you will listen and then you will do," The Boss replied as he burst into howling laughter. "Just remember now, you owe me a big one. You lost one of my girls tonight and for that you owe me and as you know, I always collect on my debts. Always."

The Boss hung up. Guz had to get things together. Pack up the girls, get them to the house and wait for the entourage to turn up and collect them. All that stood between him and the payout was a few measly hours.

The last two were still adequate girls, the deal was two thousand Euros per girl, he would still get four thousand for both, plus the passport rates and the personal goodies he'd collected from the house. There was no way The Boss would get a cut of the cash he'd collected from the villa. Four thousand Euros once converted and a passport could change his life. He'd get Rashid to fix the passport photo up and Europe was his oyster, he would be Gerhard. As his mind whirred away he glanced down at Sadik who was stooped down nursing Celile. He watched as he stroked her arm. The dazed young woman he thought he knew so well seemed to be familiar with his brother's touch as she didn't flinch. His brother, his longest standing friend was too close to his lady. His hands began to shake, how he'd like to grab his skinny brother and drag his arse across the ground and punch him, but he wouldn't. He needed Sadik to catch the girl; his meal ticket out of all of their lives. He took a deep breath, walked across to the riverside, pushed Sadik out of the way and held Celile.

Sadik stared at Guz as he stumbled back from the shove; Guz stared back, purposely caressing Celile's hair. He watched as his brother turned away.

"You," he called to Sadik. "Go and get that girl so we can get out of here. If you don't get that bloody girl, The Boss said he is going to feed your balls to his dog." It was a lie but he knew it would work, or at least save his own balls. One look at Sadik's startled eyes at the mention of The Boss was enough for Sadik and Guz knew it. He would get what he wanted, he would get the girl and pass them both over to The Boss. He would laugh as he disappeared with all their money leaving them behind with their pitiful lives. "Go on then," he shouted.

Sadik pulled out a gun and removed the safety catch. Guz watched as his little brother's fingers trembled over the trigger as he held it aside from Guz's face. He knew that his brother was trying to scare him. Guz laughed as he turned away knowing his spineless brother would never shoot him and he was right, he heard Sadik's footsteps trudging through the twigs and leaves. He didn't glance back, he didn't need to. He stroked Celile's hair. "Not long now."

"I want to go," she mumbled as she cried. He felt her try to pull away from his grasp but he pulled her back and stroked her hair. She wasn't getting away that easily.

"You will go soon my love."

Chapter 36

Eve staggered past the rock and made her way towards the waterfall. She turned as she heard a splashing sound, they were coming for her. She ran upwards to get a better view. Torchlight shone in the distance, they were coming her way. Run, she had to run. Her leg muscles burned, she placed one heavy leg in front of the other. Her damp clothes stuck to her body. She heard shouting, they were close. With all that she had left she darted away from the light, stumbling through bushes and dragging foliage around her ankles. She felt resistance, her ankle was tangled up. She shook her leg and tugged at the branches, rattling the leaves as she moved. The torchlight shone in her direction, her heart thumped as she continued to fight with the foliage. She broke free, stumbled forward then stopped. Below her there was a vertical drop, possibly forty feet. Stepping back she could feel them getting closer, she could hear them, smell them. She curled up into a little ball and pushed herself against a spiny bush. As it dug into her back she closed her eyes and held her breath. They were close, they were upon her. She could hear every step they took. There were two of them; she heard Sadik's voice, then Mehmet's voice.

Click. The sound of a gun that was ready to shoot. That sound was right in Eve's ear. She felt the cold metal press against her temple then she opened her eyes and saw what she had hoped she was never going to see that night. Sadik stared into her eyes, his hands were shaking; she felt his tremor through the barrel of the gun. Sweat dripped from his brow and dripped onto her face. Her end had arrived.

Shaking, Eve held her hands above her head and cried, "Please don't hurt me, please."

"We don't want to hurt you but we will if we have to. Do you hear me?" Eve shuffled to her knees and wailed. "Do you hear me Lady?"

"Please. I love my son. He needs me, I want to go home. Please." She felt a weakness brush over her. The fight was over; her attempts to escape were all in vain. She had failed herself, she had failed Kevin and she had failed Harry. "I love my son," she wailed. From nowhere she felt a slap burn her cheek.

"Now look Lady. You have to come with us. As I said, we don't want to hurt you but we will if we have to. Do you understand?"

She nodded. "Yes," she muttered. The realisation took her breath away; she gasped which led to her hyperventilating. She felt an overwhelming heat rise across her chest and up her neck. She inhaled then screamed as she exhaled, her whole body trembled uncontrollably. Her breath deepened and quickened and black spots clouded her vision. The moon's light was now speckled and blurred as tears gushed down her cheek. She tried to speak but the words would not come out. Opening her mouth she tried to shout but all she could do was gasp. She felt the men grab her arms and drag her along the gritty ground. With every movement a stone or a pine needle pierced her skin. She tried to move her legs but the strength had gone, she was beaten.

Moments later she felt the icy water once again. Mehmet was pulling her through the water. On the riverbank Sadik had the gun pointed directly at her. "No funny business Lady," she heard him shout. She closed her eyes as her body glided through the water, almost hoping for the end. Her breath now came in short sharp bursts and her body shook from the chill. She was cold but she felt warm, she was awake but she felt like it was nothing more than a dream. Peace almost came over her as Mehmet continued to swim. She allowed her eyes to close, her breathing slowed down. She had accepted whatever was to come.

"Pay day as they say." Guz said with a smirk as he dragged Eve's exhausted body from Mehmet.

She parted her eyelids and looked up at the man; there was no strength in her to fight them. In the distance she saw Celile sitting on the ground holding a piece of rag against her head. Behind her Sadik got out of the water after crossing the river behind them.

"Please don't let me die."

"Die. You play the game you will live and I will be a rich man."

She had no idea what he meant, but she had to play along to live. She had to please them, do as she was told. It was the only way. Kevin, she wondered if they had got him. If they had, what would they do with him? Was he part of their plan?

"I think they will be happy with this one," Guz called to Sadik. "She'll do. Probably ship her off to the Arab States or Russia even. Who knows? Who cares? But she'll be earning her keep. Did you hear that Lady? I hope you heard every word. I practised that speech in English just for you Darling."

Eve lay on her back and watched on, pleading with her inner self to regain some strength. Who will be happy? Earning my keep. Thoughts ran through her head. Was this happening to her? It all sounded very much like she was about to be trafficked. A single tear escaped down the side of her eye and meandered into her ear. Every part of her body was gritty, her eyes, her body, her hair.

"Get her onto the jeep and tie the Bitch up." Guz yelled.

Mehmet and Sadik grabbed her under the arms and lifted her off the ground, she had no control; once again they dragged her over the grit and through spiny shrubs. Trying to kick was no use. She stared up at Mehmet. "How can you let them do this to me?" She saw his face turn and she recognised the look of shame but he didn't stop, he did as he was told and fulfilled his duty to his comrades. She looked harder at his face and saw the glint of skin under his nose that she had shred with the branch and she realised that there was a big chance that he had lost all sympathy for her.

As the others passed, Celile turned to Eve and spat in her face, "Bitch, look what you did to my fucking head," she yelled. Eve stared up at the stars as they painfully dragged her and dreamed that one day she would go home. Trafficked means she would live, what that life would mean was another question. While alive she could always plan to escape, once she had some strength back she would get away. She hoped that people would question where they were and then despair set in. They had left no trail of where they had gone that day and she wept, this time the weeping was dry. There were no tears left, only sore dry eyes. 'Trust your instincts,' the old woman had said, maybe she would remember them but what good would that do? She had trusted her instincts all day and this is where it had got her.

Bang, she heard the back door open on the jeep before they flung her onto the bench in the back. She felt the rough rope bind her hands behind her back and tie her feet together. Then she felt a sharp pain across the back of the head. All went black.

Chapter 37

"Take her back to the house. Put her in the outhouse down the bottom of the garden and don't let her out of your sight." Guz yelled as he placed the jeep keys into Sadik's hand.

"We'll go now, before she wakes up." Sadik said.

"Good idea. We have five hours. I'll bring the other girl, waste the man and sort out the bodies."

"Why don't we take the other girl, Rachel now?" Celile said as she rubbed her wounded head.

"Because," Guz said as he moved closer to her, "I said I'll bring her with me."

Celile stared deep into his eyes; he knew that she knew what he was up to. So he wanted to have a private look at the girl before he brought her in. Product inspection, he knew The Boss wouldn't disapprove. It was nothing she wasn't going to have to get used to in her new future. His Celile had better things to do anyway; he had felt it in her lack of enthusiasm earlier that evening when they'd made love. But at least he'd had her, she was his and he could rub that fact into his slimy little brother's face as soon as this was all over.

"Whatever," she replied as she got into the passenger seat of the jeep.

"Mehmet, you ride in the back with the girl, keep an eye on her."

"I don't want to ride in the back, please I don't want to look after the girl," he replied.

"Just do as your old man says," Guz yelled as he slapped the young man across the head. Mehmet opened the back door and climbed into the jeep. Guz watched as he edged his way to the bench trying not to touch Eve's unconscious body. "She won't bite you," Guz said as he slammed the door hard and grinned.

He turned to Sadik and Celile. "You two, go now, let's get this thing over. I make it five hours that we have until collection. That's all the time we have to get this wrapped up. If we screw this up, The Boss will screw us up. Do you both understand?" Celile walked off and got into the passenger seat. "You need to take a car, take Sadik's car," he said as he dragged Celile back out of the jeep and thrust another set of keys at her. "I'm working with imbeciles. We can't leave a car behind; I can only drive one back."

"There's no need to pull me about," Celile said.

"Just get in the car and drive back to the house." Celile did exactly as she was told without looking back at him. He waited to see if she would look but she only turned to Sadik as she got into the car and drove off up the gravel path. "I'll see you back at the house as soon as I'm done here." Guz said.

"See you later Brother," Sadik said as he turned the engine and reversed.

Brother; who needs a brother like that? Guz turned away from him, didn't want to watch him leave. He heard the jeep trundle past. He turned to his own car and popped open the boot. He placed the loaded gun with the safety catch on in his belt and he grabbed the dirty shovel. To his delight he spotted half a roll up that he had dropped in the boot earlier that day. After lighting it he inhaled, enjoying every drag before he set to work. He grabbed a warm bottle of flat cola and took a long swig; it was just what he needed. Leaning on the dirty shovel he watched as the light from the jeep disappeared in the distance. He had to get the Rachel woman into the car, eliminate the injured man and deal with the clean-up. Three easy tasks and one that could be harder than it sounded. He had the gun; as soon as the man surfaced he would give him one straight between the eyes. He grinned as he nubbed out the roll up between his thumb and forefinger before flicking it into the boot as he closed it. He balanced the shovel against the car, he would need that soon. Now it was time for work. Five hours and it would all be over. He would be packing up to leave.

Chapter 38

Eve laughed as Harry dragged her in his little cart, she heard him giggle back as he pulled her over the bumps on the grass. It was soon time to pack up and finish for the day, time to have tea, to watch The Jungle Book and to get out the chocolate buttons. Always her favourite part of the week. She tried to sit up but her body failed to respond, maybe she had dislodged something whilst bumping over the fields. "Harry," she called. There was no answer, just another giggle. She smiled. "Harry, Mummy Eve needs some help from her little man." Again no answer. "Mummy Eve loves you, I have chocolate buttons. Harry? Mummy loves you."

Quietness fell and the light blue sky started to turn grey. "Harry," she called. "This isn't funny. Mummy Eve needs a hand." As she moved her stiff neck to the side the sky purged itself of rain that landed violently across her left cheek. The water fell until the little cart had almost filled up. Struggling to breath, Eve tried to flap her arms. Trapped in the little cart, she couldn't move; her back was still lodged. She kicked but her legs were restricted. More water? Please no more rain, she thought. She closed her eyes as the water caused her to gargle; she could no longer call for Harry. The cold water swished down her closed throat and into her lungs.

Yanked out of her nightmare Eve opened one blurry eye and coughed up a load of water. She squinted as she gazed at the small wood and concrete building she was restrained in. She felt a wetness dripping over her face and another jug of water splashed against the side of her head. She tried to move her arms but they were lodged. Throbbing pain seared through her head, a rough rope rubbed her wrists, she was bound to the wooden wall of the building. Her hands were tied closely above her head and her arm was bent sharply at the elbow. She tried to kick, her legs were also bound.

"Mummy Eve, I'm coming to help you," called Harry.

"I know you want to help me." Eve smiled as she closed her eyes again. She pictured Harry coming towards her, bounding in his childlike way, pulling his green dungarees up so that he wouldn't trip over.

"Mummy Eve." Her little man's voice became distorted. Why was he speaking in a foreign language? "Seni seviyorum." Why was Harry telling her he loved her in Turkish?

"Harry? Harry?" Eve opened her eyes and she sucked in air in sharp bursts, coughing hard as she choked on the small amount of water that was aggravating her windpipe. Had they tried to drown her? She looked around at the old structure; it was nothing but a woody blur. Drawn to her left, she turned her throbbing head. Sadik and Celile she thought. The harder she stared the clearer they became. She watched as Sadik placed a jug on the bench before grabbing the woman's hair in an almost violent way. Celile responded by lifting up his tee-shirt, her hands ran all over his caramel coloured skin and soon led to his belt. He pulled her head back by her long hair and kissed her hard as he thrust her back against the door, she responded by kissing him back hard and desperate.

Eve tried to trace the rope with her hands, hoping that they would remain diverted by passion. She yanked it with her arms hoping to free it a little, no movement. She looked down at her bound feet; they were tied together and looped through a metal ring that appeared to have been concreted into the floor. A few feet away from her, the couple began grunting as Sadik began to undo Celile's shorts. The one low light began to flicker and the couple stopped and mumbled in Turkish. Celile stared in Eve's direction before pushing Sadik off her. The man spoke to her; she spoke back, not once taking her eyes off Eve. She watched as Celile took her hair in her hands, rolled it up and tucked it into a messy bun.

Bang, the door. Both Sadik and Celile tidied their clothing up as Mehmet entered. "She's awake," he whispered.

"We know," Celile replied. "She is awake aren't you Eve?" Sadik stared at Eve. "What are you looking at?" Celile yelled as she grabbed his chin and moved his head in her direction.

"Nothing Celile. I was looking at nothing."

"Well don't." Mehmet stared at Celile. "Just do what you're paid to do Mehmet." Celile responded. The young man looked away.

"Please don't hurt me. Please, I need to get back to my son. My little boy."

"Yes we know. Harry isn't it?" Celile replied.

Eve shuffled against her binds. How did they know? "Please, what are you? How do you know my son's name?" Fine tears began to fall down the side of her dirty face.

"We are no one, just here to make some money. Your son, well you never shut up about little Harry on the journey to get here," Celile said as she stared into Eve's eyes. As the woman stepped closer Eve turned her head away.

"Where am I?"

"That doesn't concern you either." Celile walked back and forth before kneeling down to Eve's level. Eve flinched as Celile's hand brushed the wet hair from her face. "What does concern you though is the state of my head," she yelled as she slapped Eve across the face. "Look." The woman parted her hair and showed Eve the long deep scratch that the blow from the rock had caused.

Eve looked away. "I'm sorry. I was scared, you were all chasing me."

"Pass me a knife. Let's value this piece of shit." Celile spat as she held her hand out. Mehmet fidgeted and argued with her in Turkish. The woman stood, slapped the boy across the head and yanked his knife from his belt before pushing him out of the door. Sadik yelled at her, she pushed him back and held her free hand up to him. He backed down and smiled. Celile kneeled down in front of Eve.

"Please don't kill me, please," she cried. Mucous dripped from her nose and her eyes started to burn from all the crying. She watched the knife as it drew closer, pointing directly at her stomach. "No," Eve yelled as she closed her eyes. Her whole body tensed as she waited for the knife to plunge but it didn't. All she heard was a loud tear. They were cutting off her clothing. She opened her eyes and saw Celile cutting her tee-shirt first, then her swimsuit. Celile opened it up from bottom to top carefully avoiding cutting her skin. Eve wept as she sat there, powerless to stop them. Her scarring, her vulnerability revealed to her kidnappers. She knew how it looked, Kevin had been kind, had seen past it but most didn't. If they were hoping to traffic her would this be a deal breaker? Would they now kill her instead? She watched as they yelled at each other.

*****

"Oh this is just great," Celile yelled as she stood. "She is defunct. I don't suppose they are going to pay us much for this."

"How were we supposed to know? They will have her, I'm sure. She'll do for something," Sadik replied as he strolled away from the door to have a closer look.

*****

It was time to plead; Eve took a deep breath and spoke. "I'm sorry, I had an infection and nearly died," Eve said hoping to win some sympathy. "Please don't hurt me because of my scar. Please."

Celile handed the knife to Sadik and bent back down. "I suppose you will just attract a worse class of customer. Some ..... what would you say? Some pond life. And this is for what you did to my head," Celile yelled as she punched Eve hard on the cheek. The same cheek that had also been slapped and dragged. Celile pointed to a small table in the corner of the room and Sadik lifted a scarf off the table and passed it to her. Celile wrapped the scarf around Eve's head and tied it at the back, gagging her. With every breath she inhaled a musty woody dust that hit the back of her throat.

Every fibre of Eve's skin now tingled. A bruised battered tingling. She watched as the woman drew back her fist to punch again. Eve turned away and tensed up once again. Sadik shouted and grabbed her fist. Eve turned to watch as the man struggled to get the angry woman out of the building. They shouted as he dragged her to the door, they shouted as they slammed the door behind them. She still heard the shouting as they walked off until they were so far away she could hear them no more.

Above her, the dim light flickered, insects buzzed around the warm occasional glow casting shadows over the wood's grain and the white concrete floor. The chaos of the flickering, the buzzing insect noises and the creaking that was caused by her movement only served to reinforce her captivity. Helpless and bound, the only thing that she could hope for is that she wouldn't get attacked any more. She would do what they said and wait for her chance. One chance is maybe all she'd have if she was lucky. Four of them, one of her and Kevin, she rocked as far as her restraints would allow. Back and forth, back and forth.

Her life, the fairytale ending with Kevin was a distant memory. He was a distant memory. She had found love, a deep love, a trusting love and a respectful love. Love that only comes once if a person is lucky and now her life had been ruined. She wept dry desperate tears for Kevin, thinking of him, injured, alone and lost in the mountains. He would die, she visualised him being eaten by wild animals. In years to come someone might find his bones. And Rachel, what had they done with her? Had they found her or had Eve hidden her drugged body well enough? Had she killed her friend? If they had found her at least she would have a chance at life. As Eve had hidden her, what would become of her now? Both Rachel and Kevin wouldn't survive in the wilderness she was sure of that. The moment when she'd ran and she reached the edge of the mountainside; the terrain, the distance to civilisation, they would be hungry. She was sure they'd die. She bowed her head and continued to rock back and forth; as far as the ropes would allow.

Chapter 39

Bang, Kevin bolted upright. The ringing in his ears made the dark world around him feel like it was closing in. He felt around in his lap and found his glasses.

How long had he been out of it? A sulphuric smell hung in the air, gunpowder. He flinched as he tried to move, the rawness of his wound burned with every twist. He felt his leg; wetness had started to soak through his shorts. Where was Eve? Where was anyone? Where did the bang come from? As he leaned forward a branch prodded him in the side of his face, he rubbed the scratch. Nothing hurt like the throbbing in his leg. With one hand grabbing a branch and another placed flat against the tree he hoisted his body up. As he pulled, his knuckles tensed and trembled. He placed all of his weight on his good leg before stepping onto his injured leg and laying it down flat.

"I'm coming for you," Guz called.

Kevin stood against the tree as he dodged a ray of torchlight. They were still after him. Eve, he had to find Eve. He listened; there were no other sounds, not a voice, not a rustle, only the sounds of the man who was fast approaching his hiding place. He had to get back over to the jeep, try and find out what was going on. Behind him, he heard a firm step crunch on the twigs beneath, then a snorting noise followed by the man spitting. He held his position and tried hard to breathe quietly. Sweat fell down his forehead and dripped into his eyes and off the end of his nose, the humidity served to make his arms feel heavy.

The man passed him and stopped to look around. He watched the stout, gun pointing body walk off alongside the river. "I found your blood. The animals will eat you when you're dead," the man called.

Kevin glanced down and saw a blackness expanding around the light coloured material covering the wound on his leg. He was nearly down, that monster was right. He had time against him. Without a thought he fumbled with the knotted material around his leg, untied it and took a look. The moonlight only showed him so much but the sticky blackness glistened in the small amount of light that there was. He flinched as a stinging pain seared from his leg and through his body. A stream of blackness trickled down his leg. Grabbing the bloody material, he tied it back up as hard as he could. Clenching his teeth, he took a moment for the wave of pain to pass. Stomach churning, breath bad with thirst, head light, he stood closed eyes for a moment against the tree, willing the pain to subside. Why had he untied the wound?

Now, he had to go now the light had passed. He hobbled onto the path. In the distance he heard the man call again but he was too far away for the words to be identified. He shuffled alongside the river bank. As he got closer, he could hear the gushing of the waterfall. "Eve," he whispered. No answer. With every step pain jolted up his leg and waist. He had to survive, he had to find Eve and get them out of there. The last thing he remembered was slipping into a feverish sleep. The events beforehand came back to him; they were chasing Eve, hunting her down. He remembered pounding on the cars and the jeep to try and get them away from her. He remembered hoping that she would get away and fetch help. "Eve." He called again and again, there was no answer.

He thought of the few days that they had spent together. His teenage dream had come to life when Eve had wanted to be with him. Every moment that they'd shared had been the best of his life so far. He shivered as he thought back to when he felt her skin next to his back at the villa. Her smile, her warmth, her loving nature. He had to find her; he had to get her back. He needed her. Cautiously he approached the area where they were set up earlier that evening. Nothing but darkness and the sound of crickets that deceived the ear so well. At one angle it sounded like they were in his ear, a slight turn and they were all but gone. Rustling came from the surrounding shrubs, the waterfall crashed into the pool. Feeling the spray on his left cheek he enjoyed the coldness and found it almost invigorating. The vehicles were behind him, they had to be, that's where they were earlier.

"We have your slut girlfriend," he heard the man shout. Kevin's heart pounded and he could hear the blood pumping through his head. They had Eve, they had caught her. The voice was close. He turned and shuffled over the stumps and mangled twigs and headed towards the cars. Nearly there he thought as he dragged his leg over the rocks. 'Don't fall, don't trip,' he thought over and over again. "She's very nice," the man shouted followed by a loud snigger.

He turned and spotted the torchlight. The prick who was after him was probably passing the clearing at that moment and heading directly in Kevin's direction. His slow drag turned into a pain inducing jog; he had to try, for Eve. The torchlight shone straight past him.

"Trying to run with a shot leg. Not easy," the man shouted as he continued to catch him up. "Run, see how long you can run for," the man shouted as he howled with laughter. The sadistic prick had spotted him and was enjoying every moment of the show.

The car, only one car. The jeep and the other car had gone. Eve must've gone in a car, but where. "No, where the hell. Where the hell is she?" Kevin shouted. "Where is she? You prick?" A shovel was leaned against the boot of the car. A weapon, he dragged himself towards it. Bang, a bullet flew past his head and hit a tree stump. The smell of sulphur was close by. His stomach rolled and he leaked a tear as he bent over to shield his body behind the car. The torch beam got closer and closer before it flickered. He heard the man mutter to himself and bang it against his hand. The lights went out. Kevin knew that his eyes would take a moment to adjust.

"I see, we have a bit of fun. No lights," the man said. Kevin reached around the back of the car. Without being able to see the shovel, he felt his way round until he felt the wooden handle. With a swift grab he darted as low as he could back into the bushes.

"There's no way you can escape. You think you can take me down with that old shovel?" The man said. "Here's a question. You know how many people have been buried by that shovel?"

Kevin flinched as he imagined people, random people. Normal people just like them. People on days out, having fun before coming to a grisly end.

"In fact I buried one just here," the man said as he moved closer to Kevin. "I will bury you here too, next to him and his ugly wife. She wasn't like your girls, pretty. We can do things with pretty girls." The man howled with laughter before breaking into a hacking cough. Kevin kept still as he heard the man rustling near him. He smelled cigarette smoke, he was close.

Come here, come close to me, come close enough so that I can wrap this shovel around your face, Kevin thought. The man remained; smoking, spitting and laughing. He heard the gun cock as the man continued to howl.

Chapter 40

Buzz click. The flickering light went out. Eve envisaged the disappointed little moths dispersing before searching for an exit out of the building. Closing her eyes, she tried to picture the room that she had been studying for the past few minutes. She had to remember things, everything; but it was getting harder. Every small movement was punished with a jolt of pain, her muscles were stiff from the running earlier that night and the position she was bound in had solidified her stiff position. Numbness had now spread from her legs to her hips and her elevated arms felt nonexistent. Her swimsuit flapped open as she moved; she felt the bottom of her right breast slip underneath the dirty orange lycra. Open and exposed in all her shame for all to see, everything that she'd ever wanted to keep private about herself was now on display for her captors to ridicule. The room; she thought hard, don't forget the room. Eyes tightly shut she battled with the throbbing in her head to recall the room. There was a little table, maybe it could be used as a weapon. To her left, some gardening tools were hanging up on the wall. Her head flashed a pain and her numb arms tingled; she tried to wiggle her fingers but it was difficult.

'The room,' she yelled in her head; think about the room. Directly ahead there was a door, it wasn't locked. They had assumed she was well and truly stuck where they had left her and they were right. Gardening tools, shovels, a lump hammer. She shuddered, all tools they could use on her if she didn't comply. A lawn mower. Clear pots of screws and nails. Wood stain and cobwebs. Wood, lots of wood, the whole structure was built of wood with a concrete floor. Musty old wood; frail wood, oily smelling wood.

Noises, she heard the neighing of a horse close by; there had to be other buildings. Was she on a farm? All questions, no answers. Why did her head not give her the answers? What she would do right now for a couple of pain killers, a cold drink and a comfortable bed? A drink, her mind wandered, taunting her with visions of cold water. The musty rag had rubbed the corners of her mouth sore with every head movement. The material had absorbed any liquid that was in her mouth. Dryness had spread to her throat, she tried to cough but a forced croak was the only sound she could make.

A light beam jolted across her face as it filtered through a broken piece of the wooden structure. She shuffled and got as close to the gap in the wood as she could. Squinting and closing one eye she tried hard to focus on the light. A car pulled up at the back of what looked like a small sugar cube house. People were removing items from the car, lots of things. Eve squinted harder, the images were becoming clearer. Celile stood to the side of the car and grabbed a pair of shoes. Eve saw the dark silhouette of a high shoe followed by a bag. There was something familiar about the shape of the shoe, Selina. Selina's pride and joy, her favourite purchase; the purple shoes. They had looted all their belongings, all their valuables and their lives, eradicating their existence. Eve shuddered as she thought about them ransacking the villa. Had they ransacked it or quietly just removed all the evidence of whom had stayed there? She watched as their bags were flung out of the car one by one. All their belongings gone. Eve shuddered; the owners of the villa would assume that they had left. Their passports, documents, identification, bank cards and money: All coming out of the back of that car.

Eve wrenched the binds that dug into her skin to no avail; she had to get out get away. She couldn't leave their disappearance as a mystery never to be solved. Their disappearance would be met by people saying that they had left the villa, gone elsewhere, got into some sort of trouble and got lost. After all, the gang had taken their bags and belongings. She pictured the news channels at home mentioning their disappearance. It would be a thirty second slot never to be repeated and they would be forgotten forever. Harry would grow up thinking that his mother had left him. Her parents would lap up the pity from well-wishers. All this would be old news within no time. She tried to wrench the binds again, pulling hard, trying to bring life back to her numb limbs. The severity of the pain sharpened her senses, awakening her determination. Breathlessly she stopped and shuffled once more towards the gap in the wood.

Sadik slapped Mehmet, Celile unloaded something. There was no sign of the older man in the woods. Maybe it was just the three of them. She heard a shuffling sound and the main lights on the car illuminated an old woman. A bent over woman shuffling in slippers wearing a dark headscarf. Her face turned towards Celile and she shuffled across to her. Come closer, Eve thought. The old woman's features were still blurred. Celile dismissed the old woman who then began to shuffle towards the outbuilding. Maybe this woman would help her. Eve croaked as hard as she could and tried to stamp her feet as much as the binds would allow. The woman stopped and steadied herself before continuing to shuffle closer. Once again, Eve croaked as loud as she could. The old woman stopped halfway between the car and the outhouse, the lights catching her face as she turned. The old woman who was trying to sell her the sunglasses, it was her. 'Trust your instincts.' What had she known? Had they been targets from the beginning? Was she part of it or was she trying to warn them? Sadik called and the old woman ignored him.

He ran towards her and grabbed the old woman by the back of her frail arm, swung her around and pointed her in the direction of the house. The old woman shuffled away and the car's lights went out. She listened as the car doors were slammed and Sadik dragged all their bags towards the house. She relaxed her body, and sat still, listening to their movements. The front door slammed shut.

Her muscles twitched, her face tingled and her thirst grew stronger. She moved her tongue and flinched at the dry mesh like material of the scarf. The mustiness now overwhelmed her, it was almost like the stains from the scarf had become part of her. She closed her eyes, there was no point in crying, no point in screaming, every movement that was a waste of time was now a waste of the precious little bit of energy that she had left.

She tried to think back to the moment when she had been dreaming of Harry pulling her along in the little truck; it would be real in her mind for now. Stillness came over the place, the horse had stopped neighing and even the crickets weren't out. There were no insects bouncing off the light bulb and no people either. All that was left was a vacuous silence. A silence that was hard to imagine. Eve had tried to think back to a time when she had sat in total silence and she couldn't recall one.

Now, in this shed building it was her alone in silence. All she had was her own imagination to pass the time. At their mercy she wouldn't be able to go anywhere. She fidgeted, her bladder needed emptying. How that could've happened when she was so desperate for a drink, she didn't know. She fidgeted in the damp patch created from the water that they had poured over her earlier. If only she'd have known she would be so parched now, she would've tried harder to drink some of the water instead of choking on it and coughing it back up.

She heard a crunch on the earth outside the building alerting her to someone's presence. Her body stiffened as the door handle creaked. Her breaths quickened and she breathed in the musty air desperately through the scarf. Someone was coming for her, from what she could hear someone was coming alone for her.

Chapter 41

Kevin gasped for air, stabbing pains shot up his leg. The Prick's laughing got louder as he took another step towards Kevin. He could see The Prick's shadow in front of the car as the clouds passed and the moon's light shone from behind the man. The shadow neared as the hefty man moved forward a step. Kevin kneeled down and took the weight off his burning calf then shuffled backwards. He was now crouched behind the bonnet of the car. The Prick knew exactly where he was, Kevin tensed up as he heard him edge closer.

"I'm going to give her something special from you when I get back. You would call it a present. A big present, one she won't forget," The Prick said.

Kevin's heart began to pound as he clenched his teeth. Sweat dripped over his eyes and his knuckles gripped the handle of the shovel. This Prick wasn't going to get a chance to hurt his Eve. With all his strength, he jabbed the edge of the shovel directly into Guz's shins, the man yelped and fired. Kevin flinched and ducked. A branch dropped to the ground missing his head by an inch, the bullet had been fired into the sky. He grabbed the shovel then jabbed again at The Prick's shin, he watched as the metal edge tore through his trousers and gashed his leg. The Prick yelped and writhed in front of him as he grabbed the gun and aimed it at Kevin's head. Kevin kicked The Prick hard in his gaping wound and The Prick writhed on the floor before grabbing the gun. With one hand on the bonnet of the car and one on the shovel, Kevin dragged his body to a standing position and lifted the shovel above his head. The Prick lifted up his arm and pointed the gun at Kevin's face. Kevin closed his eyes, not wanting to see the bullet coming at him. He couldn't stop now, no surrender; putting up a fight was his only chance of escape. With everything he had, he brought the shovel down hard on The Prick's face, flat side on. He heard the gun fly behind The Prick and land in the hedge.

The Prick murmured and rolled his eyes back before closing them. Using the shovel as a crutch Kevin hobbled in the direction of the gun. He began prodding the ground with the tool in an attempt to part the foliage that was concealing the weapon he needed. Then he heard a crunch, metal on metal. He had found the piece. Stumbling, he fell to his knees and felt along the dusty undergrowth until he had his fingers around the gun. He grabbed it firmly and turned his head. The Prick still lay outstretched on the ground, murmuring to himself.

Gun in hand, Kevin stood and shuffled towards the splayed out man and kneeled beside him. Keys, they had to be somewhere. He fumbled in The Prick's pockets, there was nothing but a few shreds of previously machine washed tissue paper. "Where the fuck have you put the keys?" Kevin shouted as he shook The Prick. The slumped man responded with an incoherent snort. The Prick's eyes were still closed. Kevin got to his feet and shuffled back over to the shovel. He yelped as he bent to grab it; every time he moved he could feel his open wound being stretched further apart. He rubbed his sweaty face with his gritty hand before grabbing the shovel and using it as a crutch.

"Celile," The Prick stuttered.

Kevin headed towards the area where they had camped all evening, the keys had to be amongst The Prick's belongings; they had to be somewhere. As he approached the waterfall, he spotted a couple of bags positioned next to Selina's body. He flinched as he settled the shovel against the tree and leaned down to grab the bag, avoiding the skin of his perished friend. He grabbed it and shook it, there were no keys jangling in the bag. The clouds passed once again and the moonlight lit up the area beautifully. The cascading water almost took on a bluish tinge, in the distance he saw something move, a creature, a wolf like scavenger waiting for him to leave so that it could feast on his friend's body. Kevin kneeled as he continued to fish around in the bag and something caught his eye. A glint of something shiny, the sight of metal on a key ring wedged under Selina's bottom. He leaned down with his eyes closed as he grabbed the bunch of keys. He opened them once again and forced his gaze away from Selina. He pulled his body back to standing and took a step. He stopped, took a deep breath and turned before taking a step back towards Selina. He removed the scarf that had concealed his friend's deathly face.

    He placed the keys safely in his pocket and stroked her head as a tear rolled down his cheek. Her eyes were closed and her lips were slightly parted. "I will be back for you," Kevin whispered as he leaned over and kissed her gently on the forehead before pulling the scarf back over her. He turned to see if the wolf creature was still around; to his relief it had gone. Wet tears spread across his cheek; he wiped them away and started hobbling with his shovel-crutch towards the car.

    Kevin hobbled past The Prick and gave the limp man a gentle kick. The Prick's eyes opened wide as he grabbed Kevin's ankle. Without hesitation, Kevin lifted the shovel above his head and dropped it once again on The Prick's face. Heart pounding, blood pumping, Kevin swayed before steadying himself on the car boot. He had to make a break; he had to get in the car and go. But where? And, where was Eve?" Where the fuck is she you prick," he yelled as he stood there gun in one hand, shovel in the other. "Tell me where she is," he yelled again, eyes darting everywhere. His hands began to tremble and tears flooded across his face, he had lost her, let her down, fell asleep. Why had he drifted off when he should've been helping his loved one? "Argh," he yelled. He yelled again and again until his voice refused to yell any more. He had to do something, get help, get the Police.

Staggering towards the driver's door he stepped aside The Prick's still body, leaned the shovel against the back door and pulled the key from his pocket. He closed his eyes as he inserted the key in the lock. "Please work," he whispered as he turned, he smiled as all the doors unlocked. He grabbed the shovel and threw it over the top of the driver's seat on to the back seats before easing himself in. Carefully, he placed the key into the ignition, there was no way he was going to drop it or lose it now that he had come this far.

There had to be a clue as to where Eve could be. He opened the glove box and dragged out the contents, he turned the ignition and turned on the reading light; an old newspaper flopped out of the compartment. He threw it to the floor and continued rooting at the back of the box. He found the locking wheel nut and two small books. He dragged them out, two passports, he opened them up. German. Gerhard and Ilse. Another pair of victims. He threw the books to the floor; the glove box was now empty. He stretched his head around and spotted a bag on the back seat. Leaning over, he grabbed the lumpy handle and dragged it over his head and onto his lap. Again, he rooted through the bag and his hands fell upon a small bottle of flat cola. Without hesitation, he unscrewed the bottle, placed it to his lips and drank until he almost choked. A few drops slid down his windpipe and caused him to cough. He screwed the cap back onto the bottle and placed it on the driver's seat. He looked in the wing mirror, The Prick still lay there but now his left hand was flinching. There wasn't much time, he had to leave. One more delve into the bag and he was seeking out the closest cop shop.

He felt around and came across a square lump of plastic, The Prick's phone he hoped. Pulling it through the items of clothing he was looking at a satellite navigation system. "Please turn on," he whispered. The gadget failed to respond. A charger lead dangled from the cigarette lighter, he hoped it would be for the sat-nav. It plugged in perfectly. The engine was ticking along nicely and the air conditioning began to kick in. He glanced at the fuel gauge, a couple of notches above reserve. Hopefully enough to get him out of this hell hole. The light on the sat-nav came on.

The gadget beeped at him, all the commands were in Turkish; he looked at it blankly and an address flagged up. It was his only option; he clicked on the address and watched as the gadget calculated the route. Eight kilometres. He pressed a couple of buttons hoping to pin his location, he thought of Rachel still out there, alive and drugged. He had to come back, he needed to lay his friends to rest, tell the truth of what happened and get justice for them all. More than anything, he needed to get Eve; he would follow the route and see where it took him. The route was clearly mapped out, a route that snaked in and out of other snaking routes.

He reversed, making sure that he didn't drive over The Prick's body. He couldn't do what they did, harm and maim; torture and abuse. He would get his justice when the truth came out. Kevin struggled with the gears and the positioning of all the commands of the left hand drive but he was moving the car. It was happening, he was escaping. He continued to do a turn out of the clearing and towards the dirt track. The sat-nav spoke in a high voice, in a language he could not understand. It was a seductive female voice, his only option was to try and watch the route on the little screen. He was on his way out. He put his foot down on the accelerator and felt the car pull away.

Chapter 42

The door creaked open, Eve's pulse quickened. She tried to wrench the binds once more but they remained firmly in place. A figure emerged from the darkness; Mehmet. The young man looked back at the house and crept towards Eve as he held his index finger to his lips. He kneeled down and untied the scarf that gagged her.

She gasped for breath; fresh air was something she had always taken for granted. She looked up at Mehmet, hesitant to speak in case he lashed out. His eyes remained focused on hers as he reached into the back of his waistband.

"No please," Eve whispered as she looked away and wept. She imagined a knife or a gun. Had they been ordered to get rid of her? Was she of no use as a defunct person?

Mehmet grabbed her cheek and pulled her face back towards him as he held up a bottle of water. "Drink," he whispered. He held the bottle up to her lips and tilted it up. The water was warm but it was much needed. She gulped and gulped not being able to get enough. As she gulped he tipped the bottle up higher, overwhelmed by the flow she felt a gushing of liquid flush into her lungs. As she coughed violently, Mehmet drew the bottle away. She inhaled hard and coughed sporadically. "Thank you," she whispered. He nodded his head once in acknowledgment and placed the cap back on the bottle before placing it by his side. For a moment Eve sat and stared at his silhouette in the darkness. The whites of his eyes had a tiny glint every time he turned towards the door. A light, maybe a low powered outside or security light was on. He picked up the scarf and reached towards her. "Please, I need the bathroom," she paused. He stopped and placed the scarf on the floor beside him. "Please, I need to go to the toilet," she whispered. Her full bladder was causing her pain every time she moved. He stood, walked over to the door and looked outside once more.

"I will sort it," he said.

Eve watched as Mehmet fumbled around by the tools, he moved things off the shelf and rummaged behind the bench before emerging with a bucket. "Thank you. You need to untie me," Eve said.

"I can't, I would like to help but I can't. You don't understand. It is not just you that is the prisoner."

Damn. Eve hoped he might have been the one to give her a break. The moment she saw it was Mehmet she had hoped that he might help her. She fidgeted on the floor, realisation just hitting her on how humiliating it would be to use a bucket to urinate in with Mehmet watching.

"You could help me. We could get out of here together," she said.

"You don't understand. I'm in big trouble but I swear I didn't know this was going to happen, I would never have done that to Selina," he said as he stepped in front of her with the bucket.

"You haven't hurt anyone Mehmet. Don't let them make you a murderer."

"I didn't know they were going to do what they did. The plan was to steal from the Villa while you were out on the trip. I am even ashamed of that now," he said as he turned away. Mehmet held his hand to his head and began to shake. He grabbed his hair and started to breathe deeply, hitting his head as he thought.

"Mehmet, look at me. While I'm alive I can tell them that you didn't kill anyone. If anything happens to me, they will blame you though. You have to help me to escape."

"What have I done?" he said as he continued to tap his head. Eve watched the sweat beads running down his face as he passed the light coming through the open door.

"It's not too late, we can help each other." Mehmet did not respond. "I have a little boy, his name is Harry. If you don't help me Harry will never know what happened to me." Eve paused; Mehmet scraped his hand through his damp hair. "I want to become a teacher one day, I work in a school but I've always dreamed I'd become a teacher," she said. She closed her eyes for a second hoping that for one moment he could see her as a human being, one who feels pain and love, one who has a life and a son who depends on her, one who is kind, gentle and would be missed by the children she helped everyday in her job. "The children at school love me, they need me too."

"You don't understand," he said as he continued to rub his fingers through his hair.

"I do understand," Eve replied as she looked at Mehmet before allowing a tear to run down her face. "I understand that you are not an animal like the others. It doesn't matter that you wanted to steal our stuff, that doesn't make you an animal. What has happened to me and to my best friend Selina; that is the work of animals. You are not a killer. I see a good person in you," Eve said as tears started to flood down her face. Her nose became blocked up and mucous began to slip down the back of her throat causing her to cough and splutter. "Please just help me, please. You cared for Selina too, I know you did. Do what is right for her."

Mehmet looked away. He leaned down, grabbed the bucket and threw it to the floor. Pacing back and forth, he murmured Turkish words to himself.

"I'm sorry Mehmet. I'm sorry. I know this is hard for you too," Eve cried.

Mehmet turned, snatched the bucket from the corner of the room and paced towards Eve.

"I know you care," she cried as he stepped in front of her and kneeled down. He put his right arm under Eve's arm, lifted her towards him in what felt like an embrace and yanked down her shorts followed by her torn swimsuit. He pulled the damp lycra down and used his hands to fumble for the bucket. Eve sobbed as she heard the plastic scrape the floor. Her head was buried in Mehmet's hot chest, her face suffocating in his damp sweaty tee-shirt. She felt her swimsuit come down and her backside become exposed. He then dropped her onto the bucket before releasing her from his chest and pushing her backwards into a sitting position. The rope around her ankles was now so tense she felt it burning through her ankles but the worst burning was the degradation of her predicament.

"I do care, which is why I help you. I bring you water because I know you need it. I help you toilet because I know it's not right to allow you to sit in shit. I can't do any more," he said as he turned away, pushed the door closed and stood facing it. "Please do what you have to do and quickly because if I am caught here helping, I will probably get hurt too."

She sat there, needing to go but holding on. He was there, next to her, he would hear her go. Accepting this was the way it was going to be she emptied her bladder and began to sob once again.

"Have you finished?" he asked.

"Yes."

Mehmet turned and walked back towards her. He kneeled down, gently lifted her under the arm once again and reached for the bucket.

She felt Mehmet pull up her torn swimsuit, followed by her shorts before he grabbed the bucket. Eve flinched at the muffled bang at the door as she was nestled into Mehmet's tee-shirt. His arm weakened and he dropped her hard onto the stone floor. Sadik stood before them and stared at Mehmet. Eve shuffled back. "Please don't hurt me," she wept. She watched as Mehmet once again began nervously running his fingers through his hair.

Chapter 43

The car juddered over the rocky ground and the sat-nav continued to chatter away. He stared down at the screen; he was only about half a kilometre away from something that looked like a road. The road was pinpointed in red and that road was his aim. The sat-nav paused as it recalculated the route. "Where do I go?" Kevin shouted as he slammed his open hands on the steering wheel. In the rear view mirror he saw movement, The Prick was getting up. He watched the man struggle to his feet before shaking his head. The man felt his nose, his forehead and then his cheek. Through dazed eyes, Kevin stared into the mirror that reflected The Prick's eyes. He began to stagger towards the car. Kevin placed his foot on the accelerator and followed the dusty road. As soon as he straightened his leg, pain seared up his shin and throbbed at the knee then continued to shoot up to his thigh. The headlamps flickered all over the place, with every bump he was faced with more shrubs, trees and stumps; the narrow road was difficult to stick to. Patiently he followed the winding dirt track.

The sat-nav pinged then the voice returned. He checked the mirror again, he was going too slow. The Prick was catching up with him. His stagger was now straighter and his speed had picked up as his level of consciousness improved. As Kevin navigated a cluster of twists and turns he heard the bushes scratch against the side of the car. He slowed down; he had to preserve the car. Without the car, there was no way out and Eve would be gone forever. The road took him to the left, then a sharp right. He smiled as he got the hang of driving on the rough terrain at night. Glancing back in the mirror he spotted The Prick again, he was getting closer. He reached down and pushed the little knob that locked all the doors. If The Prick did catch up, there was no way he would let him in. The sat-nav kept waffling, the air conditioning blasted and the lights on the screen kept flashing. The sexy voice then made a horn sound; all part of this weird sat-nav voice that The Prick had selected. He fumbled for the volume button as he reached a short straight. Music blared out; he'd missed and accidentally turned on the radio. His heart pounded. Why was such an easy task proving to be so tricky? "Maybe it's because I've been friggin shot in the leg," he replied to his own question.

At the end of the straight there was another turn, a sharp right with a steep drop, the car took off down the hill before it levelled off and ended up hitting a clump of spiny bushes. Kevin stared out of the windscreen. Reverse, he had to reverse out. He checked the mirror, no Prick.

Kevin flinched as a pair of bloody hands began clawing at the driver's window. In his one hand The Prick held a sharp rock. With all The Prick had, he drew his arm back and began to slam the rock into the window.

Kevin extended his leg to the clutch to select reverse; the pain forced him to recoil. Crash, glass sprayed all over his hair and body then The Prick's hand reached in and pulled up the knob that unlocked all the doors.

Chapter 44

Mehmet stood and faced Sadik. Both silent, they stared at each other. Eve shuffled, trying hard to edge the top of her swimsuit down to cover the bottom of her breasts. She watched as Sadik reached for something in his pocket; she stopped, held her breath and stared. He pulled out a torch, she exhaled. He flicked the torch switch and lay it down on the bench to her left. Both men stood there in silence. She watched as Mehmet slouched in front of Sadik and began to walk towards the door while muttering in Turkish. Sadik spoke; Mehmet ignored him and continued towards the door. Sadik grabbed the back of the young man's tee-shirt and dragged him back. Eve felt a draft on her face as the young man was hurled towards her. Mehmet slammed arms first into the wall; he turned then stood against it. His hands rose to the air, a mark of defeat.

"Mehmet, please help me," Eve pleaded.

"Him, help you," Sadik laughed. "It looks like he's already been helping you," he said as he walked across to Eve and pointed to the zipper on her shorts.

"I needed the toilet."

"And little Mehmet helped."

Mehmet looked away and began to mutter once again in Turkish.

"I see he was a gentleman then, if you believe that. The little sapik, dirty boy or as you say pervert." Sadik grabbed the lad by his raised arm and flung him once again towards the door. Mehmet held his hands up and backed away towards the door. As he left he glared at Eve and shrugged his shoulders.

'Please help me. Please Mehmet, help me,' she thought, hoping that he could read her desperation and take pity on her. He could help her. He could call the police and end it all. Eve fiddled with the rope. She leaned over to her shoulder to try and wipe away the itchy cold mucous that had stuck to the top of her lip; she had hope, there was always hope. Mehmet wiped the sweat off his brow with his arm, then turned and left the room, leaving the door ajar.

The torchlight shone past Eve's face, highlighting the gap she was looking out of earlier that night. Sadik stood tall above her. What was his story? She had seen him cosy up to Celile, she had seen Celile cosy up to the man in the bushes. She had sensed their tension. The old woman; who was the old woman to him? Her age would say mother, even grandmother if she was young when she had children.

"Who is the old woman, the one in your house?" Eve asked. Her question was met with silence. "You don't want to talk, I get it. You keep me here, you stand and stare at me, but you don't want to talk." Sadik stared at her, hesitant to reply. Now he was alone with her, he had an awkwardness about him, a vulnerability. "Celile. Is she your wife or is she with the other man?" She watched as his head shook, the man turned and kicked the door shut. He took a couple of slow steps towards her before stopping and scratching the stubble on his chin. He began to pace and scratch more. "Well, is she your wife? You seem close." Eve had to push him, find out his weaknesses.

"No," he paused. "Just shut up, shut the hell up," he yelled as he darted towards her and kneeled in front of her. She felt his fast breath on her shoulder. He snorted as he inhaled. Her nerve endings prickled and she felt goose bumps emerge on her bare arms. Her head began to pound as blood pumped through her body.

"She is his then," she continued.

"Shut up," he yelled as he drew his hand back and slapped her hard. Another slap, just another slap. She had become immune to slaps. She knew now that she had touched a nerve. She had found Sadik's weakness and it was Celile.

"You like her, don't you? I can see she likes you too," Eve whispered. "You can both get through this; you can take her away now, go far away and be happy together. Let me go and we can all live."

"I said shut up," he yelled as he grabbed the scarf and began to straighten it out.

"Please don't gag me again, please? I won't say another word, I promise. I'm sorry, please," Eve thought of the mustiness, the dryness and the choking feeling she had got when the scarf was wrapped around her face, and stuffed in her mouth, touching her tongue. Without a word, he placed it across her mouth and around her head twice; then pulled it tight before knotting it. As he wrenched the scarf he caught her ear, she flinched then he slapped her again. She remained still and stared into his eyes. If he wouldn't talk to her, she would look at him. 'Look at me, I'm a person, you are hurting me. You will look at me,' she thought as she stared. He looked away, stood and walked over towards the bench. He then moved the torch until it shone directly into Eve's eyes, blinding her.

"Try staring now Bitch," he muttered. She looked away. In front of her eyes she followed the green and black blotches that the light beam had scored onto her pupils. She heard Sadik shuffle back towards her and slump down to the ground. His sticky warmth radiated onto her skin, his sweaty smell travelled up her nostrils. 'Breathe in and breathe out,' she repeated in her head, 'breathe in and out.' Through the nose only, no musty smell and no heaving. In through the nose, out through the nose. Her heart pounded as she felt his finger touch her scar. He prodded it, what was he doing? His hand moved up until it reached the bottom of her breast. He grabbed her swimsuit and ripped it a little more. She felt his cold, hard stare on her breasts. 'Please Mehmet, please call the police,' she thought. Even Kevin couldn't find her now. No one would find her. She didn't even know where she was, how long it had taken for them to get here or in which direction they had travelled. She felt his touch again and flinched.

"You have to get used to this, this is all you are now," he whispered. He was so close, she felt his warm breath in her ear and her heart cried, her mind cried as she prepared herself for whatever might happen next.

Chapter 45

The Prick grabbed Kevin's arm and tried to drag him out of the car and on to the ground. Kevin turned and spotted the gun on the passenger seat, he looked at The Prick; The Prick stared back. Both men had the gun in sight. The Prick pulled Kevin back trying to distance him from the gun. Kevin tugged back and reached out towards the gun. The tips of his fingers felt the barrel. So close, he needed another inch; he tried to pull but he was competing with the full weight of The Prick. With his right hand Kevin lashed out and caught The Prick in the eye, a brief moment gave him a lifesaving opportunity. He reached back over and grabbed the gun. With one swift movement he swung the gun over his head and struck The Prick on the side of his face. The man's grip loosened as he stumbled back.

The only sound Kevin could hear was The Prick murmuring and hissing to himself. The man, their captor was now sitting on the floor, legs bent up in front of his body, holding his bleeding head in his hands. Kevin turned the key in the ignition and all the noises of the car bounced back to life. The air conditioning blasted in his face, the radio was on full volume and the sat-nav was once again talking to him. He placed the gun on his lap as he leaned across to close the door. He had to get away, follow the sat-nav. With his other hand he reached for the radio button, the music stopped. Kevin licked his dry cracked lips as he pulled the door towards him.

The door was flung open, a sharp pain seared across his knuckles before he was met with a stare from The Prick. He had the rock and brought it down slamming it onto Kevin's knuckles again. The sweaty man let out a huge roar before latching on to Kevin's arm and tugging with all his weight behind him. Kevin's upper body slid out of the car leaving his shot leg still in the foot well of the drivers side. He extended his leg and the accelerator revved hard as a result. He drew his foot back, petrol; he had to conserve the fuel. As he was pulled again, his glasses fell off his head and landed beside him. His tired eyes struggled in the dark, he squinted to focus. The gun, where was the gun? He saw the shiny metal piece glinting before him; it had dropped beside him as he'd fallen. The Prick spotted the gun and grinned, they both propelled their hands towards the weapon. Kevin felt the metal directly below his grasp. The Prick's hand was soon entwined in his as they fought for the gun. Kevin's finger bent back and made a crack noise but he refused to give up his position. The gun was his; The Prick would not get the gun. Kevin shuffled again as he tried to free his leg from the car. It loosened and he was propelled into The Prick. With his new found freedom from the car trap, Kevin dragged his weary body across the dusty ground and smashed his fist into The Prick's already bloodied face. He grabbed the gun and swung it out in front of him, hitting The Prick once more in the side of the head.

"Stay where you are," Kevin said.

"You won't shoot me, you could've killed me before but you never did. You are gutless." The Prick laughed as he spat a mouthful of blood to his side. "Boo," he said as he began to laugh louder.

Kevin trembled as The Prick lay there mocking him and laughing. Could he shoot him? He had never shot anyone before. The only time he'd made violent physical contact with another human being was when he was seven. It was when Ryan had stolen his bike and wouldn't give it back. Ryan with all his bravado had walked up to him and said, "Make me." The only time he had hurt anyone was that day. 'Make me, make me,' those words had echoed in his mind. He shook from his knees to his hands and his face began to burn up. Ryan had laughed at him as he reached forward and started to let down a tyre on his bike. Kevin then stepped forward, grabbed Ryan's arm and yanked him away from his bike. Ryan pushed back and they were soon rolling on the floor. Ryan was much stronger and had pounded him in the side at least twice but he had saved his bike. Where his next move came from, he didn't know. He drew back and threw one blow at Ryan's nose. Blood flowed down his face and dripped onto Kevin as he lay trapped underneath him. Blood, he had caused Ryan to bleed. All the aggression between the two boys was immediately extinguished. Kevin remembered how he'd trembled even more as the blood dripped from Ryan onto his own neck and he remembered how his little bully friend had began to sob. His tears mixed with his blood and mucous, Ryan then crawled off Kevin and ran towards his home. The one and only time he had struck another human being, a moment that he'd regretted for life. Ryan had been a bully, he had deserved something, but a broken nose was extreme. Something good came from that moment though; Ryan had never bullied him again so maybe regretful was the wrong feeling. Regardless, he still felt regret. What followed was a new formed respect, a deep friendship that had lasted forever, a friendship not without its moments that had brought them here together.

 He looked at The Prick as he mockingly laughed without even attempting to move or look scared. Kevin felt around before grabbing his glasses and placing them back on. He hoisted himself up by the car door, got into a standing position and stood above The Prick.

"Shoot me then. Are you a coward? If you had my woman and had tried to kill me, I would put a bullet in your brain."

Kevin removed the safety catch and cocked the gun, could he do it? He had only seen guns fired in movies; he hadn't even used an air soft gun or been paint balling. His hand trembled.

"Look at you. If you shoot, who even knows where you would shoot me. If I held that gun to my head and said press, you would still miss," The Prick said as he howled with laughter. He was right; he was reading Kevin's body language well. Kevin shuffled and wiped his brow.

"Just shut the fuck up," Kevin yelled. The Prick was not Ryan; The Prick was an evil killer. He was someone who would wipe away his own mother for a few quid, someone who showed no empathy at all for any of his victims, and someone who would continue to do this if he wasn't eliminated or brought to justice. His shaking became more extreme. With the humidity and fear came the sweat, a sticky wetness covered his whole face, his arm pits itched and he needed to rub his eyes.

"Tick, tock, how long has she got," The Prick whispered. "You may as well kill me you know. I have failed in my mission. If you don't kill me, they will," he laughed.

Beep, beep. Kevin looked down then across for the beeping noise. As he looked down he lowered the gun, The Prick reached for the ankle of his shot leg and dragged Kevin to the floor. Kevin held the gun tightly as he tumbled.

"That is The Boss texting; he is coming for his girls soon and she is good. They will take real good care of your soft haired little girl. He is coming for her," he yelled as he dragged himself on top of Kevin.

"Not if I get there first," Kevin yelled as he brought the gun close to his body and fired. The Prick's body went limp and the entirety of his weight crushed Kevin's chest. He coughed and spluttered, pushed and pulled, The Prick was heavy. Loud ringing vibrated through Kevin's ears and throughout his body, deafened by the shot all he could do was look around. He turned his head to the left to avoid breathing in the sulphur smoke. As he coughed and spluttered he began to turn his head back. He stared at the gaping shoulder wound; he had shot The Prick in the shoulder. Blood pumped from the wound then gushed all over Kevin's shoulder and soaked into his clothing. He watched as The Prick's eyes rolled back before his head finally dropped onto his chest. Kevin pushed hard, first at The Prick's head, then at his middle. With every movement his leg burned up and his broken finger sent shooting pains through his wrist and up his arm. After achieving a rocking motion, he rolled The Prick off himself and heard him drop to the ground. His blood continued to trickle into a little well full of pine needles. Kevin watched as the little well began to fill and the pine needles floated on the top of the blood. Kevin's eyes began to well up, he had to do it. He had no choice. He looked on as the man convulsed before lying still.

    He had taken a life; he had done something he never knew he could ever do. Not expected, planned, even imagined but he had done it. His shaking hands dropped the gun. He dragged himself up again, bent down and picked up the gun. However much he hated the gun, he might still need it. He looked into the chamber, one bullet left. The ringing in his ears reached a constant high pitched screech; he looked down at The Prick once again making sure that he hadn't miraculously stood up.

    The Prick began to convulse again, foamy spittle formed at the side of his mouth, Kevin's stomach rolled as he felt his stomach jerk hard. He stepped to the side and vomited onto the ground. He had taken a life; he had taken away someone's life. It might be easy to people like The Prick but it wasn't easy to him. Enemy or not, taking a life was not something he would ever forget. He couldn't ever forget The Prick's eyes rolling, the blood pumping, the convulsing; the entire evening. Everything that had happened would stay with him for life and would be the source of all his nightmares and fears.

He thought of Eve and where she might be. "He is coming for his girls," Kevin whispered. 'Someone is coming to get Eve and take her away,' he thought. He might never see her again if he didn't get there on time. He had to get to Eve, he had to save her. He kneeled down to The Prick's level and rooted through the still man's pockets until he reached the phone. He pressed the on button, the phone lit up, no signal and the battery light was flashing. He flung the phone onto the passenger seat, flung the gun next to it and got into the car. He lifted the phone; the police, he could call the police and then he thought of Eve. If they were coming for her, the police may not get there on time, he couldn't risk it, he had to go now, right this second and not get caught up in police questioning. He had little time; The Prick had enjoyed telling him that.

He reversed the car and concentrated as he drove along the dirt track. He could not afford another crash; one more minor accident could take the car off the road. He pushed his glasses farther up his nose and watched as the sat-nav fixed on its route. He had to get to the start point, keep driving; get off the dirt track and onto a main road.

Ahead, all he could see was trees, trees and more trees. When there weren't trees, there were bushes and rocks. He checked his rear mirror and saw The Prick's body get smaller and smaller as he gained distance. He checked the sat-nav, he had successfully pinned the point he was at. He would come back for Rachel once he had found Eve. At least she was safe for the time being with The Prick out of action.

He stared vacantly out of the windscreen, in his mind all he could see was The Prick's body, he could still feel the pressure sores he had gained from his weight bearing down on him. The ringing in his ears still buzzed away. He had killed someone, he had taken a life. Nothing anyone could say would ever take that away from him. His hands shook as he turned the steering wheel into a right bend which led to the main road to Muğla that they had travelled down earlier that day. He hadn't realised they were so close to that road, had he known he would've told Eve to run up, not down. Down to nowhere. The sat-nav flashed, he was on the road and heading towards the mystery destination.

Chapter 46

Looking out into the darkness through the crack in the wall, Eve wept as she felt Sadik's hands stroke the bottom of her breast.

"I don't want to hurt you. See, I'm just touching you. It is easier this way. When they come for you, it won't be like this anymore," he said as he cupped her left breast. Goosebumps prickled across her chest and arms, she flinched as he grabbed her harder. He grabbed her chin and drew her face towards his. Leaning in closer, he smelled her face and his stubble rubbed her chin. His other hand reached in between the rope and looped around her neck, she flinched as he grabbed her breast harder. She inhaled through the gag and breathed in a load of dust. She trembled with panic before telling herself to breathe in through her nose and out through her nose. In, out. She inhaled and caught a waft of his stale odour which was made more pungent by the fresh sweat that dripped down his forehead and over his brow. "See, I'm not hurting you," he said with a gentle snigger. He drew his face back, Eve closed her eyes.

He may be able to force her to face his direction but she wouldn't let him read her thoughts. They were for her. The captors had her freedom, her life but they could never take away her thoughts; they were hers, all hers. All she wanted to think about was Harry. There was no doubt he would still have a happy life with his father. What would he grow up to be? That she may never know. She would spend her days thinking about getting away, going home and only hoped that one day if she ever got to go home Harry would still want his Mummy Eve. How long before her mother and father's disappointment would filter through to Harry, if he for one minute thought that she had gone off to start a new life and had abandoned him, he may never forgive her. A gentle warm breeze burst through the hole in the wood and tickled Eve's ear. Sadik broke away from her before shuffling around for a moment. Still with closed eyes, she heard his zipper come down before he moved in towards her again.

Crunch, crunch, footsteps on gravel. With closed eyes, her hearing was sensitive. The door burst open; Eve opened her eyes and gasped. Her heart raced and blood pulsated through her head. Sadik grabbed his zipper and tried to pull it up; it got stuck on what looked like his pants. He tugged and tugged away trying to ease the zipper but it would not budge. Celile stood before them, shaking and hyperventilating as she turned to Sadik. She slapped him hard as he kneeled in front of her before the two began arguing.

"What the fuck did you do that for?" Celile replied, then she began to rant at Sadik in Turkish. Disjointed ranting interrupted by pacing, her arms went up in the air as she raised her voice.

"You little slut," she said as she turned towards Eve. "You are nothing but trouble lady." Celile grabbed the swimsuit material that Sadik had lifted up to expose her breasts and tugged it back down. She bowed her head forward and concentrated on the shadows that were cast by the torch. The shadows of Celile pacing, Sadik standing as he tried to hold down her flailing arms. She watched as a spider scurried towards her in an attempt to flee the commotion, a spindly legged creature only after sanctuary. Eve shuffled to divert it away from her legs; the small creature changed its course and scurried off to her right. Celile yelled and tears filled her eyes as she pulled out a knife. She thrust the dagger in Sadik's direction. The man placed his arms down by his sides. She kept yelling and holding the knife up to his face. Eve trembled as she saw the blade come up and Sadik hold his hand out in defence. Celile grabbed his hand and forced the knife into his palm as she turned to Eve and nodded. With both hands free from the knife, Eve watched how the woman ran her fingers through her damp hair, her stare alternating between her and Sadik.

The knife fell to the ground onto its tip. Sadik had let it go. A moment ago Eve was sure that he would've assaulted her; she didn't know how far he would've gone or what indignity he would have burned into her mind forever but she knew in her heart he wouldn't kill her. She was not looking at a killer. Celile on the other hand had a tension, a hunger, a repressed emotiveness about her; one that was ready to burst. She was the impulsive one, possibly even the regretful one when the time came for regrets. Eve had them weighed up, it wasn't helping her cause to escape but she knew who she feared the most.

Celile bent over and wrapped the knife handle with her trembling hand. Sadik shouted and made a feeble attempt to hold her back. Eve's heart rate quickened as she tried to release a finger from her binds, just a finger. A finger would lead to some room to release another finger, then a hand. The woman's stare fixed on her as she brushed Sadik aside.

Eve closed her eyes and tried to feel the rope, feeling its direction, its twists and turns. The rope had chaffed her skin; she felt the blood drip down her arm. She heard the woman yell in a loud voice as she lunged at her, then she heard footsteps and another voice; Mehmet. It was her time now. She sobbed as she thought of her end. She had never contemplated death before since this trip but it would take a miracle to save her now. How long would it hurt for? Would the world go black or would there be a light tunnel like she had often read about? What was it like to not be able to take another breath, to fight for it, to want it but to have no choice in the matter?

A heavy weight slammed into her chest and a yell filled the room. With a hard shove Eve's arms wrenched above her and sent a muscular pain searing through her shoulders. She opened her eyes only to be met with Mehmet's black hair, a warm trickle dripped down her leg. Celile burst into tears and stepped back.

Eve had hoped that Mehmet would help and he had. He had jumped between her and the knife.

Sadik grabbed Mehmet by the arm and helped him up; the knife that Celile had plunged fell from his shoulder to the floor and rested by Eve's foot. Sadik looked at Eve, bent down and lifted the knife off the floor. Mehmet yelped and left a speckled blood trail on the floor as Sadik helped him hobble over to the bench. Eve stared into the shadows as Sadik laid the knife on the bench, grabbed an old rag from a tin on the bench top and pressed it into Mehmet's wound. The young man yelped again but took the rag and continued pressing it hard. Sadik once again grabbed Mehmet's arm and guided him out of the shed and closed the door behind him. He paced over towards the bench and faced the wall as he grabbed his hair.

*****

Celile fell to the floor, tears trickled down her cheeks and her sobs filled the room. Her compulsions had once again overtaken her. Seeing her man in a vile stupor over their hostage had broken her. He would lie, he would say he was helping her and her reply would be; what with your pants unzipped. Like Selina, he was only helping, now Eve. That scar damaged woman had nothing on her, she was ordinary, mousy, plain, pale and blotchy but she had so much more. She was loved.

Guz hadn't treated her right, Sadik was now abusing her trust and she had stabbed Mehmet, Guz's only son; she had hurt Guz's son and Sadik's nephew. Although Sadik never cared much for his nephew, she still felt that this may be her end too. When they got the money, would they dump her? She was sure Guz knew about their affair based on the little stint with the shoes that he'd pulled at the Villa. She couldn't forget how he made her feel, he wanted to tarnish her. He knew that Sadik would sense what had happened and he knew Sadik would not do a thing as he was betraying his brother also.

She gasped between sobs, her mind proposing a million solutions in a few seconds. All the solutions were becoming muddled. The only way out was to leave, they had to go now. Sadik could go with her but if not she was going alone. She would go back to Bursa, back to working farms; she had a bit of money stashed in her flat, enough to get her out of this mess. One thing she was sure of now though was that they could never be caught for what they had done. She hadn't wanted any of this, Guz organised it, Guz planned it, Guz negotiated the deals, Guz called all the shots but she was calling this one. She wiped her eyes and nose with her hand and stood. Sadik turned and took a couple of steps towards her; she could tell by the way that he looked at her that he didn't really know her. He was angry with her impulsiveness but he still wanted her enough not to slap her. She reached out her hand to his face; he slapped it down and looked away.

"Why the hell did you do that," he said with his shaking hands held up in front of her.

"I saw you; I didn't mean to hurt Mehmet. Why Sadik? Why do you betray me?" She wept as Sadik looked at her. She knew that she was nothing to him anymore. "We need to kill her and get out of here. We are all going to die, I know it."

"There will be no more killing; she is going off to wherever to be sold to whoever and we are getting money," Sadik said.

"Do you think that when The Boss hears what a fuck up this has been that any of us are going anywhere? Really?"

Sadik looked at her in silence. He looked away in thought and glanced at Eve. Celile looked across at Eve, the broken woman shaking in the corner, blood down her arms and Mehmet's blood drying up on her legs.

"I don't know what to believe anymore," he said.

Celile walked over to the bench and picked up the knife. From her back pocket she pulled out the little photo of Harry before walking over to Eve. She kneeled and held the picture out in front of Eve before placing it on the floor between them both. "At least your son is okay, that's something to be happy about," she said. She watched as Eve tried to talk behind the scarf, the woman's eyes lit up at the sight of the photo, her movements became agitated.

"What are you doing Celile?" Sadik asked.

"I'm ending this and we are going or at least I am going. You can chose to come with me or you can stay here and be slaughtered. It's over Sadik. It's all over. You can stay and watch or you can go back to the house." Celile watched as Sadik began to tremble. He walked up to her and placed his hand over the tip of the knife.

"You kill her I will kill you. Watch her and do nothing else for now. Can I trust you?"

"Can I trust you?" Celile replied as she edged the knife into Sadik's hand forcing him to let go.

He flinched and rubbed his palm. "You can always trust me. What you saw wasn't what you think. Do you not believe that I want to go away with you from all this and start a new life? I want that more than anything but we have to do this right. Think about my mother out there, she needs me, she needs you. If we run off, both she and Guz are dead. I can't let them die. So, can you trust me?"

"I might be able to trust you," she said as she turned away and stared at Eve, "or I might not."

"Please, just leave her be, just a few more minutes and we should hear something. Guz should be here soon, we can get this thing wrapped up. We have two women, a load of documents and belongings. Things are going to be fine," he said as he cupped her chin and kissed her.

Celile allowed him to kiss her but didn't respond. He would have to work hard to regain her total loyalty. "Yes, things will be fine. I will just keep this bitch entertained," she replied as she then kissed Sadik passionately and hard whilst maintaining eye contact with Eve. This was part of the game, she was good enough for her man and that wreck of a woman was nothing, nothing that wouldn't go away very soon, one way or another.

Chapter 47

Kevin steered the car in every direction that the sat-nav indicated he should go. After passing a sign for Goçova and taking a right turn the car trundled down a thinning path. The vehicle chugged and spluttered as a flashing light drew his eyes to the dash. Out of fuel; he would have to stagger the rest of the way on foot. He rolled up against the roadside and allowed the car to merge with the bushes before killing the ignition. He grabbed The Prick's bag from the back seat and filled it with the passports and the gun. As he unplugged and lifted the sat-nav, he opened the car door and grabbed his shot leg with his free hand. He released his leg from the foot well and gave it a stretch. He flinched as he elongated the limb and his finger throbbed from the break; his whole body bled and ached. He stood then opened the back door and pulled out the shovel; his make shift crutch.

     He leaned on the shovel with each step and made his way along the dusty rock lined road. The light from the sat-nav was all he had to see with. After several minutes he had reached the end of the red line, he turned off the sat-nav and placed it in his bag. Under the moonlight he stood before a long drive, at the end of the drive rested a sugar cube house surrounded by what he could only guess to be were fruit trees. On the balcony upstairs a large satellite dish rested beside a string of washing. All the windows were in darkness except for the bottom left window. There was no direct light emerging from the house, only a glimmer of a lamp or maybe a light from another room.

'One step after another,' he kept repeating in his head. Every time he moved the shovel along, he did it with complete care in order to remain quiet. With every step the hessian bag he carried slapped the side of his good leg, he was thankful that it wasn't a plastic carrier bag. One scrape of a shovel or a rustle of a bag and they could all come out and take him down. His heart beat faster. What if the address programmed in the sat-nav had been nothing more than a red herring? He could look around only to find some insomniac sat at the table thinking he was under attack when he caught sight of a bleeding man at his window; or there could be a mother nursing a baby that she had struggled to put down to sleep. As he approached the window, he leaned the shovel against the wall, careful not to make a noise. He then leaned in closer for a better look. As he watched he took the gun from the bag and placed the bag down by his feet. All he needed was the gun for now; he held it down by his side.

There was a main light on in the front room. He glared across the dark room behind the window. An old woman passed him and hobbled towards the lit up room, Kevin moved to the side where he was almost completely hidden by the window frame. He felt the flaky paint crumble off and stick to his sweaty hair line. He felt his heart rate go up as the old woman turned back and reached for a book that lay on the sideboard before walking back into the room. She turned on a table lamp which then flooded the whole garden with a strip of light. He could now see that the trees were lemon trees, the garden was wild with shrubs and dried out grass everywhere. The woman sat in an orthopaedic style chair before removing two hearing aids and placing them on the coffee table. She placed the book in her lap, put her feet on a foot rest and lay her head back in the chair before closing her eyes and rubbing her temples.

Behind the woman, Kevin spotted a long shadow on the wall, the shadow moved backwards and then forwards but never to the side so that Kevin could see who it was. The light glinted off the stainless steel corner of the sink. He had to move around the side of the house to get a better look. This had to be where Eve was being held otherwise he would lose her forever. 'They are coming for her,' those words repeated themselves over and over again in his head. He left the shovel against the wall and hobbled around the building until he reached the side wall. There was a small rectangular side window ahead. He had to get to the window, get a good look into the kitchen. Now, his worst fear was that he wouldn't recognise anyone there and that the people in the house were just normal people going about their normal business leaving him with no clues as to where to go next.

Reaching the window, he leaned against the wall beside it, bent down and tightened the material around his leg that had started to loosen. He clenched his teeth as he pulled the material tighter, it put added stress on his broken finger and his gunshot wound at the same time. The bleeding seemed to have been contained which had to be a good sign, but the pain still throbbed with an angry burning that he felt deep within him. He caught a glint of something coiled on the floor, a little coiled brown shell. He picked it up and placed it in his pocket. He had promised Eve he would help her find some shells for Harry. He paused and wiped his brow, he was going to find Eve and he was finally going to meet little Harry. Turning his head, he peered through the window and recognised the back of Sadik's head. Kevin swallowed hard, a sickening tremble travelled through his chest and rested in his stomach. He had found them; Eve had to be around somewhere. He held up the gun and watched. Where was she? Where had they taken her?

Sadik moved to his left revealing a bleeding Mehmet sat on a chair. A first aid kit lay open on the dirty worktop amongst several pots full of plant shoots. The kitchen was sparse containing only a sink, a few damaged cupboards, a table and chairs and a door that probably led to a pantry. Sadik stuck a large plaster over the wound on the top of the young man's arm and slapped him as he passed him a bloody tee-shirt. Mehmet shrieked as he lifted his arms and pulled the garment over his head. Sadik turned; Kevin jerked back and lay his head against the concrete wall. He heard a chair shuffle against the stone floor. Blood pumped through his body, as he swallowed the dryness caused him to make a click noise. He had to have a look; had they seen him?

With the gun held out in front of his chest he leaned forward and peeped into the window. He watched as Sadik walked out of the kitchen and into the room where the old woman was sitting. Mehmet had his back to Kevin and was packing away the first aid box and putting it away in the cupboard. On the table lay a gun and a knife, the very weapons they would use on him if he didn't get hold of them. He rubbed the sweat off his head with his arm and took a deep breath. Mehmet turned; Kevin drew back out of view. He heard a door open, then slam. A few feet away from him, he heard footsteps grinding stones on the path as they travelled. The noise became quieter as the feet got further away. Mehmet was taking a walk in the garden. Kevin struggled on, crouching as he turned the corner. He looked through the kitchen window, in the distance he could see the old woman's head resting on the back of the chair, Sadik was nowhere to be seen.

He tried the door handle, it opened. One quiet, painful step at a time he reached the table. He picked up the knife and then put it in his pocket, blade upwards. He grabbed the gun and held it in his other hand. He looked out of the main window of the kitchen and saw an outhouse at the back of the garden, a faint light seeped out underneath the door. Eve, she had to be in the outhouse. His heart raced, he could've cried, he had to get to the outhouse. That must've been where Mehmet had gone. As for his shoulder wound, he had hoped that it was Eve who had done that to him.

The toilet flushed and footsteps bounded down the stairs. Kevin opened the pantry door and slipped in. With barely any room, he held onto the gun and tried to breathe in to avoid knocking any tins off the shelving that stood all around him. Through the gap in the door he saw Sadik stand and look out of the window as he lit a cigarette. Kevin shifted his body and the pantry door moved a fraction. Sadik's head twitched as he focused on the window, the room's reflection filled the window. Kevin's pulse rate sped up and his hands trembled. Sadik turned his body and walked towards the pantry door.

Chapter 48

Kevin watched as Sadik turned to swipe the gun off the table, the gun Kevin was holding in his hand. He watched as the man began muttering to himself and pacing back and forth, glancing in all directions as he moved. Sadik once again looked directly at the door. Kevin withdrew back into the cupboard, surrounding him were jars of what looked like pickled chillies and fruit.

"So, did my stupid Nephew feel sorry for you Eve and untie you?"

They did have her. Sadik had just confirmed that Eve was being held by them, here. His shoulders dropped as a tear rolled down his cheek. She was here, alive and now he was going to free her and take her home away from this nightmare. He released the gun chamber of the gun he had secured in the wilderness and dropped out the single bullet before placing the gun amongst the jars of chillies. He then grabbed the new gun firmly and held it tightly with both hands. There was no way they were getting hold of a gun and trapping him again. He was free and he intended to remain just that.

"Come out and give me the gun Eve. You don't want to have an accident," Sadik said as he crept close to the pantry door. "I saw you move the door in the window Eve," he said as he sniggered.

Kevin kicked the door hard into the man's face and stepped out of the cupboard as he held the gun stretched out in front of his chest. Sadik fell to the floor and grabbed hold of his arm.

"How? When?" Sadik said as he glared up at Kevin.

"Where is she?" Kevin began to shake as he held the gun. He hobbled closer to Sadik. Sadik didn't reply. "I said where is she?"

"Oh, she?" He sniggered. "You know you can't win the game. There will be several bad asses turning up any time now to take her. If they come for nothing, we all die and that means you too. Oh you think you know how it all works, but you don't know these people," he said as his snigger turned into a vacant stare.

"I don't care about you or 'these' people. I only care what happens to Eve. The prick you left to clean me up went down easy enough with a bullet through his chest," Kevin trembled as a stream of sweat travelled down the side of his face. He might have to shoot this man, he knew he might and it was becoming apparent that they would fight to the end. He knew Mehmet was wounded but the woman, Celile. He hadn't seen her. He watched as the man digested what he had just said.

"You killed Guz, my brother?"

"If you mean, did I kill that murderous prick, then yes. I put a bullet through him, the same as what I am going to do to you." Kevin extended his arm and stared down the barrel.

"I surrender, please don't shoot me," Sadik shouted as he held his hands above his head. He shuffled on his bottom towards the cupboard.

"Stay where you are," Kevin yelled as he released the catch on the gun and pointed it at Sadik's head.

"No," Sadik shouted as he cradled his head and flinched. Kevin gripped the gun and stared down the barrel. He had a clear shot. "No," the man cried. Tears began to fall down his face as he curled up on the floor into a ball and broke down. "You killed my brother."

Kevin trembled as he lowered the gun; he couldn't shoot. He had to find a way to bind him so that he could investigate further. He shuffled backwards keeping his eye on Sadik the whole time. The old woman lay on her chair with her head back on the rest, mouth open, snoring. He felt a thud to his shot leg; Sadik had shuffled forwards and laid his foot hard into Kevin's wounded leg. Kevin fell to the floor screaming. 'Don't let go of the gun,' he thought as they rolled around on the floor. Sadik had managed to climb up on top of Kevin and hold his hands above his head. He fought for the gun, pulling at his fingers. Kevin kicked back and saw the man's face distort in agony.

"You killed my brother, I hate you. I hate you," the man yelled, spit and tears flying everywhere. He brought his elbow down towards Kevin's eye and broke his left glasses lens.

Kevin then yelped as he felt Sadik's knee bed into his wound. 'He would not let go of the gun, he would not let go,' he repeated in his head. If he let go, Eve died then the regret of not shooting Sadik when he first had the chance flashed through his mind. Why was he so gutless? One pull of the trigger and his attacker would have been taken down. If Eve died he would blame himself.

Chapter 49

Mehmet finished his smoke, entered the outhouse and leaned against the other end of the bench. He stared at Celile, she stared back. She watched as Mehmet glanced over at Eve. "Look what you did to me you bitch," he said as he wiped mucous from his nose.

"Oh just shut up you little Daddy's boy. You threw yourself in front of her so it was your fault."

"I hate you, I hate all of this. I hate you all, when this is over you are not going to see me for dust."

"Get lost," Celile yelled as she pushed the young man towards the door, opened it and shoved him out. "Stay there and keep a look out for your Dad. I need to think." Mehmet shrugged, slid down the wall and sat on the floor; legs out in front of him. "Let me know if we are needed, I'll keep an eye on this one." Celile said as she closed the door, turned then looked down at Eve.

"So, Little Miss Special, think you are so good everyone wants you?" Celile said as she traced Eve's cheek with her knife. "I forgot, you can't speak." Celile pulled down the gag.

"Please help me. I just want to get back to my little boy, he is my everything. Look at him," she replied.

Celile looked down at the photo and stared for a moment. Everything she'd ever wanted was in that picture but every man she'd ever met had let her down.

"He's only little, he needs his mother, he needs me," Eve said as she began to weep. "Please. Have you got children?"

"No, and don't think this 'poor me' routine will make me let you go." Celile said. Eve began to cry. "Why do you keep crying? It won't change anything." Celile stood and walked over to the bench. She leaned over the back of the bench and pulled Eve's rucksack up to the surface, then she unzipped it. "Water, my we did come prepared, I bet you'd love some of this," she laughed as she unscrewed the bottle and took a swig.

There was no way she was going to allow Eve to see her pain. Yes she wanted what she had so much to the point she could easily drive the knife through her flesh and end her life. She had watched Eve earlier that evening, her man had stayed by her side all night, devoted, in love. She'd never felt a love like that; she shivered as she zipped up the bag and rummaged through one of the side pockets. Anyway, her man would now be eliminated so ending it for Eve was probably the kindest thing to do.

"You know you have a message?" Celile said as she held up Eve's phone. "I suppose you'll never get to see it though." Eve's phone beeped. "Low battery, what a shame," the woman grinned, she threw the phone back in the rucksack.

Despite her conversation with Sadik she would not let this wait; she would take control like she had in the mountains. She would not let him bring her down even if it meant going alone, no Guz, no Sadik, just her, away from all this. She would go back to where she came from and start again, maybe then she would get the life she truly deserved. She gripped the knife and closed her eyes as she visualised what she was going to do.

*****

As Celile turned away Eve began to wriggle again, all her persistence was paying off. She felt her blood trickle down as she kept rubbing away, tiny strand by tiny strand, she had found a weakness, almost one finger was out. One finger, then two fingers, then a whole hand. Get a hand free and at least she would be able to defend herself from the knife blade. If one hand was free then the other should slip out. She rubbed again, the coarse rope splintered and dug into her sore, she yelped. A wave of nausea crept through her, the room momentarily swayed. She needed a drink, her dry throat was hurting.

"In pain there?" Celile said as she turned and laughed. "Let me help." Celile stepped over to Eve and kneeled down with the knife held out in front of her. "He liked you, I saw what was happening. He wanted you, despite what an ugly mess you are, that sickens me more."

"Please, he doesn't like me. He's just an animal. You don't have to be like him. He assaulted me, I didn't want it," Eve said, her voice crackling with every word. She had to get the deluded woman to see the truth. The man she worshipped did not feel the same about her.

"Just shut up," Celile yelled as she held her head, knife up by her ears. "Shut up. He does love me. The problem is that they both love me," Celile dropped to her knees and slid towards Eve so that their faces were almost touching. "Isn't that a good thing?" She grinned as she traced the knife down Eve's chin, neck and chest.

Eve felt the cold metal tickle her as it travelled down to her stomach. She held her breath and waited for the plunge. She was tired, weak and all she wanted was to go to sleep and for this nightmare to end. She smiled as she thought of her little boy. "I didn't desert you Harry," she babbled.

"I know Mummy. I know," he replied in her dream. She smiled; he knew she hadn't left him. That was enough for her, now she could go in peace.

The door burst open, Mehmet stood in the doorway. Eve could hear what she thought was Sadik yelling in the distance. Mehmet began shouting fast in Turkish; Celile looked up at him, stood and ran towards the door.

"I'll be back for you in a minute," she said as she pointed the knife at Eve before closing the door. As soon as she heard them running off down the path she began to grapple with the twine in the rope.

Chapter 50

Kevin held the gun above him, Sadik grappled with his hand. "Ahh," he yelled as he felt the tip of the knife pierce his side. The knife from the table, he tried to force his other hand between him and Sadik, he edged it forward until he felt the tip of the knife. He followed its shaft, grabbed it and slid it up between them. Kevin's head turned as Sadik punched him in the face. He gripped the gun hard but was blocked from raising it by Sadik's hand. He wrenched the knife up between them. As Sadik reached back to throw another punch, Kevin pulled the knife in front of Sadik's stomach. "Get off me," Kevin yelled.

The man's eyes widened as he felt the tip of the knife pierce his tee-shirt and tease his flesh. He jerked to the side but Kevin felt his hand clasped over the gun. There was now a gap between Sadik and the knife tip.

"I said get off me," Kevin yelled, the veins on Sadik's forehead became more prominent. The man stared back, sweat dripped off the end of his nose and landed onto the side of Kevin's neck. Both men panted, exhausted. Sadik lifted his hand off the gun leaving it clasped between Kevin's fingers before raising his hands in the air. Should he be trusted? Was he surrendering? Kevin had the gun, Kevin had the knife pointed towards Sadik's chest, yet Sadik still straddled Kevin.

    A gust of warm air filled the room as Celile barged through the door. Kevin turned to see her wild eyes as she fell to the floor brandishing a knife of her own in her hands. He watched and trembled as she brought the knife above her head and thrust it down towards Kevin's chest as she yelled words he couldn't understand. He could've brought the gun up and shot her; he could've taken the knife off Sadik's chest and tried to attack her back. He chose to drag Sadik's body directly in front of his as the knife plunged. He heard the man yell as the knife pierced his back. The full force of Sadik's weight dropped onto Kevin, blood began to trickle from the side of the man's mouth as he gasped for air. He could only imagine that Celile had reached his lung. A crackling breathy noise came out of Sadik's mouth, the man's eyes were panicked but he was helpless. For a moment Kevin was taken back to the day he was fighting with Stephen. There was a difference though. Stephen stood up and ran to his mother. Sadik could not stand up and the poor woman who may be his mother had probably slept through the whole thing. He imagined what Stephen's mother would've thought, how she would've panicked when she saw her little boy running towards the kitchen door covered in blood. He then imagined what the old lady would think once she'd awoken, seeing death, blood and crime all around her. The death and injury of people that she knew. Was she innocent? Had she been aware of their operation? Operation, there was more to this he remembered. They were coming, whoever 'they' were and he didn't want to stick around to find out. Eve? He rolled Sadik off his chest and watched as Mehmet entered and Celile sat in a ball on the floor sobbing, broken. She rocked back and forth as she stared at Sadik, not once averting her gaze.

    Mehmet yelled as he kneeled down to Celile and shook her. Kevin dragged his weary body towards a chair. Mehmet looked across at Kevin; Kevin brought the gun smoothly in front of him and pointed it at Celile and Mehmet. "Just you stay there or I promise, I will put a bullet through you both." Mehmet stood and yelled as he ran towards Kevin, without hesitation Kevin fired at Mehmet's knee cap. The young man fell and yelped as he landed in a heap. Celile remained rocking back and forth ignoring the yelping that was being expelled from Mehmet's mouth.

"I didn't want any of this," Mehmet yelled. "She is in the outhouse at the end of our land out the back. Please leave my grandmother, please. She knows nothing of this."

Kevin brought the gun down by his side. With ringing ears from the blast he had just about made out that Eve was in an outhouse. He dragged his weary body closer to the chair before pulling himself to a standing position. Celile had stopped rocking and turned her head towards Kevin. He pointed the gun at her; she screamed and continued to rock. Then she began to lash out at the cupboards, at the floor then finally at Mehmet. He grabbed her and flinched as his knee bled. The woman flapped, Kevin held the gun up towards her.

"No, please. There has been enough hurt," the young man yelled. I will deal with her. Get the woman and go." As per his word, Mehmet grabbed Celile's arms and held them down before nodding at Kevin to leave.

He hobbled across the kitchen, out of the door, then around the building where he grabbed the bag containing the sat-nav and The Prick's phone. He grabbed the shovel, his crutch and began the journey over the lumpy, weed laden garden in the dark. The only light came from the kitchen that he had left behind.

In the distance he heard the humming of an engine, 'they' were coming and they weren't too far away. He hobbled faster, needing to get to Eve.

Eventually he met a wall of darkness, his eyes adjusted to reveal a wooden outbuilding. His heart thumped and the crack in his glasses distorted his vision. He pointed the gun in front of him as he reached the door. "Eve," he yelled.

He kicked open the door to reveal a torch pointing towards the ground. On the ground lay a heap of bloodied ropes attached to a metal ring and a clasp was attached to the side of the building's frame. Aside the ropes lay a small picture of Harry and a scarf. "No," he cried. Tears filled his eyes as he dropped to the ground. It had all been for nothing. They had moved her, where he might never know. He held his head in his hands and wept as he cried harder and louder. His love, his Eve, his new life, all gone. He struggled to inhale and his heart boomed. His arm flopped in front of him and the gun's weight pulled him forward, hand first. All his efforts had been in vain. All his efforts for a dream, a life, for love, all his hope – gone.

"Kevin," said the croaky whisper that came from behind him. He turned to see Eve's bloodied and bruised face. "I thought I heard you so I ran back." He looked up at his love, her wrists bleeding, her clothing torn, her rucksack open. She pulled out half a bottle of water and held it to his mouth. "You came for me," she said as she kneeled beside him and held him tightly.

He flinched. "I'm sorry," he said as she withdrew from their embrace. "I had to shoot them Eve, I had to shoot them. But for now, we have to get out of here. There are some bad people coming now."

Kevin heard the engine come to a halt by the front of the house. Car lights lit up the lemon trees that stood alongside the drive.

"Come on Kevin. Let's go," she whispered as she helped him to stand and positioned his crutch. He held it, smiled at her and followed. She ran over to the heap of rope and grabbed her photo of Harry, kissed it and placed it in her bag.

They stepped over the lumps and bumps of the barren land that vastly filled the space beyond the house. They rested on a rock and looked back. They could see the house in the distance, warm, inviting, light; they knew it was anything but.

They watched as four burley men ran around the building, they saw the old woman come out into the garden screaming. They watched as one man held a gun out and put a bullet through her leg. In the distance they heard Mehmet and Celile scream, two more shots followed. The burley men walked out with several bags, Kevin recognised them to be their bags; the men threw them into their car. They shouted and held their hands up before getting into the car and speeding off down the dirt path.

"I'm glad you shot them. Any more time wasted and we wouldn't be here, now. We survived Kevin, we made it," she said as she cried and fell into his arms. He held her like nothing he'd held before. Their pained, battered bodies entwined without any worry of the actual pain. The real pain for him was the thought of never seeing Eve again. He should've listened to her earlier that day. She knew, she had warned them, she had sensed it, she had trusted her instincts. From now on he vowed to himself that he would spend his life trusting Eve's instincts. She was his angel, his lover, his best friend, his everything and he couldn't wait to get back to reality, to his normal life, but with her in it for the rest of his life. He didn't know if a few days was enough to decide whether you could be with someone for life but when he looked to his future, all he could see was Eve. Every other alternative just didn't exist.

"I love you Kevin," she said as she leaned forward and kissed him. The sun began to rise; it was going to be a beautiful day. Birds squawked from the trees above and he heard a cockerel in the distance.

"I love you too, more than anything," he replied as he kissed her head and stood. "For now, we have to find civilisation."

"What about Rachel? I dragged her out of the clearing and into some bushes. Did they get her?"

Kevin pulled out the sat-nav and turned it on. "I pinpointed their location. We need to get to the police and get Rachel." They began the long trek back towards the main road. Everything swayed in the distance as dehydration set in, they had to get to a road. It was already getting hot and they had no water left. Eve held Kevin's hand, steadying him as they walked.

"Wait," she pulled her phone from her bag. It was flashing an angry red. For a split moment she caught the message on her screen.

Kevin grappled for The Prick's phone; he looked down, a circle with a bar. Great.

Eve read her message aloud and smiled as the battery died.

'I'm sorry about the last message, it was uncalled for. Harry made me send this for him. 'I love you Mummy. See you when we all get home.'

Maybe Justin had a small amount of decency in there after all. She placed the device back in her bag. "Harry loves me," she smiled.

"Of course he does," Kevin replied as he squeezed her hand.

Chapter 51

"I can't go much farther," Kevin whispered.

"Yes you can, you have to. Give me the bag," she said as she took the hessian bag off him, stopped for a moment and placed it in her rucksack. It was probably only about nine in the morning but the heat was intense, about twenty five degrees she guessed and it would only get hotter. The sky above them was a cloudless blue. As they got further across the next plain she felt Kevin lean on her more. His weight was slowing her down but she persevered, encouraging him to plod on. The shovel scraped along the stones below. Dust caked over their shins and ankles. "Do you hear that Kevin," she yelled.

"I can't hear a thing. Are you with me Eve?" he asked as his eyes closed. She knew he was losing it. He was dehydrated, had lost a lot of blood and had almost fought to the death.

"I'm still here," she said as she turned to kiss his cheek. She had to drag him a bit further towards the traffic noise. One laboured step after another, one sharp twinge followed another. Eventually they reached a verge. Eve lowered Kevin to the ground; he flopped back with his eyes closed as he lay there motionless. She felt his pulse, it was faint. As she bent down she felt every ache. She rolled Kevin onto his side and staggered out into the road. The sun was coming over the hill and blinded her. She looked away flinching at the intensity of the light that had flooded her eyes. Staggering up the road she wiped her brow with her arm; a car came from behind her on the opposite side of the road and tooted its horn. Eve waved and tried to look but her eyesight was dotted from the sun. She swallowed, her mouth was bone dry. She needed some help and fast. "Please stop, please help me," she croaked as she staggered forward. A lorry came from behind and tooted its horn, Eve fell to the floor, her heart almost exploding as the sound of the lorry passed her. The tarmac scorched her knees, she yelled as she turned and sat on her bottom.

A vehicle pulled up in front of her. The smell of diesel filled her nostrils, it was a bus. A woman ran towards her and shouted in Turkish; before she knew it someone was pouring water into her mouth. She gulped, water spilled around her face and down her chin. It was the most welcome drink she had ever received in her life. She pointed towards the verge. "Please help him too, please help."

Through her eyes, she saw Harry firing his water cannon at her, she laughed. In the corner of their little garden, she watched as two men carried Kevin across the grass and beyond where she lay. She laughed as in her mind she played with her son, enjoying every moment of being blasted by the water. Such a lovely day. Her, Harry and Kevin. She heard sirens; Harry loved his police cars and ambulances. Flashing lights. Everything was going to be alright. Someone tried to prise her rucksack from her back, she snatched it back. "Police, I need to speak to the Police," she yelled as she opened her rucksack. Now it was time to tell all, about their fight for survival. A medic came towards her with a syringe. "No," she yelled. Rachel's life still lay in her hands. "Police first," she hoped that they'd understood her. The medic withdrew her syringe and called an officer over. Eve smiled, they were going home; they had won the game.

Chapter 52

Rachel rubbed her head. He mouth was dry and she had a twig stuck to her face. She gazed around; all she could see were trees, rocks and shrubs. She lifted her dusty hand off the ground and wiped it across her gritty eyes. Her mind raced back to the previous day. Had she drank too much and passed out? The strange dreams she'd had mingled with the reality of the day before. Dreams of flying, of her old house with her Collie dog called Mr. Bickerstaff. She dreamt that she had taken a load of photos of him and when she printed them off he was missing from all of them. Then a thought flashed through her mind. Ryan grunting in front of her, his hot breath. She twiddled her hair; had she had sex? Reaching for her pocket she delved down to pull out her cigarettes; great, no fags. She was stuck in some wilderness feeling like shit after some sort of bad trip with no fags. Standing, she gazed at her surroundings and staggered around. She came to a clearing, a tree. "Ouch," she whispered as she squinted at it, feeling her back at the same time. Splinters, she remembered the sex, if she could call it that. That was the last time Ryan would get his hands on her body, as she recalled he had seen to himself in record time and thought he was some sort of Casanova.

Her heart quickened as her eyes darted in every direction. Something felt wrong. She scratched her arm, her vision became blurred. What on earth had she taken? She remembered smoking some weed but weed didn't normally knock her out. She staggered towards the dirt path. "Hey guys, this isn't funny," she yelled. She stopped and gazed around. Where was everyone? "Ryan you ass, did you have some of whatever I took as well," she shouted as she approached his body that was splayed out on the ground. "Ryan?" She kneeled down and rolled him over. She shrieked and fell backwards onto her bottom as she realised her wet hand was covered in his blood. Blood, it hit her. Ryan was dead, she was attacked. She grappled with the ground trying hard to get hold of something that was fixed so that she could pull herself up. Her heart boomed causing her to see little dark speckles in front of her eyes, her stomach lurched and she vomited.

Adrenalin pumped as she got to a standing position. She wiped her lips with her arm and staggered as fast as she could towards the waterfall, she could hear the water in the distance. A memory flashed across her mind, a man attacked her. A dark haired, slightly round man. Were they all dead? Had she been the lucky survivor in all this? "Eve, Selina," she yelled. "Stephen, Kevin." No reply, all she could hear were the tweeting birds and rustling in the shrubs. The crashing of the water at the bottom of the waterfall was close. She continued to stagger, her mouth tasted rotten and she was parched to the point of feeling faint. As she reached the water's edge she bent over and cupped some water into her hand. She greedily drank it until she could drink no more then she stopped and looked behind her. She might not be alone; they might still be around, playing their sick game. Quietly, she stood and waded her way through the shrubs that led to where the jeep was parked the day before. There was nothing, no cars, no jeep, nothing. Great; from what she could recall, it would be a long walk back to any form of civilisation.

She began trekking along the grit road hoping that she could get to a main road without meeting anyone threatening. Her hands began to shake; she needed a cigarette more than anything. Her camera, what had happened to her camera? A tear rolled down her cheek as the realisation of what had happened hit her. Ryan was dead, her friends were all missing, her attacker was nowhere to be seen. Ryan, her friend. She smiled; they had got a bit silly the night before and made a bit of a dumb mistake. She imagined what would happen if he was here now, how they would just laugh it off, how he would be so convinced he was the best she'd ever had and he'd laugh. He probably would've told everyone and she probably would have never lived it down. But none of that would've mattered, she just wished he was still alive to be an idiot all the time. She wept and screamed. There was no one, she was alone. They had all left her.

She continued down the snake-like road and walked around a bend and down a slope. She stopped as she spotted a fallen tree. Beside the fallen tree was the start of a blood trail. Her heart quickened as she crept forward, following the trail until she reached a man lay in the road on his front. His arms were splayed out above his head, his knees were bent. She ran up to him, he murmured. After a sharp intake of breath she stepped back. Her attacker lay before her, he was wounded and almost dead. He opened one eye and moved a finger. She stared, fixated with his predicament. How had he got here? Who had wounded him? She had missed one hell of a night in her drugged state. Her stomach turned again, she held it down. Her head began to pound and the brightness of the sun was so intense she could barely see. The man's hand reached towards her ankle. "You can fuck off," she yelled as she crushed his fingers under her foot. She had to keep going, get away and find out what had happened to the rest of her friends.

For about an hour she staggered up the dirt path and still felt no nearer to a road but then again, she was staggering. Her muscles felt like ton weights, she eventually fell to the floor. She would sit for a minute; regain her strength. She closed her eyes and concentrated on each painful head pound. So thirsty; so dry; so nauseous.

Her camera was a good one, her nanna was the best. When she got home, if she could find her camera she would show Nanna her pictures. She definitely wouldn't tell Nanna what she did with Ryan though. The tattoos and piercings were one thing but Nanna definitely wouldn't approve of casual sex against trees. She smiled as she saw her nanna sat in the kitchen reading one of her usual crime books. Her nanna was cool; on her return she would put her book down and pull out a beer from the fridge. They would then have a long chat about how it all went. Her drinking with her nanna was what they did some nights, followed by a ping curry meal. Ping, ping, "curry's done Nanna," she whispered with a smile. The ping turned into a siren. "Oh Nanna, did you burn it? I didn't know you could burn curries in the microwave."

She felt an arm under hers as she was rolled onto something. She forced an eye open. The intense sunshine was blocked by a man in a white shirt holding a needle. She yelled. A woman ran over and smiled as she stroked her arms and talked to her in a language she didn't understand. With a smile on her face she went to sleep. Nanna hadn't burned the curry, it was done. Rachel smiled as she laid the table for them both. "Thanks Nanna, I don't say thank you often enough." Her nanna looked back at her with smiling eyes.

"You will always be my little girl."

"Can I have one of your ciggies Nanna?" Nanna smiled and passed her the packet. Rachel placed the stick in her mouth, lit it and inhaled. "Thanks Nanna."

Epilogue

The summer had passed in a blur of police interviews and media speculation. Her mother stole the limelight on many occasions with her public displays of upset. "You should write a book, you should talk to the tabloids, you should contact magazines, the money isn't to be scoffed at," she would say but not once did she show Eve any comfort or tell her how much she had missed her. Her father had turned up to meet them after they landed back in England but failed to say anything meaningful. She'd thought that just this once, given her ordeal and her visible injuries that they might want to hug her or tell her that they loved her but the most they did was what they always did, merely carried out their parental duties. To the world they were a tower of support; to her they were emotionally vacant. She'd even told them she was going back to her studies the following year to become a teacher, her mother had shrugged before continuing to tell Eve how she could make money from her story instead and not bother.

As the weeks went by, she'd started to argue with her mother again, she didn't want the papers and the interviews, she wanted to blend back into normal life, anonymously. Besides, most of the grisly details had been held back due to the ongoing trial of Guz and Mehmet Kaplan. Celile Asker had died by gunshot wound that night, Sadik Kaplan had died due to the stab wound from Celile's accidental attack. Mehmet had been luckier, when the gang shot him; they only caused a flesh wound. After a week in hospital he was moved to a prison ward.

It was looking bad for Guz her solicitor had assured her. Guz would be lucky to ever be free again and was looking at charges ranging from theft to multiple murder. Mehmet however was looking at a lighter sentence following their testimonies, they all really did believe that he knew nothing of their murderous plans and he had also taken a stab wound for Eve. She shuddered as her thoughts drew back to 'that night.' To date the Police had not managed to track down the rest of the gang, she supposed that they'd moved on, taking their illegal activities to another part of the country. Detectives however, were optimistic about some leads that they were following so maybe, just maybe there was hope.

    The descriptions that Eve gave of White Suit and Scrawny had led them into an investigation of a mafia style gang that had been operating invisibly for years in the tourist regions. The description that she gave was the best information they'd had to date. Her solicitor had confirmed that Guz and Mehmet had originally refused to talk and vowed that they would not say a word to anyone about any of it, accepting whatever would come their way. Mehmet had buckled under questioning and told investigators about the places that his father had met up with White Suit. Apparently, Guz spoke in great detail of these places when he'd consumed a few beers. After further investigations and drug busts following Mehmet's leads, they had a first name, Nicolai. Not much but a start. Eve shivered; that might not even be his real name, they may never know the real identity of White Suit. A market for women and passports would never just go away, the threat was now greater than ever. She thought deeply about all that was happening and felt tears begin to well up in the corners of her eyes. Even if they caught White Suit, there would always be another White Suit to take his place.

    Guz's sat-nav had also led to various locations that they suspected White Suit had operated from but he wasn't anywhere to be found. Most people that were questioned denied his existence; all too scared of him she expected. Guz's phone usage history was another story. The violent texts demanding girls and documents from a man he had logged only as The Boss filled his inbox. They had tried to trace these calls but the phone was found to be unregistered and was out of operation.

    Tuana Kaplan, the perpetrators elderly mother claimed not to know a thing, she had so far cooperated with the Turkish Police after leaving the hospital. Eve glanced down at the translated statement.

'They came back agitated and kept sending me out of the way, I started to read my book then I fell asleep on the chair. I suspected that they were up to no good as they kept going to the outhouse at the bottom of the land out the back but I thought they were storing their stolen goods there. I never expected them to keep a woman whom they had kidnapped in the outhouse. I knew my Guz was bad but I never knew he could do what he did." A wet trail meandered down Eve's cheek. The woman who had warned her knew her son was bad, she knew what he was capable of or else why would she have warned her. She must have known that they were potential targets from hearing her sons' discussions. Where did the 'trust your instincts' lecture really come from? She had replied with exactly that in her response and hoped that during the trial, justice would prevail. She wept as she thought of the old woman, she probably had no control over what her sons did but she must have known. Did that make her guilty? Eve would leave that question to bear a heavy weight on the old woman's conscience.

Lastly she closed her eyes and spared a moment for her friends and the others. The bodies of a German couple were dug up. Ilse and Gerhard, Kevin had found their passports in Guz's glove box and carried them around in the hessian bag, determined to get justice for them too. Having the passports made identification of the bodies easier. She shuddered and began to weep as she thought of their families, suffering like she was. Her friends wiped out forever, as if their bodies or their identities were just a commodity to be traded.

The dig is still ongoing; so far they have found another four bodies. The police are convinced that their criminal activities spanned other areas, other regions, other unused places in the wilderness. The true extent of their murderous crimes may never be exposed. Eve picked up one of the photos that was stored on Rachel's camera that they recovered in the clearing. It was the photo of her and Kevin kissing by the waterfall, the flower hat just about to fall off her head, she smiled and allowed a tear to fall.

"Mummy Eve, why are you crying?" Harry said as he looked up at her ready to go out. He played with his favourite lucky shell before he placed it in his pocket; the little shell that Kevin had kept in his pocket, keeping his promise to provide Harry with a gift.

"Mummy is just thinking of her friends, that's all Sweetie," she said as she bent down and stroked his soft hair. "I love you so much, so so much." She squeezed her son hard and wept on his tiny shoulder. She looked down, she had created a mascara smear on his pale blue jacket. The little boy hugged her back.

"I love you too Mummy."

A loud explosion went off, followed by a rocket and another blast. The porch that was in darkness lit up a bright cerise colour. She parted from her son and placed his bobble hat on his head. She wrapped his scarf around his neck before zipping up his coat.

"I see my two favourite people in the whole world are ready for fireworks," Kevin said as he entered the kitchen. Eve wiped her eyes and hugged Kevin hard.

"I love you," she said. She leaned back and smiled. He took a tissue out of his pocket and wiped her eyes before placing the case documents back into the brown paper envelope.

"I love you too, more than anything. These past few months have been the worst and the best of my whole life. If I had to do it all again so that I could be here now with you, I would without any hesitation," he said as he zipped up his coat and grabbed his walking stick.

"Do you love me too Kevin?" Harry said, his wide eyes staring up at them and his cheeky grin expanding.

"I love you too, Mini Munchkin," he said as he lifted the little boy up with his one arm and kissed his head. Eve smiled; she had her perfect little family. Harry would still go back to his Dad a lot of the time but she knew she was important to him. She had a special bond with him, a bond only a mother can have, one she'd been denied with her own mother. She had something special with

Harry, something her parents would never understand. To make her life perfect she had Kevin, her love and she knew they would have a wonderful future together as a family.

The little boy giggled as Kevin hugged him and Eve pretended to bite his ear. "Stop it Mummy." Kevin placed Harry down on the floor and passed Eve his mittens.

"Come on then, let's go and meet Auntie Rachel and watch some fireworks," Eve said as she placed one of Harry's mittens on his little hand. He ran off towards the door before she could get the other one on.

Eve smiled back at Kevin; he leaned in and kissed her tenderly. "Come on then, let's go and have some fun." Kevin walked aided by his stick towards the door, Eve smiled to herself. Her family, her life and happiness, she had everything she wanted. The only tears she would weep now were in memory of her lost friends; three special people who would always have a place in her heart, her friends who didn't make it. "Are you coming or what?" he asked as he turned back and smiled.

"Yes, come on Mummy. You'll make us miss the fireworks." She smiled; she loved hearing her son call her Mummy.

"I'm on my way Sweetie," she said as she darted to the door and turned off the light. She was now ready for a night of fun with her beautiful family.

THE END

Thank you for reading Whispers Beneath the Pines. Any reviews on Amazon or Goodreads would be much appreciated.

Further works by Carla Kovach

Flame

To Let

Printed in Great Britain
by Amazon